MORIARTY RETURNS A LETTER

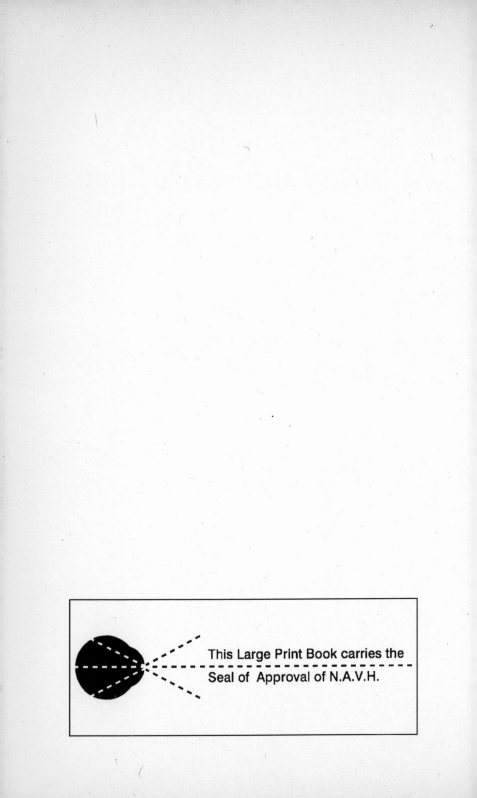

This Large Print Book carries the
Seal of Approval of N.A.V.H.

MORIARTY RETURNS A LETTER

A LETTER

MICHAEL ROBERTSON

THORNDIKE PRESS
A part of Gale, Cengage Learning

Farmington Hills, Mich • San Francisco • New York • Waterville, Maine
Meriden, Conn • Mason, Ohio • Chicago

GALE
CENGAGE Learning®

LIBRARY OF CONGRESS CATALOGING-IN-PUBLICATION DATA

Robertson, Michael.
    Moriarty returns a letter / by Michael Robertson. — Large print edition.
        pages ; cm. — (Thorndike Press large print mystery) (A Baker Street mystery)
    ISBN-13: 978-1-4104-6805-5 (hardcover)
    ISBN-10: 1-4104-6805-4 (hardcover)
    1. Holmes, Sherlock—Fiction. 2. Brothers—Fiction. 3. Lawyers—England—London—Fiction. 4. Letter writing—Fiction. 5. 221B Baker Street (London, England : Imaginary place)—Fiction. 6. London (England)—Fiction. 7. Los Angeles (Calif.)—Fiction. 8. Large type books. I. Title.
    PS3618.O31726M67 2014b
    813'.6—dc23   2013050881

Published in 2014 by arrangement with St. Martin's Press, LLC

Printed in Mexico
1 2 3 4 5 6 7 18 17 16 15 14

For William R. McKinley, USAAF (Ret.)

ACKNOWLEDGMENTS

My thanks to my editor, Marcia Markland, and associate editor Kat Brzozowski; production editor Elizabeth Curione; designer Phil Mazzone; publicist Justin Velella; jacket designers David Baldeosingh Rotstein and James Iacobelli; and copy editor Barbara Wild, at Thomas Dunne Books/St. Martin's Press.

My thanks also to my agent, Kirby Kim, at William Morris Endeavor, and Laura Bonner, for international rights.

1

LONDON, ST. KATHERINE'S DOCK, DECEMBER 1893

In the damp, stinking cargo hold of the *Queen's Gambit,* a shirtless and bleeding man stood shackled to the rough wood of the center post.

A larger, barrel-chested man stood just behind and to the side, holding a heavy, brine-encrusted rope cargo net, gripping it with both hands as though it were a sledge-hammer, eyes gleaming, eager to swing it again, as he had done half a dozen times already, and with an intent to improve his technique and get his full weight into it on the next try.

A smaller man sat at a narrow rectangular table near the door, perusing a penny publication he had stolen just a few moments earlier on the street, and a fourth man — the one the others knew as Redgil, taller than any of the other three men in the cargo hold and clearly in charge at this moment — stood directly in front of the shackled man and wondered just how much more it would take to break him.

Would he die before he revealed what they wanted to know? In Redgil's experience, and he had some in this area, the man was close to it now. That wouldn't be good. It wouldn't do to kill him right out and be done with it. Not just yet.

If the shackled man was just who he claimed to be — a great crime organizer extraordinaire, a deviser of illicit schemes, a money launderer with international resources at his disposal — then everything was fine. Redgil thought himself a great crime organizer extraordinaire in his own right, and he did not fancy competition. He could simply kill the shackled man and keep his share of their collaborative criminal enterprise, and not worry about it any further.

But Redgil had begun to suspect that there might be something else going on with the shackled man. It was just a rumor, but he needed to be sure. There was much at stake.

Redgil had in his possession a huge sum — nearly fifty thousand pounds — in counterfeit bills. The bills were too large and too many to just pass them off in small shops and street transactions — they required laundering on a larger scale, and Redgil had contacted this man, an American who had surfaced in London just recently, to find a way to get it done.

The current plan was straightforward: The shackled American claimed to have an arrangement for purchasing a cargo of whiskey, which was illegally imported from Ireland and sitting at St. Katherine's Dock, waiting for departure to the United States. The owner of the cargo, the American said, was anxious to do a deal and avoid import/export fees. He was not likely to look at things too closely. It was a fine scenario for turning Redgil's fake pounds into legitimate currency.

So the exchange would be tomorrow night. Redgil was to bring the money to the dock where the *Queen's Gambit* was berthed. He would deliver to the American the fifty thousand in counterfeit bills, in exchange for the cargo and a signed bill of lading. Redgil would then sail with the cargo to America, sell it for a handsome profit over the wholesale price he had paid with his counterfeit bills, and then he would return to London to expand his criminal operations in all the ways his imagination could conceive.

But late last night Redgil had been drinking at the bar in the Whistler pub with an acquaintance released just that day from Newgate Prison. The acquaintance complained that he had gotten nicked when the police unaccountably showed up at exactly the wrong time, late at night, when he was about to burglarize an antiquities shop on Bond Street.

The Bond Street burglary was an operation that had been planned by the shackled American. And this was not the first of these plans-gone-unaccountably-wrong Redgil had heard of.

It was true that the American had had a few successes since arriving in town a few months ago — arranging some successful burglaries here and there, with no one at home just as he said no one would be, and with loot that was pretty much as expected. Some lucrative and uneventful transactions in fencing stolen goods.

But recently Redgil had begun to hear of major operations where things would get cocked up. It was nothing conclusive, but it was certainly enough for him to do something that he enjoyed doing anyway — string someone up to a post and torture him until he expired.

12

So Redgil ordered the bulky man to swing the heavy rope again.

"Tell us!"

The American shackled to the wooden post raised his head up halfway, looked back at the London Limehouse scum that had bested him, and couldn't believe he had allowed it to happen.

Then he looked across at the table near the door.

On the table were a kerosene lamp, a bottle of whiskey sampled from the cargo (the second of the evening, and already mostly consumed), and two paper items. One of these paper items was a bill of lading, and the other was the December 1893 issue of *The Strand Magazine.*

The bill of lading had been in the American's coat pocket when he was ambushed by the other three men in the dark alley behind the Whistler pub.

The Strand Magazine was a monthly periodical that featured mainly detective stories, and this brand-new issue of it had been brought into the pub by the skinny man, who had lifted it earlier from a street vendor, just shortly before all four of these men were scheduled to rendezvous in the pub.

The American stared across at those two

paper items. One of them was the cause of his current troubles, and the other, he had begun to hope, might just possibly be his salvation.

The Strand was running a serial of stories about a particular detective. It had been all the rage in London for more than a year. The American had recently begun reading them himself — and not idly, but with a purpose. He had read all the ones that preceded this current issue, and he had even managed a glance at the first few pages of this one, earlier in the pub. He hoped this one was like the others. If it was, perhaps he still had a small chance of emerging from the cargo hold alive.

"Tell us! Who are you? What's your real name? Who are you working for?"

Redgil backhand-slapped the American across the face.

The American did not regard the slap as especially painful. The lashes on his bare back from the heavy cargo net were a different matter. That pain did not diminish; the flesh on his back got more swollen and the nerves more exposed with each fresh flailing of the net. The pain from those and the hyperventilated breathing they induced were beginning to make him dizzy.

The problem with the slaps was that they

14

jarred his head, made his brain rattle inside his skull, and he needed to be able to think. Like any other Pinkerton undercover man, he knew that if you lose your wits even for an instant, you're done.

He knew he was probably done anyway; he'd been found out. He'd been overconfident. He knew it; he knew now that he should never have taken this risk.

He'd gotten so good at manipulating gangsters in New York, he'd actually allowed himself to believe that going on loan to Scotland Yard would just be a lark. After all, they didn't even have any "real" gangs here, at least not yet. He had come across on assignment to help them keep it that way.

Within days of his first briefing at the Yard, the American had put the word out to the London underworld that he had connections none of the locals could match. Did you need to launder your hundred thousand pounds of counterfeit bills in a hurry? Did you need better rates for fencing your jewelry heist? Did you need to coordinate operations for any of the above? Then the American was your man. Especially because he was not merely an American. He was a New Yorker. The reputation of the budding gangs in New York was known worldwide. Why settle for a fledgling English gangster when you could work with the real thing?

He had started slowly, helping a few nonviolent, small-time felons to succeed in their enterprises — getting a pickpocket out of jail here, setting up a burglary there (after making sure that there would be no one at home to get hurt and that the loot would be minimal).

And then, after a string of those successes, with his reputation established, he had begun to set up the bigger fish, the real targets of the operation.

This had to be done carefully. The whole point was to nick the top-level felons or, at minimum, keep them off balance. But both the American and his colleague at Scotland Yard Special Branch knew that they could push such an operation just so far.

And that was even before the American knew he had a family to think about.

His young wife had come across the pond with him. He wished to God now that he had persuaded her to remain in New York. He had promised her this would be his last field operation, the crown of his career. There would be no more after this, he had said, he would return home and take a desk job, and then they would start a family. He had wanted her to stay safely behind until then.

But she wouldn't hear of it. She had come with him.

And then she had become pregnant.

And all at once, everything had become crystal clear for the American agent.

He'd been taking too many risks. He would stop. He had been overconfident. He would not be so in the future.

But that epiphany had come too late. He was stuck now in this cargo hold with three mean men, each of them stupid in the way mean-spirited bottom-feeding criminals are stupid, but one of them — the one the others called Redgil — was just slightly smarter than the others, smarter in the way that people who make it their business to cheat and steal and hurt get smart in doing so. Just the sort of lout that the American had come across the pond to nab.

But instead of the American and the inspector grilling the felon at Scotland Yard, it was Redgil doing the questioning in this hellhole.

"Tell us! How did they know?"

Another backhand slap. Just an insult, nothing more.

The American agent wished that someone would untie his hands just for an instant, so that he could return a proper response — but he knew it wouldn't happen. Not unless he could get them off their game.

He looked across again at *The Strand Magazine* on the table. He tried to remember everything he had read in it.

The man with the net got ready to flail it again.

It was now or never. The American agent let his head fall again, this time deliberately. He would play it for all it was worth.

He muttered under his breath. If you want someone to believe a lie, you need to make them work to hear it.

"It was that bloody Holmes," he said.

"What? What did you say?"

Redgil slammed the American's head back against the post.

And the American began to laugh.

"Fools. You bloody, stupid fools. Do you really think I would sabotage my own operations? Think! Why would I do that?"

Redgil seemed puzzled by the laugh. He responded, with natural and justifiable suspicion: "You could be a copper. You could be working for the Yard."

"Balls. If I were working for the Yard, you'd have all been in the nick a month ago. And so would everyone else in the Whistler pub. Use your head, man. This was Holmes's doing."

"I don't know who you're talking about."

The American channeled all of his pain into a laugh that was as loud and arrogant as he could make it.

"He thwarts me at every turn! It had to be him! There's no one at Scotland Yard with a mind like that!"

The skinny man — the one who had brought the magazine into the pub, the only one of the three who could read, the American had guessed — jumped up from the table and ran over eagerly, within a foot of the agent's face.

"You don't mean . . ." He paused, eyes wide, and he spoke in a whisper: "Sherlock . . . Holmes?"

"What do you think?" said the American. He said this with a sneer, his voice dripping with contempt. Presentation wasn't everything, but it was most of it.

"What are you talking about?" said Redgil to the skinny man. Then he looked over at the brute with the fishing net, who shrugged.

But the skinny one nodded affirmatively. "Sherlock Holmes," he said, fully out loud this time. "I've heard of him. Sherlock Holmes! Holy Mother of God, if Sherlock Holmes is on to us, we're done!"

The man tied to the post did not move his head. He did not move his eyes. He did

19

not even breathe. If you want the fish to take the bait, you must stay completely still.

"An old wives' tale," said Redgil. "There is no Sherlock Holmes."

"No, no," said the skinny one. "I read about him. He's real." The skinny man ran to the table, grabbed the copy of *The Strand Magazine,* and brought it back like a puppy to the leader. "They can't print it if it isn't true."

Redgil took the magazine, opened it, stared into it — looked stumped for a moment — and then he tossed it contemptuously back at the skinny man.

It hit the damp wood floor with a nasty-sounding splat; the skinny man ran quickly to pick it up, and did his best to wipe the muck off.

Redgil never liked it if someone else might be right. Especially he didn't like being corrected in front of an audience, and the shackled American, at the moment, constituted an audience.

"No, no," said Redgil, rather grandly after a moment's thought, but not with genuine confidence. "Just because it's printed doesn't mean it's true. It has to be what they call . . . what they call . . . published . . . published, that's it . . . in a newspaper. Then it's true. But this is not a newspaper. This

— this is just something where some git made stuff up!"

The American agent fought through his pain and focused. This was the final hurdle in any scam. The moment when the mark's basic common sense would try to take hold of him and let him realize exactly what was going on, and if that happened, then his basic instincts would take hold as well, and if that happened, with scum like these, then it was all over. The game was up, whether the mark had figured out all the details or not. He would be done with it and just cut your throat.

The American agent and Inspector Standifer at the Yard had always known that at some point the very success of the sting operations would begin to make the American's cover identity suspect. Someone would want to know, as the lead bunghole here wanted to know, right now, why plots kept getting foiled.

The agent couldn't keep blaming it on bad luck. He couldn't keep saying that a couple of bobbies just happened to be walking by when the heist went down, or that one of the conspirators must have talked in his sleep to his paramour, or gotten drunk and let something slip in the pub. He needed an explanation that was all-encompassing. He needed a scapegoat. He and the inspector had tried to come up with one.

And then, a few weeks back, he had been at Scotland Yard when a letter arrived. A letter that the Royal Mail had seen fit to carry directly into the inspector's office.

It was a confession letter.

That, by itself, did not make it a rarity at Scotland Yard, or even unusually important.

What made it important was that it had not been addressed to Scotland Yard. It had been addressed to someone else.

And it wasn't the first. There had been others — confessions to crimes, tips about crimes, questions about crimes — all addressed to Sherlock Holmes, and being delivered to Scotland Yard.

To the Special Branch inspector, such letters had been just a curiosity, and sometimes an actual annoyance.

But the American agent saw an opportunity.

Like everyone else in the English-speaking world, he knew the name Sherlock Holmes quite well now. And he had seen how eagerly the crowds would gather around the street vendor every month for each new issue of *The Strand*.

But more important, he had now begun to hear the name Sherlock Holmes muttered in fearful whispers in the Docklands' dirtiest, toughest pubs, by men with souls as hard and mean as lobster claws, huddled around pub tables like children around a campfire and scaring themselves with tales of the bogeyman.

This, thought the American at the time, could be useful.

And so he had invested sixpence and picked up last month's issue of *The Strand* and read "The Adventure of the Naval Treaty."

And then he had backtracked and read all the others, all the way back to *A Study in Scarlet.* He wanted to know who this fictional detective was, and why even streetwise felons seemed to want to believe him to be real.

The American thought he understood.

Bleeding and barely conscious, he was now going to put it to the test. He had no other choice.

His tormentors in the cargo hold were practically begging for some reason to believe that the failures of their vicious, shortsighted schemes were due to some other cause than their own personal faults. He would give them one.

He was ready. He looked up at his interrogator.

"What are you smiling at?" said Redgil, and he gestured for the brute to deliver another lash from the cargo net.

"Oh, yes, you are the smart one," said the American quickly. And then the lash of the whip came anyway. He held back his scream, he did his best to control the frantic, involuntary hyperventilation that the pain induced, and then, after several agonizing, dizzying seconds, he maintained consciousness. He looked up.

"Yes, the smart one," he said, forcing the smile again. "I knew that about you. You're right. That rag right there is just *The Strand Magazine.* Not a newspaper, where everything is God's own truth. No sir, not a bit of it. It's just a magazine full of halfpenny stories. Stories that everyone repeats. In every pub. On every dock. That every whore and pickpocket and stockbroker in London knows about. But all the same, it's just stories. You are absolutely correct."

"Right, then," said Redgil, buying the flattery, but suspicious of where it was going.

"Except it isn't just."

The thick man with the net whip raised it again, eyes gleaming, and looked at Redgil.

But Redgil hesitated. Too many of these and the shackled man would actually just die; he would go into shock or bleed out; he didn't look to be far from it now. And he still hadn't revealed what he knew.

Redgil raised his hand to stay the whip.

"What do you mean?" he said.

The American took a moment to spit blood out onto the floor. Then he looked up, calmly and contemptuously, at Redgil.

"The stories in this magazine are not something some writer made up. They are biography. You know what biography is, don't you? It's not fiction; it's fact. The stories are a biographical account, written by an educated man, a doctor, this John Watson. He's writing biography — actual reminiscences — about this detective he knows. If you'd been reading them all along, you'd know that. The very first one said right up front 'a reprint from the reminiscences of John H. Watson, M.D.' It's fact. And he's not just a doctor; he's an army doctor. You know they wouldn't have let him write things that aren't true."

Redgil was suspicious, but he looked again at the skinny man. The skinny man nodded emphatically. "That's right," he said. "I read that in the very first one. A reminiscence. By John H. Watson, M.D. Late of the Army Medical Department."

"So there you are," said the American agent to Redgil. "Read it for yourself, if you like." Then he added, "You can read, can't you?"

That remark brought another slap across the jaw. The American knew that would happen; he was already pretty damn sure Redgil couldn't actually read. The slap confirmed it, and it was worth the inconvenience — because now he had made the leader of the little group defensive about what he didn't know, and anxious to prove he knew more than he did.

"Sure I can," said Redgil. "Of course I've read them. I've read all of them."

"Then think about it. Who could possibly make up such things? Figuring out the meaning of the five orange pips? Deciphering the note written by the Reigate squires? Do you really think some git of a writer in a penny magazine could make those things up?"

Redgil looked back at the skinny man, and the skinny man, proud of his own knowledge, shook his head emphatically.

"All right," said Redgil slowly, turning back to the shackled American. "I suppose they're not made up." And then, to prove that he figured this out of his own accord, he added: "This Mr. Watson being an army doctor and such."

"Of course not," said the American. "Only

26

a true genius could decipher those clues. And only the greatest of minds could deduce and unravel the plots I have laid. Only a man with an intellect that rivals my own. But great minds have great egos, and the great weakness of Mr. Sherlock Holmes is that he cannot bear to work in anonymity. And so he allows his feats to be published. And that's what you see in *The Strand Magazine* — biographical accounts of his actual doings, with only an occasional detail altered here and there."

"All right," said Redgil, still pondering that possibility. "But just because Sherlock Holmes is real — that doesn't necessarily mean he's the reason your plans didn't work, now does it?"

"Hell, he's thwarted more of my plans than I can count!" said the American. "I set up a burglary just last year that would have shook the world if Sherlock Holmes hadn't figured it out."

"Prove it," snarled Redgil.

"Look it up yourself," said the American. "It's in last month's issue."

The skinny man came running over.

"You don't mean the Naval Treaty?" he said, quite eagerly.

"Bloody hell yes, except it wasn't just a Naval Treaty. They change things you know, even in biographies, when they write them up. But I was behind it, it was no simple burglary, and it would have worked, too, if Holmes hadn't sussed out where the document was."

"So all the crimes that Sherlock Holmes solved in these . . . these biography things that Dr. Watson writes," said Redgil, "they were all schemes of yours?"

The American hesitated. He wasn't claiming that at all; it could be too easily disproved. But he couldn't be seen to be backing down. He needed a denial that didn't sound like one.

"All?" he said. "Well, that's a mighty big word. Your crimes of passion, someone's long-lost love surfacing in a quest for vengeance, snakes crawling down ropes — those had nothing to do with me, although I'll admit that snake thing might have come in handy. Mine were just the ones where a lot of money was at stake, and even one or two of those accounts had nothing to do with me. That Red-headed League thing?"

The skinny man nodded enthusiastically. Clearly, he had read them all.

"Not mine," said the American. "Not my style. If I'd been starting a Red-headed League, it'd have been only women could join, if you take my meaning. But the important point here is, the few failures I have had, and there have been very few, have all been due to Holmes."

"So you say," said the leader, rubbing his chin. "So you say." He looked over at the magazine on the table. "But I'll wager that if we take a look in the one that came out today, whatever the Sherlock Holmes story is —"

"Biography," said the American.

"Whatever the hell it is, it will have nothing to do with you."

"Fair enough," said the American. "I'll wager a quid."

"No," sneered the leader. "You're wagering your life."

"Fine," said the American. "Just bring it over here. I can help you with the long words if you want."

The skinny man eagerly ran forward toward the American agent, the magazine in hand.

"Stay back!" commanded Redgil, before the skinny man could get too close. "Don't let him see what's in it."

The American shrugged, though it hurt to do so. "Well, we can't settle the bet if you won't open it up."

"You read it," said Redgil to the skinny man. "Read it aloud."

The skinny man opened the magazine. He was quite eager about it, but he wasn't a fast reader, and it took almost a full agonizing minute for him just to locate the story in the magazine.

"I found it!"

"Well, read the bloody thing!" commanded Redgil.

The skinny man began to read aloud: " 'The Final Problem,' " he announced.

"What's that mean?" said Redgil.

"That's the title," said the skinny man. " 'The Final Problem.' "

"Well, get on with it," said Redgil.

The skinny man began to read.

" 'It is with a heavy heart that I take up my pen to write these the last words in which —' "

"Wait," said Redgil now. "Just how long is this going to take?"

The skinny man shrugged. "I read the last one in just two days," he said, with some pride.

Redgil shook his head. "Take your damn magazine over there," he said, pointing at the little table. "When you've figured out what it's about, assuming it happens before the sun comes up, then give us the short version."

The skinny man did as he was told, and

went to the table, his eyes fixed on the page of the magazine even as he walked.

Meantime, Redgil picked up the bill of lading, brought it over to the American, and stuck it in front of his face.

"Sign this. Make it over to bearer, so I can present it to the ship's captain and take possession."

The American shook his head. "That's not our deal. I'll sign it over when you bring the money to the dock and I get my twenty-five percent."

"Of course you'll get your cut. Why wouldn't you? You will. I promise. You have my word. As a gentleman."

The American just snorted defiantly.

Redgil nodded to the brute, and the rope came down on the American's back again.

The pain ran in shivers down his back, into his legs, and then back up again to his head, nearly causing him to pass out. He fought to stay conscious. He raised his head and looked directly at Redgil.

"You are making a very serious mistake," said the American. "I am not alone. Do you think I work with no one but you, that I have no confederates? I have schemes in place everywhere in this city. You know that. I don't take credit by name, but it's me that makes it happen. You know and I know that you cannot cheat me and leave me alive. But my operatives are everywhere, and if you kill me, I will be avenged."

Redgil just sneered when the American said those things. But the skinny man — still slowly working his way through "The Final Problem" in *The Strand* — looked up now when he heard the threat. He looked back down at the text he was reading — then across at the American — and then at the text again.

Then he got up and came over, the opened magazine in his hand. He stared at the American.

"What is your real name?"

The American looked up. The skinny man's face had a look not just of suspicion but also something very much like awe — as though he were wondering whether he should bow down in front of the American before it was too late.

Once more the skinny man looked at the text he had been reading, and then up at the American and then back at the text again.

Page two, thought the American. He's reached page two. It was just far enough.

"If you're reading that," said the American, nodding toward the copy of *The Strand,* with all the quiet menace he could muster, "you damn well know what my name is."

The skinny man's eyes grew wide. He stepped back from the American as though the man was a bonfire that had gotten too big. He turned toward Redgil.

"What now?" said Redgil.

The skinny man displayed the magazine in front of Redgil, and jabbed his finger at the relevant page.

"Moriarty!"

"What are you talking about?"

"He is Professor Moriarty! The Napoléon of crime! It says so, right here!" The skinny man read aloud from the magazine, pointing at portions of the text and displaying them in front of Redgil's face, to Redgil's great annoyance.

" 'He sits motionless, like a spider in the centre of its web. . . . He does little himself. He only plans. But his agents are numerous and splendidly organized. Is there a crime to be done, a paper to be abstracted, we will say, a house to rifled, a man to be removed — the word is passed to the Professor, the matter is organized and carried out.' "

Redgil, growing more impatient by the second, ripped the journal out of the skinny man's hands. He shoved it in front of the

American's face:

"Well?" he demanded. "Out with it. Is this you, then?"

With an intense effort of will, the American agent got his breathing completely under control. He composed his face completely. He even stopped sweating. He looked at Redgil directly and calmly and then smiled a very cold, minimal smile and said:

"You may hope that it is not. Your hope is in vain."

"Oh, bloody hell," said the skinny man. "We are done, we are done. His agents will do for us all!"

"Shut the bloody hell up!" shouted Redgil. "I need to think."

To make that process easier, apparently, he turned away and pushed on his own forehead with the palms of his hands as if to force a thought. He stroked a reddish birthmark that ran parallel with his jaw on his right cheek. Then he turned back and stared for a long moment at the American.

And then he motioned the other two men in the room — that is, everyone who was not shackled to the post — into the far corner. He spoke in a whisper, almost softly enough that the shackled man couldn't hear.

"Maybe he is Moriarty, and maybe he

ain't. But we can't cut him loose, either way. We've already gone too bloody far. But no one has to know it was us that did it. First we get him to sign the cargo over to us, and then we throw his body in front of a bloody train or something."

The man with the rope grunted. The skinny man nodded eagerly.

Then they all three came back to the shackled man.

Redgil thrust the bill of lading at him.

"I don't give a damn farthing who you really are," said Redgil. "You sign this! Make it over to bearer, so that I can present it to the ship's captain and take possession."

The American glared up at Redgil, and said:

"I need a writing surface."

Redgil looked puzzled for a moment.

"Surely you don't expect me to sign in thin air?" said the American, with a nod toward the little wooden table.

Redgil considered it.

"Well, we sure as hell ain't cutting you loose," he said. Then he turned to the skinny man. "Bring that table over here."

The skinny man picked up the kerosene lamp and handed it to the man with the rope, and then cleared the remaining items from the little table. Then the skinny man brought the table over and set it down next to Redgil and the American.

"I can't bend down that far," said the American, standing up straight, still shackled to the post. "Little problem with my back."

The skinny man ran back and got the little three-legged stool that went with the table. He set it down in position for the American.

"May I?" said the American to Redgil, in a voice dripping with sarcasm.

Redgil growled something unintelligible.

The American slid down, both hands still tied to the post, and sat on the little stool. He positioned himself at the table as if for afternoon tea, and looked up at Redgil.

"If you want me to sign, I think you'll need to untie me. One hand, at least."

Redgil looked at the bloody, battered wreck of a man who claimed to be Moriarty, and decided he could take just that much of a chance. He motioned to the man with the rope to cut one arm loose.

The American flexed his fingers and wrist, as if to get the circulation running again.

Then the skinny man dipped the pen into the inkwell and held it in front of the American's face. A black drop of ink fell from the metal pen nib onto the table, where a small pool of the American's blood was already beginning to soak into the wood.

The American took the pen and, with as steady a hand as he could manage, he began to sign an endorsement on the bill of lading.

"There's a good lad," said Redgil.

The American had one hand free, the hand holding the pen. And time was up.

He signed. But he did not make the endorsement to bearer, as Redgil demanded. He made it to someone else. Come hell or high water, and one of those was surely about to come, he was going to maintain his newly invented cover story. If it didn't save his life, it might save someone else's.

Now, with his free hand holding the pen, the American used his shackled hand to push the signed bill of lading across the table to Redgil. And then the American allowed his head to drop, as though finally succumbing to unconsciousness.

Redgil sneered at the American, picked up the document, and turned away.

In the three months that he had been working with Redgil's team, the American agent had never allowed any of them to see him do anything more physically impressive than launch a chewed wad of tobacco into the spittoon from a distance of four feet. No bar fights — he avoided them. No climbing along second-story windowsills to complete a burglary — he left that to the skinny man. No pickup games of cricket in the street, though he had dearly wanted to, because he'd played damn good stickball growing up in Hell's Kitchen.

With his shirt off, they might have picked up a hint that he was something other than just a planner of crimes. But if there was one characteristic of this lot that was stronger than their suspicion, it was their arrogance. And that was only compounded by the fact that they thought he was now about two breaths away from death's door.

Of course, at this point, that was pretty much his own assessment as well.

All the more reason he had nothing to lose.

The small table — no more than three feet by two — was in front of him; he was seated on the little three-legged stool they had brought over at his insistence.

Two feet away, directly across the table from the American, Redgil was unable to read the bill of lading, and so, as the American had expected, he was turning to his left, to show the signature to the skinny man.

At the other side of the table was the bulky man, who had left his original position behind the post. That was lucky. He still had the cargo net in his hands.

The American's left arm was still shackled to the post. Only his right hand was free, and he could only do damage within a radius of about six feet. He twirled the pen in his hand and waited.

"Bloody hell," cried the skinny man, reading the bill of lading in his hand. "He signed it over to Moriarty! He endorsed it to himself!"

The skinny man and Redgil both came back to the table, and Redgil leaned in angrily toward the American, intending to grab him by the throat.

The agent thrust forward with the pen.

Redgil was the most dangerous of the three men, and the American knew he had to kill him at the outset. He was aiming to put the pen not just into Redgil's right eye, but through it. But in the American's woozy state he missed — not by much, but for his target it was the difference between life and death.

Or at least the difference between life with partial blindness as opposed to death — the thrust was still pretty damned close. Redgil screamed in pain and rage, blood streaming from just below his right eye, and his hands went to his face.

The skinny man stepped back, but not quickly enough. The American stood, grabbed the stool by one of its three legs, and swung it hard into the skinny man's jaw.

Now the American felt the slashing sting of the rope net, and not just on his already-flayed back, but on his face and arms as well. This meant the bulky man had done what the American needed him to do — stayed in close to swing the net.

Before the bulky man could recover from his forward motion in swinging the net, the American pivoted to his left, grabbed the bulky man by the hair on top of his head, and using the man's own weight slammed his head down into the table.

But now where was Redgil? He was no longer in the American's field of vision, which meant he must have circled behind, where he could attack with his knife from the protection of the post to which the American was shackled. That was a damned shame. The American knew exactly what Redgil would do now, and he tried to turn to prevent it.

But too late.

2

SCOTLAND YARD, A FEW DAYS LATER
Inspector Standifer of Special Branch was in his new office, at the newly constructed Metropolitan Police Service headquarters. It was a splendid building, five stories of red and white brick, and with his recent promotion the inspector actually had an office with a window.

But he was too worried to enjoy the surroundings. He got up from his chair and paced to that window; he looked down at the pedestrians and the clattering hansom cabs on Victoria Embankment, in the same way that someone waiting anxiously for a train looks down the tracks — but he saw nothing hopeful.

He went back and sat in his chair, just as a letter carrier from the Royal Mail arrived. The young man stood hesitating in the doorway.

"Well, what is it then?" said the inspector.

"It's another letter, sir. Addressed to — well, you know."

Standifer sighed. He had more important matters on his mind, but he accepted the letter. He looked at the address and nodded. And then he carefully paused before opening the envelope.

He had established a protocol for these. He felt obliged to follow through on it, even if no one in authority from the Royal Mail ever came around to officially check.

"This letter is addressed to 221B Baker Street," said the inspector. "Have you attempted to deliver it there?"

"I have, sir," said the letter carrier from the Royal Mail, who knew the ritual quite well. "But there is no 221B Baker Street."

"This letter is addressed to a Mr. Sherlock Holmes. Did you attempt to locate that person so that you could deliver it to him?"

"I did, sir. But I found no Sherlock Holmes to whom it could be delivered."

"Very well then," said the inspector. "Scotland Yard will accept the letter on his behalf."

They had gone through this ritual several times in the past two years, ever since the publication of a short novel called *A Study in Scarlet,* by the now-famous Arthur Conan Doyle.

At first, the inspector knew, the lads at the Royal Mail had just looked at the name of the addressee, held the letters up to a lamp, and had a good laugh. Most of the letters — a request for more details about the proper use of plaster casts for footprints, an inquiry regarding the monograph by Mr. Sherlock Holmes on tobacco types and their origins — they simply sent on to Arthur Conan Doyle himself.

But then the confessions had begun to roll in. Small crimes, mostly, but it wouldn't do to ignore them. And those letters the Royal Mail brought to the Yard.

The Inspector had never put the protocol in writing — he wanted deniability, as he wanted deniability for so many things since becoming head of Special Branch.

But he did follow it. And now he said to the Royal Mail carrier:

"Did you carefully steam the sealing wax until it was soft, then open the letter and look at it, and then carefully seal it back up so that no one would know?"

"Of course not, sir. The Royal Mail does not open people's private correspondence."

"Then did you hold it up to a lamp and try to peer through the envelope?"

"I may have done, inadvertently."

"And based on what you inadvertently

saw, you think it belongs here?"

"Yes, sir."

"Then you think it mentions a crime?" said Standifer.

"It not only mentions one; it confesses to it," said the carrier.

Now they were done with the protocol.

"Let's see it, then," said Standifer.

The Royal Mail worker willingly surrendered the letter; Standifer opened it without further ceremony and took a look:

Dear Mr. Holmes:

I want you to know, first of all, that I would never had done it if I'd had any choice in the matter. But the bookies were after me for fifty quid, and for another ten every week that I didn't pay, and those are not blokes you want to mess with, if you understand me.

And so I did it. I am very sorry for it. But it was only one mistake. Surely you won't send a young lad like me to Newgate, just for that?

Well, all right. I know I can't fool a man like you, the world's greatest detective, so I won't even try. I'll own up to it, right up front: It wasn't the first time.

But I truly believe that if only I'd had a better upbringing, I'd never have done any of it at all. I know it must seem to you like a very poor excuse, but Dad left when I was only five, and my mum was always lacking in what they call the maternal instincts. Who can blame me for turning out the way I did?

Be that as it may. I want you to know that I have reformed. I won't do any of it ever again. Here's the twenty quid that I took from the pensioner's purse on Shaftesbury Street. I hear she's recovering nicely.

Please don't send me to Newgate.

Yours Truly, An Anonymous Felon

Oh, what's the use — my name is Evan Berkshire. You'd only figure it out anyway.

But please don't send me to Newgate.

Yours Truly,
Evan Berkshire

"It's a growing city," said the inspector to the postal worker now. "One of these days I suppose they'll expand the Marylebone district a bit, and then there might very well be a two-hundred block in Baker Street. What will you do then?"

"I'll deliver the mail to where it's addressed, sir. If I ever find a Mr. Sherlock Holmes, I'll deliver it to him. If I ever find a

221B Baker Street, I'll deliver it there. But since I can find neither —"

"You deliver it here. Very well," said Standifer. "Thank you, that will be all."

But the letter carrier remained in the doorway.

"Was there something else?"

The young man produced another letter from his bag.

"I hope not, sir. But I fear it."

The inspector opened the letter and began to read.

And then he took a deep breath and sat down.

With the opened letter still in front of him, he said to the letter carrier:

"When you pass Sergeant Turner's desk on the way out, send him over, will you?"

"Certainly."

"And say nothing to anyone else at all about this one."

"Yes, sir."

The letter carrier exited. The inspector remained seated, staring at the letter, for the next two minutes, until Sergeant Turner arrived in the doorway.

"What is it, sir?" said the thirty-year-old sergeant.

"Close the door," said the inspector, and the sergeant did so.

The inspector shoved the letter across to the sergeant. The sergeant looked. The letter was handwritten, it was signed with a flourish by someone named Redgil at the bottom, and it read as follows:

Dear Mr. Sherlock Holmes:

Some say you are real. Some say you are made up.

I'll tell you straight off that I used to be with those in the second camp. But I recently learned otherwise.

However, as I'm sure you know, *The Strand Magazine* says that you are now dead. You have plunged over the Reichenbach Falls, which I'm told are a terrible sight, to your doom — along with the legendary Professor Moriarty.

If it is true, I am glad of it, if you'll pardon my saying so.

But if it is not true — and indeed I suspect it is not, because no bodies were recovered, not yours, and not Professor Moriarty's, and there were no witnesses, just your handwritten note, if indeed it was yours, wedged on a rock on the ledge — so if this is just a clever ruse on your part, and you are even at this moment lurking in London to take advantage of poor blokes like me when we come out of hiding — I want you to know of the great favor that I have done for you.

Professor Moriarty is now in fact dead. For I have killed him.

How can I prove that, you say? How do I know the man I killed was Moriarty?

Well, for one, he said he was. Just before I did him in.

And I put him in some pain before he expired. No extra charge for that.

I will not tell you my address or real name, of course, but I am known as Redgil. You can reply to me in *The Times* if you like. And all I ask of you is this — should Scotland Yard contact you regarding me and my endeavors, kindly decline. You may hear rumors. Kindly ignore them. What is fifty thousand pounds, after all, in the grand scheme of things? You have royal scandals and the fates of nations to worry about. Turn your attention to such other matters, and let the little fish like me swim through. That will be best for all concerned.

Live and let live is my motto, Mr. Holmes. If you stay out of my way, I shall stay out of yours.

Now the sergeant became as somber as

the inspector. He put the letter down.

"This man named Redgil, and this thing about fifty thousand pounds . . ." he said quietly.

"Yes," said the inspector. "That's the counterfeit operation our American operative was infiltrating."

"And what it says about 'pain before he expired' . . ."

"Yes, Turner, they tortured him, I don't doubt it at all, if that's what you're asking."

The inspector said that quite sharply, and then looked up at the young sergeant.

"Sorry," he said. "It's been a long morning."

The sergeant sat down in the chair opposite the inspector's desk. He stared at the letter, at the inspector's somber face, and then back at the letter again.

"So what's all this about a Professor Moriarty?" said Turner. And then, quickly, very softly, "I suppose . . . our man was growing delusional under the duress?"

The inspector shook his head. "Not at all. In point of fact, he and I had been considering something like this earlier."

"What do you mean?"

"Our American agent was so persuasive as a criminal recruiter that aspiring perpetrators flocked to him even more rapidly than we had hoped. We originally intended to just round a few of them up every couple of weeks or so — spaced out, you see, with time enough between each so that no one would make a connection. But there were too many, too quickly. We realized that a felon might get nicked, meet another in jail, they'd tell each other how it happened, and next thing you know, they realize that they've both been working for the same man. And once they discover that — well, these fellows aren't bright, but even they would smell something wrong. So we needed a cover — something to explain why the nastier felons kept getting caught. Someone to blame it on. Just last week we began considering the use of Sherlock Holmes for that."

"You mean you seriously considered getting criminals to blame their failed plots on a character in *The Strand*?"

"The criminal element believe him to be real. So yes — a fictional character as the scapegoat for what our agent was doing in reality. Of course, if we'd known Conan Doyle was going to kill his character off, we wouldn't have considered it. But we didn't know. And if we could make Redgil and others think their plans were being foiled not by a snitch in their midst, but by an intellect so powerful that he could foil their plots by simply reading the morning paper and deducing the details of their criminal actions — well, yes. Why not?"

Turner nodded. "All right. But I've heard of Sherlock Holmes," he said. "I haven't heard of this Moriarty character."

"You will. He just popped up in this month's issue. I'd never heard of him, either, before that. But as you can see from the letter — anyone who can be persuaded that Sherlock Holmes is real is likely to believe the Moriarty line as well."

Now the inspector pushed the Redgil letter aside in disgust. "Real enough that they'll do something like this."

"I understand that our American agent has a wife," said Turner.

"Yes."

"And that she's with child," said Turner.

"Bloody hell," said the inspector. He hadn't known.

He paused for a long moment, pondering all that.

And then, having decided on a course of action, he stood.

"Steps will need to be taken," said the inspector. "We can't have these rotters finding out about his widow, or they'll be after her, too, to see what he might have told her.

And it won't matter that he told her nothing."

"Yes, sir. But they don't know her name, do they?"

"No, they don't. And we're going to keep it that way. We're going to preserve her husband's cover."

"You mean the notion that his name is Moriarty?"

The inspector nodded, and said, "You used to work Forgery, didn't you?"

"Yes, sir. Still do."

"Did you get good at it?"

"I'm not sure what you —"

"Don't play dumb with me, Turner. When a smart cop works a particular beat, he acquires the same skills the crooks have. So I'm asking you — how are your skills?"

"Passable, sir."

"Good. You'll need to alter a few records. They're asking if the man they killed was Moriarty, and I'm going to let them think it was. In case they check, that's what the death certificate has to read. You may need to visit the passport office as well. The records have to be made consistent with his cover."

"I get you, sir."

"I'm going to reply to this letter with a posting in *The Times*. I'm going to sign it

'S.H.' I'm going to tell them that both Holmes and Moriarty survived the Reichenbach Falls, but now that these louts have indeed killed Moriarty, they'll have hell to pay when his minions learn of it. I want them on edge. I want them to believe the lie our agent told every bit as much as they believe the fiction in that magazine."

"Sir?"

"*The Strand,* Turner, *The Strand.* Pick it up. That's a good lad. There it is, 'The Final Problem.' Except for our claim that both Holmes and Moriarty survived the Falls, every trace we leave of our man must be consistent with what you see in there."

"Will do, sir."

"And Turner . . ."

"Sir?"

"Once you've finished with that . . ."

"Yes, sir?"

"We'll never speak of this again. Not to each other. Not to anyone. Ever again. Understood? I'm in trouble enough with my superiors as it is."

"Perfectly, sir."

"On your way then."

The young sergeant exited.

The inspector sighed and sat at his desk. He picked up his own copy of *The Strand,* opened it, and stared for a long moment at the story it contained.

"You were becoming a great help to us, Mr. Doyle. And now you're becoming a great bother. Our fault of course — we should have told you what we were planning. But perhaps someday you'll help us make amends."

3

A FEW DAYS LATER

Inspector Standifer had the window closed against the brisk December morning, but he was having a better day than earlier in the week.

He was beginning to worry about the Irish Problem. And the Anarchist Problem. These were improvements on worries over the grubby counterfeiting gangs he'd been dealing with, and much more likely to bring positive recognition from his superiors. He was beginning to feel that he was indeed on his way up.

And then he heard Turner's annoying knock. The young sergeant opened the door and stuck his head in.

"There's a woman to see you, sir," said Turner.

"Name?"

"She said, and I quote: 'Apparently that is a matter of some dispute.' "

That could not be good, thought the Inspector.

"Bring her in," he said.

The sergeant stepped out of the office for a brief moment; then he opened the door again and admitted a young woman. The inspector recognized her immediately.

It was the American agent's wife. His widow.

She was perhaps as old as twenty-four, a petite figure, with jet-black hair, and emerald green eyes that made you want to stare but a little afraid to do so.

And — it was apparent now — she was indeed with child.

His heart sank. It was enough that the murdered American agent was leaving a widow. It was too much that there would be a fatherless child as well.

The inspector stood up to greet the woman.

"Do you remember me, Inspector?" she said.

"Certainly, Mrs. —"

He knew her real name — her husband's real name — but she interrupted too quickly for him to speak it.

"Moriarty," she said. "Or so they think, apparently, at the coroner's office."

"Please sit down," said the inspector, pull-

56

ing out the chair for her. "I will explain about that. I had hoped," he began, then faltered. "I had hoped that you would not feel the need to — to view him until the undertaker has finished."

"View him?" she said. "Is that the term we use? Is he an exhibit now?"

"I'm very sorry."

"He is my husband, Inspector," said the woman, quite calmly. "And I can well understand that you would not want me to see how he died."

The inspector took a breath and tried to think of something comforting to say. It wasn't easy.

"The results of a train accident," he began, "are . . . are very difficult to look on. But for the victim of the accident, they are at least . . . instantaneous."

"Please," said the woman. "Do not try to tell me that the marks I saw on my husband were from a train."

The inspector wanted to just drop his head into his hands and hide. For lack of anything better, he fell back on official protocol.

"Please accept my sincere condolences. If there is anything the Yard can do —"

"Anything the Yard can do?" she said, repeating his words in an amazed tone.

He could say nothing in response.

"Well then," she continued. "I have already received the very sound advice that perhaps I should leave London and return to America just as soon as possible, and I have also received my paid ticket for doing just that. Second-class, I see," she added, taking the ticket out of her purse. "I suppose I am indeed grateful it isn't steerage."

The inspector stood, thrilled for there to be any aspect of this at all for which he could still make amends.

"I'll get that fixed straightaway," he said, with perhaps too much enthusiasm.

"Inspector Standifer, sit down!" said the woman, and it was a command.

He sat.

She stared across at the inspector for a long moment, and then she said:

"I shall not leave London — nor indeed shall I even leave your office — until you explain to me how my husband died with half the skin of his back flayed to the bone."

The woman sat back in her chair, her chin tilted up, and her eyes, just slightly damp, fixed in a direct stare on the inspector, who shifted ever so slightly in his chair.

"I . . . I am not at liberty to say."

"Then I am not at liberty to leave."

"It will not ease your pain to know this."

"Nothing will ease my pain, but I will know what happened, regardless of the inconvenience it will cause you to tell me."

The inspector might have been able to hold the line if she had not added that last part. She had shifted the topic from her own situation to his in an instant, and his situation was indefensible. He wondered if she was born with that negotiating skill or had acquired it.

He looked back at her direct stare and decided that she was born with it.

"How much," said the inspector, with a long sigh, "did your husband already tell you?"

"That he was working undercover and that he was working for you. And that he was very proud of what he was doing."

The inspector nodded.

"With reason," he said. "I will tell you what I know."

He was breaking protocol by doing so, but he knew that she would not be deterred. And perhaps by telling her, he would make her understand the danger she was in and she would become the more willing to leave London at once.

"Your husband infiltrated one of the most dangerous counterfeiting gangs in London," said the inspector. "He made them believe that through the resources he could provide to them — resources that were in fact coming from Scotland Yard, though of course he did not dare let them discover that — they would be able to expand their operations beyond their most insanely criminal fantasies, exporting their counterfeit currency and contraband goods not just to the Continent, but to the United States as well.

"He convinced them that they could exchange their counterfeit fifty thousand pounds for a cargo of premium whiskey, in the hold of the *Queen's Gambit,* which is docked at this moment at St. Katherine's, in preparation for a departure to New York City this evening. He signed a document executing the contract for that — for which they obtained a bill of lading from him — and all that remains for them to do, they believe, is for them to show up at that dock with the counterfeit money, present that bill of lading, and set sail for America with fifty thousand quid worth of whiskey — and that's wholesale value.

"But the gang became suspicious. We pushed this operation too far. They suspected your husband was not what he seemed, and that's why they — why they did what they did to him. I am so very sorry."

The lady's eyes were looking glassy now, as though she were somewhere far away, perhaps in that cargo hold herself, in place of her husband.

Then she focused.

"So they tortured him to get him to confess that he was working for Scotland Yard."

"Yes."

"But he did not confess."

"No. And in a last-ditch attempt to distract them, I believe he tried to convince them that the reason for all the failed plots was a character of fiction described in this magazine."

He showed her the copy of *The Strand*. She picked it up, glanced at it, and then put it down dismissively.

"But they didn't believe *that,* of course," she said.

"Well — in fact they did. I believe at some point he had them convinced — that all the clever criminal schemes he had devised for them were being foiled by the consulting detective known as Sherlock Holmes. That Sherlock Holmes is real, that Dr. Watson is his biographer, and that Arthur Conan Doyle is merely Watson's literary agent for getting the bloody stories published. And finally, your husband let them believe that he himself — keep in mind, he never told them his real name — was in fact the Professor Moriarty described in this latest story. He went so far as to use that name in signing the bill of lading. And it all might have worked. I believe it was working."

"Why didn't it?"

The inspector picked up the magazine, gripping it as though he could find something in it that would change what had happened, and then he just dropped it on the desk.

"These scum are extremely dangerous even when they do believe you. But it probably didn't help that this monthly issue only came out last week. I'm sure your husband was winging it and just didn't know."

"Know what?"

"That at the end of the story, both Sherlock Holmes and Moriarty are killed."

He picked up the magazine and tried to turn to the appropriate page.

"They fall into a watery chasm in a place called Reichenbach Falls. It's right here, someplace near the end —"

"Please," said the woman, placing a hand on the magazine to stop him. "You needn't show me. You're saying that this story got my husband killed?"

"No, no. It very nearly saved his life. And

in fact it made it possible for him to preserve his cover. But in the end, they . . . I'm very sorry, but they intended to kill him whether they believed him or not. We received this letter from them."

He handed her the letter that the man named Redgil had sent to Sherlock Holmes.

She took a long moment to read the letter. Then she folded it and placed it on the desk in front of her. She looked up at the inspector.

"How will justice be done to these men?" said the woman.

"Dear lady," said the inspector. "It is being done as we speak. And when it is all complete, I promise to send to you a full accounting."

"Send to me?"

"To your address in the States."

The woman took a moment to absorb that. She didn't seem as though she was going to object to the idea, and it certainly made no sense for her to stay. But clearly something was on her mind.

Now she leaned forward, looking directly at the inspector, the muscles in her face set so hard to keep herself from trembling that it seemed she would simply shatter at any moment, and without any trace of the bravado she had shown a moment before she said:

"Inspector, how are I and my child to live?"

This gave the inspector pause. Then he said:

"Surely the New York City Police Department has provisions —"

"There is a life insurance policy that my husband was able to purchase, and there is the New York City Police Department's Widows and Orphans Fund."

"Ahh," said the inspector, hoping that meant everything would be taken care of, though in his heart he knew better.

"Inspector," said the woman again, "how are we to live?"

There was a long moment of silence. The inspector had no answer.

Then there was a knock on the door.

"Not now," said the inspector. He was too much a gentleman to use the interruption as an excuse to extract himself from an uncomfortable conversation. He considered it, but didn't.

But the knock was repeated, and then the sergeant on the other side of the door, sounding quite urgent, said, "Turner here, sir."

This was different. The inspector knew what this would be about.

"Come in," said the inspector, and Turner did so.

Turner seemed a bit excited, slightly out of breath, but he stopped himself from speaking when he saw the woman sitting there.

"Sergeant Turner," said the inspector, "this is Mrs. —" The inspector stopped himself before speaking her actual name. "Mrs. Moriarty."

The sergeant's face grew somber; he nodded toward her. "I'm deeply sorry for your loss, ma'am."

"Thank you, Sergeant."

Turner looked at the inspector to see if he should continue.

"It's all right, Turner," said the inspector. "You can report. The lady asked how there will be justice; she will be interested in what you have to say, and I want her to hear it. I'm rather anxious to hear it myself."

Turner gave the inspector a doubtful look.

"Proceed, Sergeant," said the inspector.

"Very well, sir," said Turner. "We assembled at the *Queen's Gambit* before dawn, just as planned. I put Jenkins in the cargo hold, Dawson in concealment at the stern, and Wilkins behind the crate stacks near the bow. I went on board to take the captain's place. We waited for Redgil to arrive, and he did, with both his men, just past dawn as we expected."

Turner paused now for a breath, and the inspector showed just the lightest trace of a grim smile. He was going to relish this next part, and he wanted the widow to hear just how thoroughly the Yard had expedited the justice she so rightfully demanded.

"Go on," said the inspector.

"Redgil ordered his first confederate to bring two canvas bags on board. The confederate did so, opened the bags, and I ascertained that they were indeed full of packages of five-, ten-, and twenty-pound notes — enough to total close to fifty thousand pounds in all — and all of them counterfeit, though of course I didn't let on that I knew that."

Turner took a breath.

"And?" said the inspector.

"I informed Mr. Redgil, on behalf of Scotland Yard and Her Majesty's Special Branch, that he was under arrest for counterfeiting and murder. At that same moment, Wilkins likewise informed the confederate who was stationed at the bow. Unfortunately, that confederate resisted, and Wilkins was obliged to strike that confederate several times on the head with a truncheon. That confederate has since expired. At that same moment, Dawson came forward with his own truncheon from the stern to place the second confederate under arrest, who we anticipated would resist as well, but unfortunately Dawson slipped on the slick surface of the deck — he's never been on a ship before, he has told me since; I know I should have inquired about that beforehand — whereupon the second confederate pulled a six-round revolver from his inside coat pocket, and fired off two rounds, in my direction, before Jenkins came up from the cargo hold and struck that suspect several times on the head. With a truncheon. That confederate has since expired."

Turner paused and looked at the inspector, apparently expecting some specific follow-up question at this point. The inspector just looked back expectantly.

"And?" said the inspector, finally.

"Both shots at me missed, sir."

The inspector nodded impatiently as though that were a given, and said:

"And Redgil?"

Turner straightened his stance, as if on parade inspection.

"Sir, during all that, Redgil jumped overboard. I heard the splash, and we kept close surveillance on all points where he could likely surface — but we did not find him."

"Bloody hell!" The inspector leaped up and slammed his hands on the desk.

Turner stood straight as a telegraph pole. "He may have drowned, sir. It is possible."

"And I may someday become prime minister, but I don't advise that you bet your pay on it!"

Turner held his position as the inspector circled him.

Then the inspector paused, looked at the widow sitting by his desk, and, with Turner still standing there, he said to her:

"I am sorry."

The woman looked up at the inspector as if to ask what for. Then she looked at Turner, who dared do nothing but just stand ramrod still and look straight ahead at the wall.

Then she looked back at the inspector again.

"Oh," she said. "You were hoping that the sergeant would manage to kill Redgil, and in so doing make up for the loss of my husband, as if they were chess pieces on a board, and things could be evened out by the exchange of one for another. I see."

Now the inspector, deeply embarrassed that he had indeed been thinking that, turned almost as red and sweaty as Turner.

"Inspector," said the woman, overstepping her bounds with no apparent hesitation whatsoever. "Perhaps the sergeant can be excused now?"

The inspector quickly nodded and told Sergeant Turner that he was dismissed.

Turner opened the door, but before he could exit, the woman spoke again.

"Sergeant —" she said.

"Yes, ma'am?" said Turner, snapping to attention again.

"Thank you very much for your efforts," she said, with all sincerity.

"Yes, ma'am, thank you for saying so." And then he exited.

The inspector went back to his desk and sat behind it, avoiding eye contact for a moment with the widow sitting in front. Letting her hear directly of the justice being done to the man who had tortured and murdered her husband was the best card the inspector had to play, and it hadn't played nearly as well as he had hoped.

And now the woman was still in London, and also still sitting at his desk and racking him with guilt.

He tried to think of another approach.

"I think," he said after a moment, "that with this Redgil still on the loose, it is all the more reason for you to leave London as quickly as possible. He doesn't know your real name, and that's the name under which you are booked to America; so far as he knows your husband was named Moriarty, and even if he goes to the trouble of checking the official death certificate, it will confirm that; I made sure of it. Passport, death certificate, bill of lading — everything regarding your husband now shows the name Moriarty. So if you leave the city now under your real name, you can do so safely; Redgil will never be able to find you, even if he tries. But if you stay here — well, there is no telling what a criminal might try to do, or what he might somehow have learned that could lead him to you."

The inspector paused now. He wasn't at all sure the widow was even listening to him.

But now she looked up.

"Inspector," she said, "if I understand you and the sergeant correctly, my husband, under the cover name Moriarty, signed a contract to purchase the cargo on board a ship, with the alleged intent — for purposes of his cover story — of sailing with it to the United States for sale."

"Yes."

"And the bill of lading now shows that the owner of that cargo is someone named Moriarty — again, consistent with the cover story of your operation."

"Yes."

"And that cargo of whiskey is worth fifty thousand pounds."

"Yes," said the inspector. "That was the wholesale price of it." He began to worry what she might be getting at.

"Was it contraband?" she asked now. "That is, was it illegal goods that the Yard just happened to have seized earlier in some other operation and just happened to have on hand for this one?"

"No," said the inspector quickly, and now he really wondered where she was going with these questions. "Scotland Yard does not traffic in stolen goods. Not in my division. The cargo was bought and paid for by the Yard, for use in this specific operation."

"So I presume that now that the operation is over, the whiskey will need to be sold so that the funds can be restored to the coffers of whatever governmental authority administers them, but it will probably be at a loss, unless the Yard plans on going into the whiskey-retailing business, is that not so?"

"Yes," said the inspector, nodding grimly. "The Yard is not a whiskey retailer. The expense of the operation will be noted in the record. As will the fact that the main target escaped. My superiors will not regard this as a success, and I will be held accountable. But that is not my first concern at the moment, nor should it be yours."

The woman smiled and nodded, almost condescendingly. Then she said:

"What I propose, Inspector, is this: I shall take possession of that cargo as my husband's widow — as Mrs. Moriarty. You shall sign an affidavit to that effect, in case anyone of an official capacity should ever inquire. I shall sail with the cargo to New York City, as my husband's cover story said that he would do, I as his widow, with the inherited cargo, in his place. On arrival, I will sell the cargo at the best retail price I am able to get, and I will return to you — to Scotland Yard — the full wholesale purchase price that was paid. But all the profit above that I shall keep. I and my unborn child."

The inspector stared at her.

"Inspector," she continued, "by doing this, you will restore to the Yard all the funds that it has expended. Furthermore — and more importantly, I suspect — this will make it possible for you to maintain my husband's cover story even after his death, thereby diverting attention from other operatives you have in the field, who are working undercover in similar activities. You do have others in operation, I presume?"

"Yes," said the inspector. "But I was going to pull them all out. I was going to shut them all down. And given what happened to your husband —"

"That is your choice, of course. Given the price my husband already paid, I thought perhaps you might want to see what could be salvaged of your operations. That you might want to have the gullible criminal element in London continue to believe that there is a consulting detective named Sherlock Holmes who is thwarting the best-laid plans of even a criminal genius such as my husband — the late Moriarty. And if you're concerned about the outcome described in that magazine — what was the story called? 'The Final Problem,' was it? Well, I would just point out that when someone in fiction plunges into a waterfall, however fearsome, and their body is never recovered, fictionally or otherwise — well, anything is possible in the future, is it not? Perhaps if you were to make a polite request of the author —"

The inspector stood. He was trying desperately to think of a solid objection to her plan.

"My dear woman," he blurted in desperation, "do you actually know anything about whiskey?"

"I know that my husband began drinking something called Macallans's since he arrived here and he liked it. I myself neither drink, nor smoke, nor gamble at cards or horses. I do not participate in any of the recreational pursuits that men engage in, except for one that I do enjoy, and that one was and is reserved for my husband. But I am good at numbers, Inspector, and you can rely on me to make good use of that cargo."

"Mrs. . . . Mrs. Moriarty," said the inspector, pleadingly, "if you do indeed take on that name, I shall not be able to protect you from whatever Redgil does in the future."

The widow stood.

"I shall be in New York City, Inspector. Do you know anything of the Irish in New York City?"

"A little. I know what your husband told me. It was partly on that experience that we hired him."

The widow smiled.

"I am Irish myself," she said. "New York City Irish, as are all my family there, of course. And if Mr. Redgil should wish to come to Hell's Kitchen to reclaim his cargo, he is very much welcome to try."

The widow moved toward the door now — but then she stopped and turned very deliberately back to the inspector.

"The letter that this Mr. Redgil wrote to you — may I have it please?"

"Really, no. I'm afraid not. We must keep it for our records."

The widow Moriarty nodded. "As you wish," she said. "I was just thinking that perhaps someday it might be returned to him. But please be so good as to sign this additional document and add it into the place where you keep your official records."

She handed the inspector a one-page, typewritten document. He read through it quickly, and then looked up at her.

"I don't understand," he said. "You are deliberately keeping the name Moriarty so that you can depart with the cargo. So why do you also want a document stating that your husband was not Moriarty and was in fact working for Scotland Yard?"

"Because I don't want our child or the future children of our child growing up without knowing who their father really was."

"You can tell them that yourself."

"I do intend to. But the future is uncertain. I want it documented here at Scotland Yard — so that the Yard will remember the price that was paid in pursuit of this fiend named Redgil, and so that if anyone should ever ask in the future, the proof will exist."

The inspector didn't want to sign such a thing, and he tried to think of a way to dissuade her.

"Aren't you worried," he said, "what might happen if the document should ever fall into the wrong hands — if Redgil should ever learn of your identity . . . and find you?"

"I trust you completely not to let it fall into the wrong hands," said the woman. And then, quietly, she added: "And perhaps it is Mr. Redgil who should worry if our paths should ever cross."

The inspector sighed. "Well, let's try not to let that happen," he said. He scrawled his signature on the document, and he called the sergeant back to the office.

"Turner will take care of it," said the inspector, and he handed the signed piece of paper to the sergeant.

"Thank you, Inspector," said the woman. "Good day. I don't suppose we shall meet again."

And then she exited the office.

Turner was about to exit the office as well, with the documents in hand, but the inspector stopped him.

"Where are you going with that?"

"To the archives for filing," said the sergeant.

"Not bloody likely," said the inspector. "Didn't I say that I want no record of this?"

"Yes, sir."

"Well, then?"

The sergeant thought about it, but he didn't know what to say. He was merely following procedure — and what the woman had requested.

"Make sure first that the widow has left the premises," said the inspector. "Then take that document out back and toss it in the incinerator. The letter, too."

"As you wish," said the sergeant. He tried not to let his expression show what he thought of the matter. He exited the office.

The inspector breathed a sigh of relief and sat back behind his desk. This had not gone well. But at least it was over.

Outside the closed door of the inspector's office, Sergeant Turner paused for a moment and considered whether he should knock and openly revisit the issue with the inspector.

There was a protocol about such things. The letter should go in the filing cabinet that the Yard had already set up for such correspondence. And the signed document should go in the records department, to be saved for the archives or until hell froze over, whichever came first.

Somehow, it just didn't seem quite right to burn either of them.

The sergeant walked out into the corridor. He paused and stretched a kink out of his neck, as if that might make the issue go away. But it didn't.

And then, instead of walking down the stairs to the incinerator — he went up the stairs to the archives.

4

LONDON, 1944

The American army captain on Marylebone High Street walked in full uniform, and with a limp that was so obvious that he no longer tried to conceal it.

In October of 1944, this hitch in his gait told the locals all they needed to know about him, and he was greeted with smiles and "g'morning, guv" by everyone he passed.

It had not been quite so when he first arrived in England several months earlier. After four years of holding off the Nazis on their own, after enduring the bombs and the deprivation, and the deaths of civilians and soldiers alike, there were some who viewed the Americans as arriving a bit too late to the party.

But not so now, not after the invasion had begun at Normandy. Everyone knew the price that was being paid, and everyone knew where the American army captain had been to sustain his wound.

And he was older than most, close to fifty, even allowing for the aging from war — which meant he had not been drafted, he had volunteered, and clearly some of the Londoners he met on the street understood that.

He had never before been to this city himself. But he knew his parents had spent some time here, before he was born. And today — the last day before he would be sent home with his wound — he had an errand on their behalf.

He entered the lobby of the Marylebone Grand Hotel and a young woman at the reception desk greeted him.

Just as he started to tell her his name, an air-raid siren went off. He stopped speaking, and they both just froze in place for a moment, as the siren went through one repetition, and then another. They looked at each other. He was too battle hardened to run at the mere sound of an alarm. And, he realized, so was she.

She made no move to head for a shelter, and so he didn't, either.

The siren stopped. They both listened for a moment, for the guttural, chugging sounds of a V-2 engine overhead.

They didn't hear one.

The young woman breathed a sigh of relief, and then smiled.

"I'm sorry, Captain, I didn't catch that. What did you say your name is?"

"My name is Moriarty."

"Yes, thank you. I'm very sorry for the interruption. I don't like these buzz bombs one bit, do you?"

"No."

"I hope you don't get them in America. Now let me see if we have who you're looking for: Redbull, Redfern, Redgrave — oops, backing up, it would be before that, wouldn't it — Redgil, Redgil. Ah, here we are; it — No, sorry, false alarm, that one's Redfil. So, so — let me see. . . ."

Now she looked up apologetically.

"I'm very sorry. There doesn't seem to be a Redgil here."

"I see."

"You're sure you have the name right?"

"Yes."

"Well, I'm very sorry that we don't have one. Is it possible that he's a guest at another hotel in the area?"

"Possible. I just assumed he'd be at this one because he owns it."

"Oh? Oh dear no, I'm afraid you're mistaken. The owner of the hotel is not named

Redgil. His name is Redfern. He's the original founder, you know."

"Yes, I know. An elderly gentleman, isn't he? Birthmark on his right cheek?"

"Well, yes, that does rather describe him. Late seventies, I would say, but quite spry. Still likes to get out in the afternoon for a pint, whether the Jerries are dropping things on us or no. May I ask why you need to see him?"

"I promised my mother years ago that I would pay her regards to him — if our paths should ever cross."

"Close friends, are they?"

"Not exactly."

"Perhaps you should check with her regarding the name?"

"She passed some years ago. But it doesn't surprise me that the name might have changed. Where does Mr. Redfern take his afternoon pints?"

"It's the pub just two doors down. In fact, if you're lucky, you might find him there now."

The American captain thanked the young woman, stepped back into the street, and began walking toward the pub.

It was the only one visible on the street. There had been two more before the war began, in the next block — but most of that block was rubble now.

As matter-of-fact as the Londoners tried to be about it, he could still see it occasionally in their eyes — a brief shadow would be cast over the street, a cloud would pass under the sun, a flock of birds would startle up from a tree, and the Londoner would not turn to look, would refuse to do, would not give in to that instinct. Bloody hell, you couldn't hear the rockets until it was too late anyway, and if by some miracle you looked up and saw the fleeting blur, the disturbance in the air, it would mean that you were already dead. Or you weren't. There was nothing you could do about it either way.

Still, occasionally, on some subtle movement or sound, or even an imagined one, the eyes would look up.

The captain reached the pub and went inside.

Two gentlemen, perhaps as much as sixty years of age, were standing at the bar with their pints. A married couple of about that same age were in a booth with fish-and-chips. None of these were old enough to be the man he was looking for.

A middle-aged woman behind the bar came over as soon as the captain approached.

"What'll it be, luv?"

"Just a pint of ale," he said, out of courtesy. "I'm looking for someone. The gentleman who owns the hotel down the street?"

"He's upstairs," said the woman. "At the snooker table."

The captain took his pint of pale beer and ascended one flight of wooden stairs to the billiard room above.

It was a loft structure, with two walls, and a wooden railing that overlooked the bar below.

At the front of the room, nearest the stairs, was a snooker table, with a rack of wooden cues on the wall and a small black chalkboard for writing scores. There was no game in progress, and two small children, a girl of about five and a boy of about nine, played with the piece of hanging white chalk, drawing designs on each other's hands.

Farther back in the room, in the shadows beyond the well-lit snooker table, two men stood in one corner, one of them taking aim at a dartboard.

The captain stepped carefully around the two children and moved toward the back of the room.

He stopped at a respectful distance from the dart throwers. The man not currently throwing a dart acknowledged the captain's presence with a nod that indicated the captain would be invited to the next game, if he chose to participate.

The captain stood by and waited his turn.

One of the two men, the one who had just nodded, was in British uniform; he was in his late thirties, perhaps forty. The other, the man currently throwing the darts, was some thirty years older.

A father and son was the captain's guess. Probably it was the grandchildren who were playing with the chalkboard.

The captain had two children of his own, just now grown to adulthood, and a young grandchild as well.

He hadn't seen any of them in almost two years. Perhaps that was why, as he was looking at these young children now, they reminded him of his own.

And at this moment, the American captain hoped that the man throwing darts was not in fact the person he had come looking for. Perhaps the woman at the hotel had been mistaken about the hotel owner's destination. Or perhaps that man had come here and then gone and this was someone else entirely.

It wasn't as though the captain could not do what might need to be done. After Normandy, he knew that he was capable of doing anything that was necessary.

But he had had enough of death and dying.

What he was thinking of doing now was to just walk back down the stairs, catch a bus to Victoria Embankment, and talk to someone again at Scotland Yard. That would suffice. He could leave it with them. And then he would just go back home to New York and resume his life. It might be just that simple.

But first he had to be sure. He couldn't just stride into Scotland Yard, tell them a tale his mother had told him, and expect to be believed. He had tried that once already, immediately after getting out of the hospital, and the officials he talked with had not been of much help. There was a war on, after all. They were not much interested in a crime that he claimed his mother said had been committed against an American in London some fifty years ago.

The officer at Scotland Yard had said that they had more pressing concerns.

And at this moment, the American captain was inclined to agree. He drank the remainder of his beer in one long draught and set the empty glass down on the table, and was about to leave.

"Your turn, mate."

The older man was pulling the darts out of the board, his back to the American.

"Thanks," said the American. "But I need to be on my way."

"We'd love it if you'd stay for a game, Yank," said the younger of the two dart players.

This was a friendly invitation between peers, one Allied officer to another, and the only reason the Englishman addressed him as "Yank" instead of "Captain" was because they were in a pub and the formal titles were dropped in favor of being sociable. There was an etiquette to be observed, a basic courtesy, and the American had no excuse that was good enough for him to decline.

"Sure," he said.

The English officer gave his handful of darts to the American.

"But watch out my dad doesn't cheat you," he said. He winked when he said that, and then he went to check on his two children at the chalkboard.

The American stepped up to the throwing line, holding the three darts in his hand. He had played the game once or twice before, on his first arrival in London. He was pretty sure he had a grasp on the rules.

He waited for the older man to finish collecting his darts from the board.

The older man turned — and now, for the first time, the American saw the right side of his face. In the light from the lamps above the dartboard, he could see it clearly — a birthmark, a slashing reddish line, just above the man's jaw.

The American froze. And stared.

The older man caught that stare, and returned it with an inquiring glance. The American looked away, and the older man came back to the throwing line.

"And what is your name, Captain?" said the older man. And then, with the American not responding immediately, he pointed toward the board and said, "Your turn now, you see."

This was a challenge.

"Moriarty," said the American. "My name is James Moriarty. After my father."

With that, the American threw his three darts in rapid succession, each perfectly on target.

He went to collect his darts from the board. When he had done so, he turned, and saw that the older man was staring at him — staring at his face in the light of the dart lamp, just as the American had stared at the older man's birthmark a few moments before.

The American came back behind the

throwing line, and the older man, finally averting his gaze, stepped up. He got ready to throw, though to the American the older man seemed to still be trying to look at him out of the corner of his eye.

As the older man prepared to toss his first dart, the American said, "And what is your name, then?"

The older man tossed his dart, just as the American answered his own question.

"Redgil, isn't it?"

The dart went wide. The older man, with the two remaining darts clenched in his fist as if they were ice picks, turned to face the American.

And then, suddenly — so suddenly that only the survivors would ever be aware of it — there was a disturbance in the air.

The V-2 flying bomb struck in the street, directly in front of the pub.

At the Marylebone Grand Hotel — the nearest occupied structure, other than the pub itself — the walls shook, mirrors broke, and plaster fell, but within moments all half-dozen occupants and staff had found one another in the lobby and determined that no one in their building required immediate medical attention.

Once they knew that, every one of them,

staff and guests, went out into the street and down to the site of impact to see how they could help.

Bonnie, the young desk clerk, ran toward the location of the blast.

Remnants were everywhere in the street. Bonnie nearly tripped over the pub's wooden logo sign. If it had been any more of a direct hit, there would have been nothing left at all of the pub or anyone in it. And as it was, there wasn't much.

The entire front façade and wall were gone, as well as the side of the building facing south.

All the tables and booths from the first floor were a shambles, but the bar was still standing.

Sharp fragments — from a wall mirror, from lamps, from a slate chalkboard — were everywhere.

Bonnie stood in place for a moment in front of the devastation, her ears still recovering from the sound of the blast, and tried to determine in which direction to move to help.

The barmaid, dazed but apparently uninjured, was being helped out from behind the bar by the two older gentlemen who had been drinking their pints there a moment earlier.

Johnnie, the bellhop from the hotel, just a few months short of being seventeen and not yet old enough to be in the service, was already moving toward the flattened bar booths to assist the injured middle-aged couple who were stirring there.

Bonnie knew the street and its occupants very well, and she tried to think of who else was likely to have been in the pub. She knew of at least four people — no, five, if you included the American who said he was going there — who should have been inside.

Mr. Redfern, the hotel owner. His son. And, dear God, the two young children.

If they weren't below in a booth and they weren't at the bar, then she knew they all would have been in the loft, where the hotel owner played darts.

Above and to her right, all but one of the supporting structures for the billiard loft had been blown away. The wooden frame of the floor leaned precariously downward, touching the ground floor in front of the bar.

The snooker table, a traditional full-size model, twelve feet long, six wide, and weighing a ton, was at a forty-five-degree angle — one corner perched on the portion of the loft floor that had survived, and the diagonal corner resting on the ground below, where it had fallen with enough violence to break off the two supporting legs in front.

Bonnie began to move through the debris in that direction.

She saw blood on the shards at her feet.

Then she heard a child crying.

And she saw movement.

They had been concealed by the fallen loft floorboards at first, and by the still-teetering snooker table, but now she saw them — three human figures.

The hotel owner — and his two grand-children.

Bonnie stepped forward to help.

Mr. Redfern appeared to have already shaken off most of the dust and debris. He ushered the smaller of the two children — the one who had been crying, the five-year-old girl, who was crying still — toward Bonnie.

Bonnie took the girl in her arms, and then briefly paused. At her feet, just a couple of yards away, were two bodies. One had very clearly been struck by the falling table, the other perhaps by something else, but there was no question that those two adult males were dead.

Bonnie covered the little girl's eyes as she carried her away from the scene.

Bonnie knew the man killed by the fallen

snooker table was the girl's father; the other man was bloodied with severe head trauma, but Bonnie knew from his uniform that he was the American captain.

Now Mr. Redfern walked out with the nine-year-old boy. The boy was still covered in chalk dust and splinters of wood and plaster, but apparently without major injury. Unlike his younger sister, he wasn't crying. He just stared, in shock, as his grandfather led him out of the rubble.

"He saved me," said the girl, through sobs, and struggling in Bonnie's arms. "He pulled me away from it."

"I know, darling," said Bonnie, assuming the girl was referring to her father. "I know." Bonnie cradled the girl's face and tried to keep her from looking back.

5

CANVEY ISLAND, THAMES ESTUARY — PRESENT DAY, 1998

Lawrence Cheeverton had been running his little boat in the broad estuary of the Thames for more than twenty-five years, and he had fished out many things, but never anything like the catch he'd pulled in one night last autumn from the river proper.

He'd been on his way back home from the farmers' market at Blackheath, where he sold the eels and sole and sea bass that he had hauled in that morning.

It was night on his way back, because after selling his catch he'd spent several hours, and all of the day's profit, in the pub at Blackheath before heading home.

This was an indulgence he'd been allowing himself more frequently, and especially on that one night in autumn, because it was just one week before his sixtieth birthday.

It had begun to occur to him that time

might be running short.

He no longer felt young. Physically, he felt that he might still be able to run the boat, and throw the nets and haul them in, for another twenty years or so. That is, barring injury, of course.

But in other respects, it had begun to occur to him that time might be running out. And it was the very experience of drinking at the pub that was telling him that.

For the first three or four pints on these evenings when he tarried, there would be good company — other fishermen like himself, and a couple of locals from the market, all tossing darts, or standing at the bar and telling the most entertaining lies they could.

But then the crowd would thin out. One after the other, his drinking companions would announce their last round, because they had to get on home, even though it wasn't even last call yet. "Why leave so early?" Cheeverton would complain, and he had wondered why he was always the last one standing.

Then he had realized what the difference was — the others all had someone at home to go to.

Not anyone scenic necessarily, mind you — he had seen some of their wives in the pub. But that wasn't the point. The point was, there was someone.

He had been married once himself, some thirty years ago. He had been young then, at an age when working twelve hours a day on the water made him appear strong and vigorous, rather than old and worn, and at an age when his talk of someday owning a small fleet of boats of his own almost sounded plausible.

So plausible, in fact, that he had once been able to impress a lovely young woman in her early twenties, who had also grown up on the island and could be impressed by such things, and who had not yet thought of what better prospects she might have if she took her youth and beauty to the city.

When he actually managed to marry that girl, everyone in the town had recognized what a catch she was for someone like him. There were many hearty congratulations on his good fortune, and more than a few remarks on the side regarding how long it was likely to last.

For three years, things had in fact gone all right — until one particularly unproductive season, and a series of foolish financial decisions on his part, made her realize that his talk of his own little fleet would never be achieved, that at best he might someday be able to buy an old secondhand boat and eke out his living on it (which indeed was what had come to pass), and that she would never be more than a poor fisherman's wife if she stayed.

He had almost been able to see those thoughts go through her mind at the time; they registered in her eyes in the morning; they slipped out at times when both he and his wife had a few pints in the pub.

And then one cold afternoon he had trudged up from the dock, smelling of fish and bait, his knuckles scraped raw, his fingers with a new set of slivery cuts, his palms roughened with another layer of calluses — and he found she was gone.

After a couple of trips in vain to London to persuade her, he realized that there was no bringing her back.

He was himself still young then. He had that going for him anyway, for a time. Blond and tanned, as lean and muscular as a shark, he was still a popular figure in the pubs about town; he could do a passable imitation of one particular Australian movie star when occasion required.

But the next lovely lass did not come along right away, not that year, nor the year after. And Cheeverton gradually discovered that while at first the problem was that the local girls did not sufficiently impress him, eventually the problem had become that he did not sufficiently impress them, either.

And then thirty years slid by, to that evening last autumn. Blond and tanned had long since become gray and leathered, and gravity and pints had done what they do. Even so, he was playing darts with a rowdy crowd in Blackheath and everything was fine for a while; he was managing to forget that his sixtieth was approaching with no hint of planned celebration.

But then the evening wore on, and the crowd thinned. So he took a seat at the bar and stared up at the big-screen telly, where a soccer match was over and the late-night news had come on.

The anchor toff on the screen was reporting that there had been some sort of a row over at the Tower Bridge. A Black Cab had driven past the barricades and warning lights, just as the two separate bridge spans were rising to let a high-masted yacht pass beneath — and the cab had actually managed to get stuck between the two spans as they parted. The bridge spans won that contest, and the vehicle got torn in two.

There were two people in the cab at the time — one passenger, and the driver.

The passenger in the cab was Laura

Rankin, a London actress in her early thirties, whom Cheeverton thought he might have heard of once or twice before, even aside from the unusual event of the cab getting stuck on the spans of the bridge.

That actress had managed to escape the cab just in time, and was in the hospital.

But the twenty-five-year-old female cab-driver — who, according to the telly, was suspected of actually abducting the actress and doing some other bad things as well — was less fortunate. She had plunged into the Thames.

"That's why I never go into the city," said the barmaid, a well-rounded woman of about fifty.

Cheeverton, lost in his thoughts, just stared at the telly and nodded.

"Perk up, mate," she said. "It's last call."

"Then what?" he said.

"Then go home to your wife, like everyone else." She said that without thinking, and then she caught herself — she did not know Cheeverton; he had only been in occasionally on her shift; but she was usually more perceptive. He wasn't wearing a ring. And there were other signs; he had that look about him. It wasn't good practice to remind paying customers why they were still hanging about and spending their money in the pub at closing.

"Home is home, anyway," she offered. "I know lots of gents would prefer to just have the peace and quiet."

Marlowe, the only remaining gent in the pub other than Cheeverton, came up to the bar now to get his last pint. He looked up at the telly screen, which was showing a taxi company pic of the woman who had been driving the Tower Bridge cab.

"A shame," said Marlowe. "That's a lovely bird right there. Too bad she's fish food now."

"She's wanted by the police," said the barmaid. "She killed a man, they say. Maybe two."

Cheeverton looked up at the telly now, at the shape of the woman, and it reminded him — in a general sort of way — of the shape of the young woman who had married and abandoned him thirty years ago.

That was the past, of course. He knew such shapes would not come his way again.

"Still a shame," he said, out loud.

As the two men stood waiting for their beers, Marlowe put an advert card — peeled from the inside of a phone box in London — on the counter in front of Cheeverton. In glossy pink, yellow, and purple, it showed a very buxom bare-breasted young woman, advertising her services. There were some specifics.

"Last time I was in London," said Marlowe, "I rang this one."

Cheeverton looked down at the card. He'd seen such adverts many times before of course; nearly every phone box in London was plastered with them. He had rung some of those numbers and tried some of those services, not infrequently, at an earlier time. But those ladies were expensive. And patronizing them did not seem to recapture what he felt had been lost.

"What's she mean by that bit there — 'genuine GFE'?"

"Genuine girlfriend experience," said Marlowe.

"But just exactly what does she do? It says she wants twice as much when that's included," said Cheeverton.

The barmaid had extricated herself from the conversation, so the barman came over and put the last pints down in front of them.

"It means she fixes your breakfast in the morning, don't it?" said the barman.

"No, it doesn't," said Marlowe. "It just means she'll smile when you take her to dinner and she'll try to make everyone who sees you believe she's for real — that she's with you voluntarily."

"You mean you have to take her to dinner?" said Cheeverton.

"Not likely anyone will believe it anyway, with you lot," said the bar lady, passing by.

"Even with GFE, you still fix the breakfast yourself, and she'll just eat some of it if she wants," said Marlowe.

"In my book, that's not much of a girlfriend experience then," said the barman, in what sounded like bragging, and then he went to put up the chairs from the tables.

Cheeverton finished his pint and departed the pub. He wasn't at all sure that he felt any cheerier now than when he had first arrived.

He walked to the dock, where he had tied up his boat. He got on board, cast off, started the engine, and puttered off into the fog.

And a short while later, he began to feel better. He was on his boat, he was on the river, back in his element and standard routine, and that helped a bit.

The tide was on its way out; with the current in his favor, he was making good time. Within a few minutes he was past the Thames tide barrier. There was no wind, and no other river traffic that he could see. The motor on the little boat chugged in a regular rhythm, and the water parted in front of the bow in a regular pattern.

The self-pity induced by too many beers was beginning to ease. He reminded himself that the sunlight on the estuary in the morning would always be there. And there was still hope that he might someday get a new boat.

And a pint was still a pint.

And then, chugging along ten miles below the Tower Bridge, he saw it.

Saw her.

Moonlight on white skin in the dark gray water.

It caught his eye and made him sputter the little boat closer.

And now he could see her clearly, though it was such an unusual sight that he did not believe it at first.

It was a woman. Her body was completely nude, floating vertically in the water, her black hair spread outward and upward, as though reaching for the surface.

Cheeverton immediately shut off the motor and turned the rudder to bring the boat around.

He reached over the gunwale and grabbed the woman under her shoulders. It was not an easy angle for lifting; she was light, relatively speaking, but the water was heavy. Still, he managed to lift her enough to get her into the net. He cranked the net to pull her out of the water and onto the boat, and then he got both arms under her and lifted her out of the net.

He was certain that she must be already drowned. Almost certain.

He laid her out flat on the long wooden board that was used for preparing bait.

He'd been on or near the water all his life, and he'd seen CPR done more than once. He'd never done it before himself, but he knew how, and he did it now.

And it worked.

Her eyes opened — emerald green, glinting like scales on a live fish in the water — with an expression that Cheeverton would have described as astonishment. She immediately tried to inhale, on reflex, and then her upper body bent forward in spasmodic, painful jerks as she expelled river water from her lungs.

He did his best to help, as she alternately threw up water and drew in air. And then, when the spasms subsided, he picked her up again, his arms under her bare thighs, her breasts within inches of his leathered face in the cold night air, and he carried her below.

She had not spoken, hadn't even tried. Neither had he. He could see her eyes dart-ing back and forth in wild surprise, as though trying to understand where she was. He laid her down on the bunk.

She looked to be in her mid-twenties. She had a perfect shape. Just for a fleeting instant, Cheeverton recalled an image of what life was like thirty years ago.

He got a gray woolen blanket and threw it over her; she would freeze otherwise.

"You are on my boat," he said, as he tucked it in around her. "You are safe now."

She still said nothing, but she stared back at him, her eyes focusing, and her breathing began to even out.

And then — because it was almost automatic, because he knew without having to think about it that it was the proper thing to do — he went to his band radio to call the Thames emergency patrol.

It shouldn't take them long to get there; he'd been seeing patrols up and down the river during the day, because of that thing on the Tower Bridge.

But then he stopped. He had turned the radio on; he had tuned the dial past the static — but he didn't place the call.

He remembered the face he had seen on the telly back at the pub — the lovely female cabdriver who had plunged into the Thames.

And he was pretty sure he knew who he had.

He put the shortwave radio mike down and returned to the interior cabin where he had placed her on the cot. He looked in. She was breathing more calmly now. She was awake, and no longer in obvious distress. She propped herself up slightly on her elbows, and she stared back.

To Cheeverton, those green eyes seemed to be looking at him in a way that no woman had looked back at him in a very long time.

Or perhaps ever.

He decided not to call the Thames patrol just yet.

Instead, he started the boat's engine and began motoring as quickly as he could through the night, heading for his home on Canvey Island.

He made Earl Grey tea in the galley and took it below to his catch, and was glad to see that although she still seemed unwilling or unable to speak, she quite willingly drank the tea.

He went back topside. They were almost home. He knew this, even in the dark, because they were passing the town of Croydon — which, unlike Canvey Island, still had an active oil and gas refinery; the gas vents were alive with fire, glowing bright orange as he cruised past.

He stayed on the south side of the river long enough to dodge the oil tankers heading out from Croydon; then he turned the rudder and motored at a sharp angle to the north side, to Canary Creek.

He reached Smallgains Marina well before dawn. That was good. He was glad to be there before anyone else was getting ready to shove out that morning.

He dropped anchor and tied the boat up.

Then he wrapped the woman more securely in the gray blanket; he pulled a wool cap down over her head, almost completely obscuring her face. He told her and himself that it was to keep the cold out, which was true, but it wasn't the only reason.

Then he picked her up and half-walked, half-carried her nearly a mile to his little wood-frame house, near the industrial section of Canvey Island Harbor.

His arms were aching as he carried her inside. He set her down in the only cushioned chair, the one he used himself for watching the telly.

She was fully conscious now, and out of danger, and as he settled her in he talked to her — much as he had begun to talk to himself in recent years when at home — describing his actions as he did them.

"There," he said. "This will keep you warm. And now I'll fry us up some nice bacon; you'd like that, wouldn't you? And we'll have stewed tomatoes, and beans, and toast. And orange juice, if there is any. Ahh. Yes. There is."

She didn't say anything in response. But he proceeded to do just as he had said, cooking up a large breakfast and putting it before her on a little folding table, all the while prattling on about who he was, and how he had come to live there all his life, and a little but not very much about his ex-wife.

She appeared to be listening, or at least paying attention — her green eyes followed his every move.

She did not speak a word. But when he put the breakfast in front of her, she dug into it ravenously.

As she did, he went into the bedroom. That was more or less instinctive, but once in there he realized it was because he had to figure something out.

There was only one bedroom. And there was only one bed in it. It was a full-size bed, not a queen, not even a double; it was only as much of a bed as had made sense for him, living alone.

He suddenly realized that he dared not

put her in it. He wasn't sure why, given that this should only be for a few hours or so. But even so, his chest tightened, as though he had created a great dilemma for himself.

And then he thought of the small folding cot, the spare one for the boat, that he kept in the storage room next to the kitchen. He went there — her eyes following him again, as she looked up from the stewed tomatoes and beans — and he found the cot, mercifully.

He pushed the telly into the corner and managed to make just enough room to put the narrow cot against the wall.

And then, a short time later, he set her down on it.

She was asleep almost instantly.

Cheeverton went back into the kitchen, ate what remained of the bacon and toast for himself, and tried to think things through.

Once more he thought about calling the Thames patrol. Again he decided not to. If he called now, he would have to explain why he hadn't just called right away when he found her earlier. He supposed he could claim that his radio was out of order. Still, it would get complicated.

He was now harboring a wanted woman. A fugitive. He was almost sure of it.

But perhaps she hadn't really done any of the things she was wanted for. From just looking at her, it was quite difficult to imagine that she had done them.

Cheeverton didn't ring the Thames patrol. Perhaps he would do so later. Not now. He would sleep on it. There was no harm waiting until morning, and so he did.

And the next morning, when she woke, she began to speak. This was good, thought Cheeverton — perhaps it would help him decide what to do.

But all she did was ask questions:

"Where am I?" she said. "Who are you? How did I get here?"

Those questions seemed natural enough, at first. But when he told her that he had fished her out of the river and then she asked, "How did I get in the river?" — well, then he began to wonder a bit. She should remember how she got in the river.

"Don't you know?" he said.

But she had not answered; she just stopped talking and lay back and closed her eyes.

As she lay there, Cheeverton studied her calm face and he wondered if perhaps she was not the person from the news reports at all. Or even if it was her, perhaps the telly reports might have gotten it all wrong.

Perhaps she was not the criminal that they all said.

Perhaps she was just misunderstood.

Later that morning, Cheeverton went out and got a newspaper, brought it back, and then he fixed another breakfast for her.

While she ravenously devoured the toast and bacon and tea that he brought her, Cheeverton opened up his morning copy of *The Daily Sun.*

And then he quickly shut it. He stared across at her, just to be absolutely sure, and then he opened the paper again, but this time more carefully, below the table, out of her line of sight.

It was all right there in the paper. Her name, her color photo, and everything. More than Cheeverton really wanted to know. This was her.

Her name was Darla Rennie. She was twenty-five years old, according to the tabloid. It had dubbed her a schizophrenic savant, because although she clearly had some difficulty distinguishing personal fantasy from reality, she was also a sort of genius at learning things. But she had gone off her meds, believing and proclaiming herself to be the great-great-granddaughter, on her mother's side, of someone named Moriarty — yes, the paper said, that Moriarty, the Professor Moriarty from the Sherlock Holmes stories. And while under that delusion, she had become obsessed with a barrister, one Reggie Heath, who currently occupied the location at Baker Street where 221B would be, if it truly existed, and whom she believed to be Sherlock Holmes and therefore responsible for the death of her ancestor Professor Moriarty at the Reichenbach Falls, and as a result of that obsession she had murdered one of Reggie Heath's clients and had made an apparent attempt to abduct Laura Rankin — ending, as everyone now knew, in Darla Rennie herself plunging from the Tower Bridge into the Thames.

"What is in the paper?" said Darla Rennie, wiping her mouth and looking up at Cheeverton.

"Nothing," lied Cheeverton. He tried to glance down and look at the paper he was holding beneath the table, because there were more details there — something about how the client was murdered, and other things, which Cheeverton felt in his gut he probably should read.

"Are you sure?" she said.

"Yes," said Cheeverton, without finishing the article. He quickly closed the tabloid, and tossed it out of reach onto the kitchen counter. "How are you feeling this morning?"

"Better," she said. "I was so hungry. May I have coffee?"

He brought her coffee. And now she began talking eagerly, in a torrent. But still none of it was about her. It was all questions — first about Cheeverton, and then about the village nearby, and then about pretty much everything else in the world, seemingly at random. He had never known anyone who asked so many questions, and he had never answered so many in his life. She might as well have been a mermaid, for all she seemed to know of the world.

And suddenly Cheeverton understood, so clearly — from the things that she asked and the things that she could not respond to when he asked questions back — that she simply did not know who she was.

Within a few days she seemed to be completely recovered physically, and quite aware mentally — very bright in fact — even if she didn't know her own identity.

It had become a problem now to know what to do. The police were looking for her. Everyone in the Thames basin, it seemed, was talking about her.

Cheeverton did not think it would do to take her to the pub with him. Even if she was not specifically recognized, for her to be seen with him would cause the entire town to talk. He would have to explain her presence — and he had no explanation to offer for this woman half his age. At least none that the town would accept without it becoming a focus of public attention.

So he told no one.

A full week went by. Remarkably, she gave no indication that she wanted to leave. She seemed perfectly content to go out with him onto the river in his little boat every day. It was almost his normal routine. They would rise well before dawn — earlier than the other Thames fishermen, because Cheeverton did not want to encounter anyone on their way to the dock. She would help him cast off and mind the engine, and perform other basic tasks, although she showed no interest in the fishing itself. She would just sit near the bow and watch, like a small terrier that he had once years ago.

In the full morning, with other boats on the river, Cheeverton would keep an eye out for any that came too close. Once, Thaddeus Sizemore's boat had appeared out of a fog bank, just fifty yards or so off to starboard, and then had suddenly turned and come in Cheeverton's direction.

"I think you'd best go below now," he'd

said then to the woman, and she had done so quickly, and without another word.

Sizemore had brought his boat up alongside and asked Cheeverton how productive his morning had been. Sizemore had never done that before; he was older and even more taciturn than Cheeverton, and unlike most of the small net trawlers, he rarely volunteered anything about his own catch, or inquired about anyone else's. But on this day he had come over full of curiosity, to the point that Cheeverton finally just started the motor on his own boat and moved on.

That evening, in the pub, Sizemore stood at the bar and kept looking sidelong in Cheeverton's direction. Had Sizemore seen her? Cheeverton couldn't be sure, but he was taking no chances, and he left the pub after his first pint.

Months had flowed by in that manner. Cheeverton had pulled her from the Thames in early autumn, and now it was solid winter.

Had she warmed to him? He couldn't tell. She had not indicated any desire to venture from her little cot into his bedroom, though he himself lay awake agonizing about that fantasy nightly. But neither had she shown any restlessness or a desire to leave.

Until just recently.

The wind was cold and the water was cold, but even so, she had begun to walk down to the deserted shore in the late afternoon. She would walk barefoot, though there were sharp shells among the pebbles, and then she would sit on the damp sand-bank and just stare out for hours, until the sun set. He had no idea what she might be thinking.

And now, just in the past couple of weeks, she no longer wanted to go out with him fishing on the boat. She wanted to stay behind, and though he knew there was risk in that — that she might be discovered — it didn't feel right, or wise, to deny her.

And then, just a few days ago, she had asked him for bus fare to London.

He asked if she knew how to get about in the city. She said that's what buses are for.

And it had become clear to him that her remaining amnesia was, apparently, only regarding her own personal specifics — she might not know her own name, or where she was from, or what she had done in the past, but she had no difficulty now with any of the details of the world around her.

He gave her the fare. But he asked her to promise that she would avoid their little lo-cal village — she would just go to the bus stop and get on the bus, and if she should encounter anyone along the way she would not stop to talk to them.

She had agreed.

And when he returned from his boat late that afternoon, he was greatly relieved to discover that she had returned home.

The same thing happened the next day. And the next day as well — but this time, when he returned from his boat, she was not already there at their home. He had to wait. And the next night, he had to wait even longer.

He would ask her where she had been, and she would tell him, but without much editorial comment at all:

She had been to the British Museum. She had taken the bus all the way out to the National Archives. She had taken the tube to Baker Street and gone for a walk.

Did she see anything she liked at the British Museum? He had never been there himself, except once in a group trip in primary school.

She shrugged.

Why did she go to the National Archives? Not much to see there, really, was there? He had never been there, either, but it sounded like just a lot of dusty old paper.

She shrugged. She said it was a very large place and she wanted to go back there again.

What did she see on Baker Street?

She looked down at her fried flounder, put a bit of it on her fork and then in her mouth, smiled slightly — and shrugged.

She hadn't quite said so, but he was almost certain now — she was remembering who she was.

What all the consequences of that would be he didn't know. But he knew what one of them would be — she would leave or she would be found out, but either way, he knew she would soon be gone.

He began to wonder how he would endure such a loss again.

6

A FEW DAYS LATER, IN BAKER STREET
"I'm tired of places with bright sun and
warm turquoise water and fine white sand
that pleasantly tickles one's toes without
sticking to them," said Laura Rankin. She
was sitting on the mahogany desk in Reggie
Heath's law chambers office, she had her
shoes off, her red hair on the verge of being
undone, and she wiggled those freckled toes
as she said it. "I'm ready to go someplace
dour."

"Your aunt's manor house in Newquay
certainly qualifies on that account," said
Reggie. He supposed he could understand
why Laura was bored with white sandy
beaches; she had been on a location shoot
in the South Seas for several months during
the past year. But he had not.

"It's not a manor house; it's a genuine
castle," said Laura. "I mean, not the type
intended for repelling military invaders and

such, but imposing enough to intimidate poor peasants who dared to hunt deer in the woods. Though my aunt Mabel says she's pretty sure the original Earl of Darby never once tried to stop them. Just in case he ever did, she volunteers her time now for lots of good causes. But anyway, it is a castle, and if you don't believe me now, you will when you realize there's still no indoor plumbing on the top floor. And the estate has its own trout streams. You can fly fish."

"I don't know how to fly fish," said Reggie, "and I don't plan on spending our engagement trip with trout."

"Well, I suppose that's not what I have in mind for you, either," said Laura. "But my aunt is my last living relative, and there is this family tradition to uphold. We have a coat of arms bolted in above the main fireplace, with a Latin or Gaelic motto, I forget which, inscribed at the bottom, that says: 'Everybody has to get engaged in the castle and get drunk after.' I mean, words to that effect, anyway. It's all very imposing, almost as much so as my aunt, and I really can't fly in the face of either one. Don't pretend you didn't know this about me."

Reggie did know that about her. But as much as he would have preferred tickling her toes on the white sands of the beach she had just described, his expressed annoyance at the prospect of traveling instead through dark and foggy moors in the dead of winter was almost completely feigned, and mostly just for her entertainment.

The fact was, after coming so close to losing Laura in so many ways in the past two years, he was now so relieved to have it all settled — he was now so completely committed and eager — that she could have insisted that they spend the night in the dungeon of the blasted castle and he would have happily agreed.

Two years ago, on a dry, windy Los Angeles movie lot, she had — well, dumped him, he had to admit — for not being able to make up his mind, let go of some ghosts of his past, and commit.

In the year after that, with Reggie consigned to a sort of Laura-less purgatory, she had very nearly said yes to Lord Robert Buxton — the publisher of *The Daily Sun* and owner of a vast media conglomerate, a man infinitely more wealthy and powerful than Reggie could ever hope to be.

And then, just this past September, Laura had very nearly been driven off the Tower Bridge and into the Thames by Darla Rennie, a schizophrenic young woman who had gone off her meds and believed Reggie

Heath to be Sherlock Holmes and therefore responsible for the death of a nineteenth-century ancestor named Moriarty.

As it turned out, it was the young woman herself who plunged into the Thames, never to be seen again. So that obstacle, complete with its delusions, had been carried out to sea. Problem solved.

And in the months since, Laura had worked through her remaining Buxton issues — saving the life of the pompous ass in fact, thereby making it easier for her to say no to him. Problem solved there, too.

Even so — Reggie knew life to be uncertain. And it seemed to him of late that the world wanted nothing more than to break him and Laura apart — even if one or the other of them had to be destroyed to do it.

He was determined not to let that happen. If anything — or anyone — did try to bollux things up for them now, that would-be bolluxer would be dealt with in short order. Because Reggie was now on the lookout.

"Beware the moors," he said now, lightly. "I'm pretty sure that's the Gaelic they write on the walls at most of those castles."

Laura leaned in toward Reggie, pushing aside some legal documents.

"Sometimes they write: 'You shall bring

no work with you,' " she said, warmly, in his ear.

"I kept my calendar clear," said Reggie. He cleared his throat and continued. "I have no court appearances until the Wednesday morning after. Some stockholder suit nonsense. I'll have plenty of time to prep for it after we return on Monday. So I won't bring my work if you won't bring yours."

Laura sat back just a bit.

"How on earth would I bring my work with me?" said Laura.

"You'll bring no scripts to read."

"Well, that's easy. Agreed."

"And no paparazzi or gossip reporters. And no fans, other than me. And you won't take calls from your agent."

This list of objections was more or less in priority order. The society press had not been kind to Reggie since word of Laura's pending engagement had been leaked. The gossip column headlines were not all exactly the same, but they all asked the same implicit question: "Is She Too Good for Him?" and emphasized her career stature in comparison with his. The *Daily Sun* column had been especially obnoxious, with opening lines like "Will the barrister's briefs be big enough to keep the lady satisfied?"

Reggie's chambers were in fact not doing

badly, but in the press at least it was difficult for anyone in a noncelebrity occupation to match up with a rising film star with a blockbuster hit.

"I'll do my very best," said Laura. "They say the weather will be lovely. And you won't even have to drive. I cleverly designed our itinerary so we can take a train the whole way there, with a couple of stops just for the fun of it. Do you think they still provide sleeping cars for short trips?"

"Sleeping is next to trout fishing in how I do not plan on spending my time."

"Big talker. We'll see. Anyway, if they don't, I can sit on your lap all the way there and perhaps initiate a scandal. Or something like one."

She slid across the desk toward him on that, which made an entrancing sort of swooshing sound and caused her skirt to ride back from her panty hose.

But then her mobile rang. She settled back from Reggie a bit, picked up the phone, said hello, and then she covered the receiver and whispered to Reggie:

"It's my agent. He must have heard you talking; I've no idea how he does it! But we're not on our way yet, so this doesn't count."

Then she said, to the agent on the phone:

"Yes, we'll be completely unreachable for three whole days. I know that's outrageous. . . . No, I can't. Nothing until I return. . . . No, you can't, and if you do, I won't pick up. . . . No, I'm not giving you the itinerary, either. We'll end up at my aunt's castle at the end of the week, there will be a big to-do, everyone knows that, the media shall have their opportunity at that time and place, and that's all anyone needs to know. . . . Yes. So sweet of you to call, but don't do it again. Cheers."

She shut off the phone and turned to Reggie.

"Well?" she said.

Reggie nodded. "Fair enough," he said.

Laura slid in closer again.

But now there was a rap on the office door.

"What is it, Lois?" said Reggie, loudly and in a warning voice.

"Mr. Rafferty," said Lois, wise enough to stay on the other side of the closed door. "I'm so very sorry. He said it's quite important."

"He always says it is —"

"I'm so very sorry," Lois called out desperately, because the door was opening anyway — and Rafferty came right in.

"Heath! So you are in, after all! Good

morning, Miss Rankin."

Laura got up from the desk, and straightened her skirt.

"It was on its way to being, Mr. Rafferty," she said, and she gave the man a look that would have frozen him, if he had been aware enough to catch it.

Reggie glared at Rafferty, who just remained standing there in front of the desk as though oblivious that he had interrupted anything at all.

Rafferty was a grayish man, always in a grayish suit, and slight enough in stature and build that Lois, though not tall herself, really should have been able to block his path, if she had tried harder. Reggie made a mental note to have a talk with her about that.

"I need your assistance, for an hour or so," said Rafferty. "And I expect we'll need a dolly."

"Excuse me?"

"Dorset House has been invited to contribute an exhibit for the grand opening of the newly restored Marylebone Grand All En Suite Hotel and Exhibit Hall."

"All en suite is it, really?" said Laura.

"That's what they claim," said Rafferty.

"My, this is an event then."

"Perhaps you've noticed all the hubbub

over on Gloucester Court for the renovation?" said Rafferty to Reggie.

"Yes."

"Well, now it's completed, celebratory invites have gone out to all of us locals, and unfortunately, Dorset National Building Society was delighted to accept."

"So?"

"It is indeed an event," said Rafferty, pulling up a chair, uninvited. "Not only is Dorset National Building Society participating, but so is another bank down the street, and so is the Sherlock Holmes Museum, and the Regent's Park Preservation Society, and the pub on the corner, and the American burger place with the clown, and —"

"I get the idea," said Reggie. "It's the biggest thing since the Queen's Silver Jubilee. What's it to do with me?"

Rafferty looked at Reggie and sighed, as though this was a shared disappointment.

"I'm afraid Dorset National, for its part, wants to contribute an exhibit of the letters. Apparently that beats the pants off the alternative proposal, which would have been a series of bulletins illustrating how interest rates have changed over the years."

Reggie raised an eyebrow.

"Do not ask which letters I'm referring to," said Rafferty. "You know which letters.

The Sherlock Holmes letters. The letters that people still write to him, ignoring that he is fictional and would have expired long ago either way. The letters that get delivered to Dorset House because we occupy the entire two-hundred block of Baker Street, and which you are responsible for because you agreed to take a lease on this floor for your law chambers."

Reggie sighed. He knew all that, of course. Responsibility for the letters was more or less ingrained in his life now, although he did his best whenever possible to shuffle them off to his younger brother, Nigel, in Los Angeles.

But Reggie was beginning to get used to them. He didn't even mind any longer that once or twice people had even suggested that he *looked* like Sherlock Holmes — or the way they imagined Sherlock Holmes should look. He knew he didn't. And he knew they only mentioned it at all because of the letters, and because he was tall, and perhaps just a little angular.

And more important, he knew that Sherlock Holmes was never lucky enough to embark on an engagement trip with Laura Rankin. Reggie personally was having much more fun these days than Sherlock Holmes ever did, fictional or otherwise, and intended to keep it that way. So long as the letters didn't interfere with that, he had no problem with them.

"All right," he said to Rafferty. "But my question still stands — what does this pending exhibit have to do with me?"

"I need you to help me move the cabinets."

Reggie had to think about that for a minute. He had thought this would be some legal matter, or a leasing issue, or something unimaginably worse.

He said, "Seriously?"

"Yes," said Rafferty. "Of course seriously."

"Why not just have Building Maintenance handle it? Or hire a professional? Or have the hotel itself do the transport, given they're so keen for it?"

"Out of the question," said Rafferty. "This is not an ordinary matter of moving furniture, Heath, as you should realize. These are the letters to Sherlock Holmes. Many people know that they exist, but only a small circle know exactly where we keep them. I don't want that publicized, and I think we all know from recent experience the sort of thing that happens when we allow strangers on the top floor."

"I don't suppose this can wait a few days?" said Reggie. "I'm going out of town, but my brother Nigel arrives day after tomorrow. You can reach him at my penthouse number. He could help you. And except for you, no one likes the letters more than he does."

"It has to be done today," said Rafferty. "I got the large dolly from Building Maintenance and some packing boxes. It's all upstairs. I wasn't able to arrange a rental truck, but with both your car and my hatchback I'm sure we'll be able to —"

"I'll help," said Laura cheerfully.

"I would hardly ask you to move heavy boxes, Miss Rankin," said Rafferty, "but I'm delighted to let you supervise, if you like."

Reggie looked at Laura, who was smiling and didn't seem at all nonplussed about the task.

"We can spare you an hour," said Reggie. "No more."

"I'm sure that will take care of it," said Rafferty.

"Very well," said Reggie. "I haven't helped anyone move furniture since university, but if that's what you want — let's get it over with."

They took the lift to the top floor. Rafferty took out a bundle of keys from his pocket, sorted through until he found the oldest and oddest of the bunch, and used that one to unlock the storage room.

The door opened with a musty scent. Rafferty reached up and pulled the chain for a single overhead bulb.

There were at least a dozen full-size cabinets in the room, each of them almost as tall as Reggie.

"Not all of them, I hope?" said Reggie.

"Dear me, no," said Rafferty. "I insisted that we would display nothing recent — nothing that you or your brother has responded to, Heath, or, for that matter, anything within anyone's living memory. We're not going to take a risk with privacy issues, or any sort of liabilities. We'll lend the contents of just two cabinets — this one, containing the early letters that began to be delivered here when Dorset House was first built, and also the smaller one over there in the back corner."

Reggie went back to take a look.

"The label says: 'Pre–Dorset House,' " said Reggie.

"Exactly," said Rafferty. "The letters began in the 1890s, long before this block of Baker Street even existed. Scotland Yard received most of them back then. But when Baker Street was extended and Dorset House was built, that created an actual 221B. All the letters started coming here, and Scotland Yard sent over everything it had accumulated years earlier. They needed the space, I guess. In any case, I'm sure the hotel people will find the letters historically very quaint — and it won't cause us a bit of trouble."

"So you say," said Reggie. He positioned himself behind the farthest cabinet, and got ready to maneuver it out of the narrow space.

"Careful, Heath, mind the floor," said Rafferty. "That's what the dolly is for."

"It's what a moving crew is for," said Reggie. "And yet, here I am doing it."

7

More than an hour later, Reggie's Jaguar
and Rafferty's hatchback both pulled up in
front of the hotel. Reggie and Laura got out
and helped Rafferty unload a cabinet and
boxes, and then Reggie wheeled the dolly
toward the lobby entrance.

The elderly bellman prepared to open the
door for him, but a thirtyish-looking supervisor intervened.

"Deliveries around the back, please," he
said.

"We tried that," said Reggie. "But it's
blocked. There are two cargo vans there
already."

"Well, yes, I know there's a bit of a queue,"
said the supervisor, with a sort of shrug.

Reggie checked his watch. The task was
already taking longer than advertised.

"We are delivering these materials at the
request of the hotel," said Rafferty, sound-

ing offended on behalf of the letters themselves.

"Yes," said the supervisor, "but isn't it
possible for you to wait your turn?"

"Another possibility," said Reggie, "is that
you will continue to block our path and ac-
cidentally end up wearing one of these
boxes as a hat."

"Boys, play nice," said Laura.

Reggie gave that approach some thought,
but before he could try it out a more
authoritative figure came out from the
supervisor's office.

She was tall, in her mid-fifties, and as
carefully tailored and impeccably maintained as the hotel lobby itself. She took a
moment to size up the situation, and then
focused on Laura.

"Laura Rankin! Is that you?"

"So pleased to meet you," said Laura,
extending her hand. "Unless we have already, in which case I hope you're doing
well."

"No, we haven't, but of course I recognize
you. My name is Helene, and I'm the
manager here." She turned to the doorman
supervisor. "Charles, help them with those
boxes, will you?"

"No thank you," said Rafferty quickly.
"Heath and I can handle them without

problem."

"As you wish," said Helene.

Reggie and Rafferty began to wheel the boxes in, and the hotel manager walked alongside Laura.

"I wish someone had told me you were coming," she said. "I would have —" And then she stopped. "Oh! I just realized. This is the week of your trip to the castle, isn't it?"

"Excuse me?" said Laura.

"I read about it in *The Daily Sun.* Oh my, are you staying here tonight?" Her eyes lit up, the color flecks in her pupils flashing like paparazzi cameras and pounds sterling. "I didn't realize. Someone really should have told me. I didn't see our hotel listed on your itinerary."

"No, we're not staying; we — do you mean *The Daily Sun* actually published my entire travel itinerary?"

"Yes," said the hotel manager. "Didn't you know?"

"No," said Laura. "I suppose I'd better have a chat with someone there."

"Yes, there must be boundaries, mustn't there?"

"There soon will be," said Laura. "Can you point us to the exhibit room? Where the Sherlock Holmes letters go?"

"Yes, of course. I'll take you there myself," said the woman, and then, to Reggie and Rafferty, "Just follow along, please. It's right this way."

She escorted them through the lobby and across the main reception area, beneath the skylights, and past golden draperies, gigantic indoor palms, and tourists and locals seated at high tea.

They went up the carpeted ramp to the mezzanine level, where a perimeter corridor had the truly prime display space, which a visitor would have to traverse to get to the other exhibits.

And right at the top of the mezzanine stairs was a video display. It seemed to be triggered by a person stepping in front of it. Or else it was just lucky timing that it lit up and began a show as soon as they reached the top of the ramp:

"Welcome," said the expensively dressed, sixtyish man in the video. "My name is Harold Redfern, and I'm CEO of Marylebone Grand Hotels. This hotel, our flagship, has been in my family for generations, and I personally thank you from the bottom of my heart for joining us in this, our centennial celebration of its founding."

"It's just like Disneyland," said Laura. "If we go down the stairs and come back up, will he start again?"

The hotel manager smiled slightly. "That's my brother," she said. "I manage the family chain of hotels, and he sits in the board-room, makes executive decisions, and man-ages public relations. You can never get him to stop talking when you want him to. So you just come this way, and his voice will fade in the distance."

They moved on down the corridor.

"On these main walls," said the hotel manager, "we have displayed the memora-bilia and documents from the hotel's own history. And along the way here, each of the members of the merchants association has its own individual exhibit room."

She paused now outside an empty room.

"Here you are," she said. "This one's yours. You have the center easel and all four walls of this room at your disposal, to display what you'd like. Enjoy! Would you like me to send over some additional staff to help out?"

Reggie was about to say yes, but he wasn't quick enough.

"No," said Rafferty, immediately. "We'll muddle through on our own, thank you."

"I'll just stop by in a bit to see how you're getting on then," said the woman.

"We'll just be hammering away," said

Reggie, as she exited down the corridor. "Don't mind our noise."

"I think," said Laura, "that I saw mini-cheeseburgers being set out in the exhibit room we just passed, the one with the clown. Can't you smell them? I think we should stop for a snack on our way out."

"I wish they had given us a more traditional neighbor," said Rafferty. "Sherlock Holmes is many things, but he's not American cheeseburgers."

"You wouldn't say that if you'd skipped breakfast," said Reggie. "Let's get these bloody things unpacked."

Rafferty took one set of letters to one side of the room, and Reggie and Laura took another set to the other.

Laura and Reggie began to take out the letters from the 1890s box.

"I'll read them and decide which ones we want," said Laura. "You hammer them onto the wall."

"Fair enough," said Reggie.

"Here's the first one: 'Please send to me your monograph on how to determine a person's occupation, quirks, and whether he is a blackmailer, based on the wear on his coat sleeves,' " read Laura.

"Good for a start," said Reggie.

"We can put that one by the door," said

Laura. "Next letter: 'I have a map to the treasure of the sunken sixteenth-century Spanish galleon *El Conquistador*. If you will only decipher the code for me, I promise to send to you twenty-five percent of all the net proceeds upon recovery of the treasure, except for the royal rubies of Nepal, which I reserve for myself.' "

"Not a very generous offer," said Reggie.

"So it goes on the side wall," said Laura, and she pulled out another letter.

This time she paused for a moment, rereading it silently. Then she said:

"I have committed an evil murder, and I am confessing, complete with my name and signature."

"What?" said Reggie.

"Well, that was just a summary. The highlights are: 'Dear Mr. Sherlock Holmes:

" '. . . I want you to know of the great favor that I have done for you.

" 'Professor Moriarty is now in fact dead. For I have killed him.' And so on and so on. And then the person adds, 'I put him in some pain before he expired. No extra charge for that.' "

Laura held the letter out for Reggie to see. "Murder and torture," she said. "Charming, isn't it?"

"Well, that's all right then," said Reggie.

"If someone had confessed in print to an actual murder, I would have expected Scotland Yard to do something about it, and not just stuff it in a box. But given what they've confessed to is killing a fictional character —"

Rafferty, at the other end of the room, raised his head and looked over for a moment, but then he just continued on with his own batch of letters.

"Let's put it in the center display, where everyone can see it," said Laura. "In place of this other one, which is just to Sherlock Holmes from some Nigerian prince."

In a few minutes more, all the designated wall spaces were covered. Rafferty put the boxes of remaining letters back onto the dolly, and Reggie prepared to wheel it back downstairs.

"You both go right ahead," said Laura. "I'll catch up. I'm going next door and get us all some mini-burgers."

Reggie and Rafferty wheeled the dolly out, and several minutes later Laura joined them in front of the hotel.

"Sorry I was delayed," she said. She carried a sack of little burgers in red-and-white paper wrappings, which Rafferty declined but Reggie gladly accepted.

"It was the oddest thing," said Laura.

"The hotel manager stopped by to have a look as I was leaving, just as she said she would. I stayed politely for a few minutes, so that she could finish thanking us properly. She walked along the wall, nodding approvingly at how we made only a little mess at hanging the things, and then she came to the center display — where we had put up just that one letter, from someone claiming to have killed Moriarty — and she turned white as a ghost."

"What, I angled it wrong?" said Reggie.

"I hardly think that was it. One would have thought that she had some personal stake in the matter. She smiled when I first pointed the letter out to her; she actually took a moment to read the whole thing. And then, all at once, her expression changed completely. She didn't even stay to inspect the remainder of the display. She said that she suddenly remembered an urgent appointment, she turned on her heels, and she just rushed out of the room as if the fire alarm had gone off."

"That's a hotel for you," said Reggie. "Always experiencing a completely predictable crisis. And usually in a way that inconveniences you and makes money for them. I've never been in one where they didn't forget that I requested a room with a view, or insist that I have to put up with construction noise outside the window, or a lack of heat, or a temporary suspension of the free breakfast deal they promised."

"That's not how things usually go for me at a hotel," said Laura. "I always find the staff are quite nice."

"That's because you have good hotel luck. I have bad hotel luck."

"Well, I hope they balance out from now on. In any case, given the look on her face, if your rule holds true, I'm glad this hotel is not on our itinerary," said Laura.

"I'll just be glad when the bloody exhibit is over and we get the letters back where they belong," said Rafferty.

As Laura tossed the bag of mini-burgers into Reggie's car, she glanced over at Rafferty. Then she looked at Reggie and raised an eyebrow.

Reggie shrugged. Like Laura, he had never heard the man whine before.

8

On the mezzanine level of the Marylebone Grand Hotel, with all the exhibits finally in place (even the Sherlock Holmes letters brought over by the Dorset House folks, who seemed to have never done this sort of thing before), a young tour guide positioned herself at the top of the stairs, right next to the automated video exhibit, and waited for the video to finish.

She wanted to get it right. The hotel manager, a very intimidating woman, had rushed by a few moments earlier, all in a huff — and now, for some reason, she seemed to be watching, having positioned herself at the opposite side of the mezzanine, only partially concealed by a potted palm tree.

The tour guide didn't know why the hotel manager was watching, but whatever the reason, she knew that now was not the time to botch it up.

She had enough of a crowd now to begin. There was a thirtyish woman with two toddlers, a few older pensioners, a group of half a dozen schoolchildren and their teacher, and, for the third time in a week, a woman of about twenty-five, with green eyes that were startling in their intensity, even at a distance of several feet.

This woman had been present for each day of the exhibit, and she had stared so long on the first day at one particular display that the tour guide, new to her job, had actually gotten nervous, and gone to the trouble to inform security at the end of the tour.

Nothing had come of it though. The woman had not misbehaved. She had simply returned again the next day, as she had again today.

The tour guide began the presentation.

"Welcome to the centennial celebration of the Marylebone Grand Hotel," said the tour guide. "You are here at a very special time for us, and so we have assembled a very special exhibit — not only to show you the history of the hotel itself, but also to give you the flavor of our business community here in Marylebone, and I don't mean just the American mini-burgers."

A couple of the adults in the group chuckled appreciatively. The scent from the burger exhibit, for good or ill, was wafting out into the corridor.

"Which are made especially for our celebration, today only, and are complimentary, I might add, at the conclusion of our little tour."

That got an appreciative response, and the guide continued with the tour, stepping just inside the first exhibit room.

"Most of the documents and photographs in our exhibit have never before been seen by the public. In this room are letters written over many years to Marylebone's most famous resident — Sherlock Holmes."

The woman with the green eyes spoke up. "He's not real, you know," she said.

"Excuse me?" said the tour guide. On each of her previous visits, the green-eyed woman had asked the tour guide when the exhibit of the Sherlock Holmes letters would be in place. Now, for the first time, it was.

"Sherlock Holmes is not real," said the green-eyed woman again, as if it were a revelation. "He's a character of fiction."

There were a couple of titters from the schoolchildren, and a tolerant smile from one of the pensioners.

"Yes, of course," said tour guide. "But

these are the letters, even so, should you want to have a closer look later."

The tour guide didn't actually intend to take the little group through the whole room; it was only a ten-minute tour, and she needed to keep them moving on down the corridor — especially with the hotel manager still watching from behind the indoor shrubberies. Probably the manager wanted the tour to focus more on the displays that were specific to the hotel itself, and so the tour guide wanted to get along to it.

But the young woman with the green eyes didn't budge; she seemed stuck on the letter in the center Sherlock Holmes display, and was now standing directly in front of it, with the rest of the group gravitating into the room along with her.

"Moving right along," said the tour guide. "If you'll just come around the corner here and into the corridor, you'll see the first of our displays for the history of the Marylebone Grand Hotel itself."

The group hesitated.

"Moving right along, then," said the tour guide again, and this time she used her authoritative tour-guide command voice.

The little group, including the green-eyed woman, finally responded, and moved just a few steps from the letters exhibit to the first display in the corridor. And it was a good thing, too, because the hotel manager was still watching.

"Yes, that's right, thank you," said the tour guide. "Now, here you see the original partnership document for the founding of the hotel — exactly one hundred years ago this month. You'll notice the slightly old-fashioned form of communication — hand-written, as many people still did in those days who did not possess one of those newfangled gadgets known as typewriters."

Most of the group didn't seem to care much. Only the green-eyed woman, again, seemed to think this document was something remarkable. A group of tourists like her would be the perfect audience — if only the tour was scheduled to last the whole day.

But it wasn't. The guide tried to put an end point on this display and move on to the next.

"The entire agreement, written and signed by all the parties, on just one page. Talk about a simpler time!"

Again, a couple of polite smiles and chuckles from the adults, and that was the best that could be hoped for.

The tour guide herded the little group on

down to the end of the corridor. Or at least most of them. The green-eyed woman was lagging behind again, standing all by herself and staring at the handwritten partnership agreement that had created the hotel.

Fine. The tour would have to go on without her. The guide moved everyone along briskly, past several more documents in the corridor. Then she stopped, gathering everyone in front of a newly placed photograph on the wall.

"As you'd expect in the life of any great lady, there were dark days as well as bright ones. Here you see a photo of the hotel in October of 1944, when a V-2 flying bomb struck between the hotel and the pub down the street. The photo was taken not very long at all after the blast, by a guest from the hotel. In the upper right, here, you can see the members of the Fire Brigade still on the scene, with the fire just then put out, which of course was always first priority. There were twenty-three bomb hits on that one particular day, and though everyone pitched in to help, full cleanup did not take place immediately — there was always another place that needed more urgent attention."

This was the last display in the guided tour, it had just been received from the

National Archives and put up that morning, and the young tour guide knew full well that of all the documents and photos on the mezzanine, there were none with comparable gravitas. She paused and let everyone take a look.

Two of the pensioners stepped up closer, saying something softly about it and nodding to each other, as though they understood it firsthand.

It was a black-and-white photo, only eighteen inches wide by twelve high, and not visually spectacular. It showed a portion of a twenty-foot-wide crater where the bomb had made direct impact in the street. Firemen and bystanders stood to the right of that, and in the center, behind the crater, was where the front of the pub had once been.

There had been a billiard loft above the pub, but most of that level had been blown away; the remaining floor tilted downward, with a heavy, full-size snooker table leaning at a forty-five-degree angle from the loft floor to the ground.

To the right in the background was the pub bar, with its draft beer spigots still intact somehow. A bartender was very deliberately standing behind the bar, passing a glass to a patron who was very deliberately standing there as well — in a pose intended to convey that come hell or high water or bombs that fell in the dead of night or the glorious energy of the day, Londoners would carry on as though it were all less an inconvenience than the weather.

In the foreground — facing the camera, having apparently paused for just a moment at the request of the photographer — was a tall, thin man in his mid-seventies. On either side of him, each holding one of his hands, were two children — a boy about nine years old, and a girl of perhaps five.

"Who are these children? Do we know what became of them?" said one of the pensioners.

"Indeed we do," said the tour guide, with a proud smile. "The older man in the foreground was in fact the founder of this very hotel. And the two children you see there next to him — well, you may well have already seen them on our premises or on the video today — because that little girl is our hotel manager, and that little boy is CEO for the entire chain."

With that, the tour guide gave them all a moment to study the photo further.

The face of the man in the photo was defiant, almost glowering back at the camera. Courage in the face of violent adversity would have been anyone's first interpretation, though his expression wasn't quite the same as any of the others.

The girl whose hand he held appeared to be on the verge of physiological shock.

The boy standing on the other side of the older man showed something else — alarm, fear, rage, it was hard to tell which of those was winning out. Whatever he had seen, in the tour guide's opinion, it must be something no child should — but she saw no need to point that out to the observers. It was a war photo, after all.

The firemen in the photo seemed to be looking at something not in the foreground — something mostly concealed by the corner of the heavy slate and mahogany billiard table that had come crashing down to meet the pavement, something that perhaps the photographer had not even noticed when the shot was taken. Something that most people would not notice now.

But the young woman with the intense green eyes seemed drawn toward it. As soon as the pensioners gave her room, she stepped up for a closer look. Much closer. She stared for a long moment.

And then she turned toward the tour guide.

"Who is this on the ground?" she said.

"Excuse me?"

"Here," said the young woman. "Behind the snooker table."

The tour guide stepped in and took a look.

The tour guide was quite young and her eyesight was perfect, but even so, it took a moment of study. And then she saw it as well.

Behind the snooker table, covered so much by fallen gray plaster and hazed over so much by the graininess of the photo that it was almost indistinguishable, there was a body. The edges of a military uniform — an American uniform, given the olive jacket and tan trousers — were just visible.

"Oh my —" said the tour guide.

She knew the hotel would never have posted the photo had they known. It was simply not appropriate. There is hotel history, there is the war history, and there is showing respect. She immediately turned, facing the little tour group, blocking their line of sight to the photo.

"And that concludes our little tour for today, thank you very much for attending."

The tour guide remained standing there, until the little group disbanded. Then she hurried off in the direction of the hotel manager, who was still standing behind the potted plant at the far end of the mezzanine.

As the tour guide hurried off, the green-eyed woman returned.

She stood for a long moment, staring at the photograph, before she, too, finally turned and walked back down the corridor, toward the exhibits that the tour group had already viewed earlier.

And then, as the green-eyed woman moved on, Helene, the hotel manager, came down the corridor to have a look for herself.

The tour guide had alerted the hotel manager where in the photograph to look, and it took just a moment for her to verify that yes, indeed, the tour guide was correct — there was a body visible, just partly. The photograph would have to come down.

But the hotel manager stared at the display for a much longer moment.

She had never seen this photograph before. She had been aware of its existence for years; she knew that someone at the National Archives had suggested it for the exhibit, and she had not objected; she had not been able to think of a good reason to do so — not even when the hotel's marketing group conceived the idea of distributing copies throughout the entire hotel chain for display during the centennial.

But she had never had any desire to look at the photo herself. She simply did not want to. She had been there. It was not a historical artifact to her. It was personal.

And she just hadn't felt any need to see it.

But she had to look at it now, and she did so. She looked at her own face in the photo. At that of her brother. And at that of her grandfather.

And then, finally, she took the photo down, frame and all.

She carried it under her arm and began to walk down the corridor, heading for the lift that went to the top floor.

And then, before she got to the lift, she stopped. She was still in the mezzanine corridor, where other documents from the hotel's history were on display — and directly across from her was an empty display frame on the corridor wall.

A document was missing — gone from its frame.

It took her just a moment to realize which one it was. It was the partnership document — the original signed agreement from 1898 that had created the hotel. Someone, in the past few minutes, had to have stolen it.

Helene pondered that.

And then she turned and hurried to the lift. As she got in, she rang the head of security — but she got only his answering machine.

Bloody hell, of all the times for him to be out.

Several moments later, at the front of the hotel, Helene came out from the lobby. She commandeered the hotel's luxury limo, and told the driver to take her to corporate headquarters in Canary Wharf.

She arrived there, took the lift to the top floor, and went directly to her older brother's office.

"He may be in conference," said his personal secretary in the waiting room. "I'll ring him to let him know you're here."

"Ring all you want," said Helene. "I'm talking to him now."

She opened the closed office door and went on in.

Forty minutes later, Helene left her brother's office and took the limo back to the hotel.

Her state of mind was such that after several minutes the limo driver, as professionally discreet as anyone in the business, actually broke the code and asked her what was wrong.

She just shook her head, made no other answer, and closed the limo partition.

9

THE NEXT MORNING

At Baker Street Chambers, Reggie had just arrived at work, and barely had time to set his takeaway coffee down on his desk, when the phone rang.

Reggie picked up.

"Heath! Glad I caught you in."

It was Detective Inspector Wembley, though the reception was poor.

"How are you, Wembley? You sound faint."

"I'm on my mobile. On Canvey Island. There's something here that you will want to see, Heath."

Reggie had no idea what that might be. He had no criminal cases pending. "You know I'll be out of town with Laura as of Saturday," he said.

"Yes, I read the papers," said Wembley. "It's all the more reason you'll want to see this now. I suggest you drive out, Heath. I'll be around for another hour or two with

Forensics."

And then the connection cut off.

Reggie got in the Jaguar and drove to Canvey Island, on the Thames Estuary.

The air was cold, but the sky was clear, and it was difficult to imagine things dark and dangerous while driving through sheep-dotted hills and blue vistas. No doubt Wembley was exaggerating the sense of urgency.

Reggie took the turnoff, and he saw below him the little hamlet of Canvey and, just beyond that, the sea.

He drove through the village, past a pub at one end as he entered, and then past another at the other end.

He pulled over and got directions from a woman at a bus stop, who seemed ready for the question. She told him to drive on another quarter mile toward the estuary and then turn right before he got to the marina.

He did that. He drove up a small rise. The estuary was clearly visible from here, and the water was not as calm as it had seemed from a distance; it was choppy, with dark cobalt angles in continual motion.

He drove down into a dell and took another turn, off the narrow paved road onto an equally narrow unpaved one.

He was approaching a small wood-frame cottage, all by itself in the dell. No fence.

There was an old lorry with a wooden flat-bed.

And there were two vehicles with the official insignia of Scotland Yard parked in front. One of those was the van used by Forensics, and Reggie recognized the other as Detective Inspector Wembley's sedan.

Reggie parked and walked up to the front porch. If he hadn't already known that a small, lone house this close to the estuary would belong to a fisherman, he knew it now from the scents that came from the wooden structure.

A forensics official was unpacking some equipment from the van. Reggie recognized her — a woman, in her forties, named O'Shea. She glanced over as Reggie approached.

"Good morning, Heath," she said. "Wembley's inside."

"Do you know why he rang me?" said Reggie.

"I guess he'll tell you," she said. "Put these on before you go in, please."

She tossed a pair of thin disposable booties to Reggie.

Reggie stepped up onto the narrow wood porch, put the booties on over his shoes, and pushed the door open.

He paused at the entrance, to let his eyes

158

adjust to the dark room and get some light through the opened doorway. There were windows on two walls, but the solid, grease-stained vinyl blinds were pulled down.

"Don't touch anything."

That was Wembley.

The detective inspector was kneeling carefully on the floor at the opposite end of the room. At his feet was a chalk outline of a human form, and near that was a pool of dried blood.

That end of the room served as the kitchen, and it was a narrow space; there was a steel sink and faucets, and an old, chipped white enamel stove with black grills. There was a small table with two plain chairs.

Reggie stood in the portion of the room that served as the general living area; there was an old green cloth sofa immediately to his right, with a small end table and lamp. To his left, an old television set and a tiny wooden bookcase were crowded together in the near corner; a narrow, collapsible cot was set against the wall. There was a door to the bedroom. At his feet, the dark oiled floor timbers extended from the porch into the front room and then into the kitchen.

There was a residual scent of some sort of grilled meat; Reggie looked down and saw that on the floor, just inside the doorway and next to the sofa, was a half-empty, white paper sack of something from a fast-food restaurant.

At the opposite end of the sofa, between it and the kitchen, was a broken floor lamp.

Reggie moved closer to the kitchen. He saw two unwashed dishes, accompanying utensils, and a tea strainer in the sink. A frying pan and greasy residue on the stove. A teacup and a couple of beverage glasses on the counter; some spilled instant coffee granules; a loaf of bread, the wrapper of which had not been properly closed.

Reggie looked about, but only casually. He had been asked not to touch anything, and in fact he had no reason to do so. It was not his case.

And he did not envy Forensics the task of trying to identify all the biological substances absorbed by the floor in that kitchen.

"And don't brush up against anything either," said Wembley. "I don't want them to have to distinguish your camel hair overcoat from every other fiber in the place. You should have taken the bloody thing off before you came inside."

Reggie said, "It's cold, Wembley, and I don't intend to touch a thing. I just want to know why I'm here."

The detective stood.

"The body is already on its way to the lab," said Wembley. "His name was Cheeverton. A fisherman, sixty years old. A neighbor was walking by yesterday evening, on the way to the pub around six; saw the front door open, checked, found the body and called it in. According to the neighbor, Cheeverton lived here alone."

"But I would guess he's had company recently," said Reggie.

"Yes," said Wembley. "Possibly a working lady. The neighbor said he rarely had guests, but O'Shea found a phone box advert in the bedroom, and a woman's hair in the loo sink. Hey, don't touch those."

"I'm not touching them," said Reggie, looking at receipts and ticket stubs that the forensics team had sorted out on a plastic tray. "But which of them — the fisherman who's lived here all his life, or the working lady — do you suppose would have been taking the bus out to Kew and doing research in the National Archives?"

"That's a fair question," said Wembley. "And if he set up a cot in the living room for a working lady, I think he was a little unclear on the concept. But what I want to show you is over here."

Wembley came over to the front of the room and switched on the little table lamp next to the couch.

On the floor underneath the couch, a two-foot rectangle had been marked out by the forensics team. One of the dark boards had been pried up. Wembley knelt down by the loose board, lifted it, and withdrew from the space beneath it a small tin box. He turned and took the box out to the porch, where there was light and a forensics table, and Reggie followed.

"Was that board already removed when the body was discovered?" said Reggie.

"No," said Wembley. "It was loose — O'Shea found it on her first walkthrough — but it was still in place. Your casual observer wouldn't have noticed. Put these on."

Wembley gave Reggie a pair of thin vinyl gloves, and then he opened the box.

There was just one item inside: a folded piece of newspaper, cleanly cut, and not yellowed.

Wembley carefully lifted it out and handed it to Reggie.

Reggie unfolded it. It was from *The Daily Sun*. It was less than a week old. Reggie had not seen this little article himself, but he had heard of it just recently. It was from the gossip pages, and the headline read:

It was a smart-ass description of their engagement trip to Newquay, to be followed by the announcement at the family castle, before Laura would have to jet off again to another film shoot. A honeymoon-in-advance, as the paper called it. The article included an itinerary, complete with dates and destinations and the obligatory speculation on whether the prospective groom would have the stamina to make it to their destination.

It was a rude thing to publish, but it was not surprising, given that it was Lord Buxton's paper.

"I presume the article itself is not news to you," said Wembley.

"No, it isn't," said Reggie. "I happen to be aware that Laura and I are announcing our engagement at the castle. I'm even roughly aware of the itinerary, and naturally Buxton would tweak us about it in his paper, both because that's what he does for a living and because Laura said no to him before she said yes to me."

"Right," said Wembley. "What I thought you'd want to know is that apparently this fisherman saw fit to clip out that article and only that article, save it in a tin box, and hide it away under the floorboards of his house."

"Before he got stabbed to death in his kitchen."

"Exactly," said Wembley. "Now, I lead a quiet life, myself, Heath. Not like you. But just personally, this sort of thing would worry me."

"So you think this dead fisherman was a celebrity stalker? Or one half of a couple of stalkers?"

Wembley shrugged. "Everyone has their fantasies, Heath. I just thought you'd want to know."

"I appreciate it," said Reggie. "I suppose the news media will be here shortly?"

"They're on their way," said Wembley.

"Do you suppose you can keep Laura's name out of it?"

"I'll try," said Wembley.

"May I keep this?" said Reggie, holding the news clipping.

"What are you going to do, frame it? No, of course you can't keep it. O'Shea will take it back to the lab, along with everything else."

They both turned and looked toward O'Shea, who was looking back at them from the truck. She smiled and waved.

Reggie put the clipping back in the box.

"You'll let me know what she finds?"

Wembley nodded. "It might take a few days. You could be on the road. I suppose we can call your hotel if necessary."

"Yes," said Reggie, "given that my itinerary is public knowledge. You can try my mobile, but there might not be a signal where we're going."

Reggie got back in his car and drove away from Canvey Island. He was anxious to get back to London. His trip with Laura was only days away, this was not his case, and he wanted nothing to do with dead people.

10

Reggie didn't want to have to tell Laura that a clipping of their travel itinerary had just been found in a concealed location at the scene of a murder.

And so he didn't. Not that evening, anyway. He thought he knew what to do about the situation, but he didn't think she'd like it, so he waited.

But in the morning, as he was sliding a perfectly grilled slice of French toast out of the skillet and onto Laura's breakfast plate, the telly was on, and it delivered the news for him, announcing the murder on Canvey Island, and describing details in even more lurid detail than was actually visible at the scene. The telly reporter went for a contrast between the allegedly sleepy seaside town and the grisly, blood-soaked murder scene, and the fact that evidence suggested that someone at the murder scene was obsessed with a well-known, but as yet unnamed,

London stage actress who was about to embark on a romantic excursion.

"Why is it always a kitchen knife?" said Laura. "You'd think we as a nation could occasionally be a little more creative than that."

"Whatever is at hand, I suppose," said Reggie.

"And who is this actress they're talking about? I'd hate to be her. All those teen slasher flicks notwithstanding, what could be worse than knowing that a crazed lunatic is stalking you on your tryst?"

Laura paused even as she said that.

"Not knowing?" volunteered Reggie.

Laura looked at him.

"Is there something you're not telling me?" she said.

Reggie told her.

Laura poured syrup over a single bite of French toast.

"I really like these corner pieces," she said to Reggie. "You get them so nice and crispy."

She ate that crispy, syrup-soaked bite and mulled things over for a moment.

"Well," she said, "I suppose I should be flattered that I've finally arrived as a celebrity. Though I would think commercial fishermen are not your typical scrapbook-ers."

"Scrapbooker?"

"It's what fans do these days."

"I thought we referred to such people as stalkers."

"They're only stalkers if they pin your photo to the wall and draw a red bull's-eye on it. Or if they jump the hedge and show up on your back porch invited."

"Well, this is close enough," said Reggie.

"But it's moot, isn't it? You said the poor man is dead."

"Well, yes. But we don't think he was completely alone in that house. Someone else was there, or he wouldn't be dead now."

"So we're saying there was a little nest of Laura Rankin worshipers holed up in a fisherman's little house and now one or more of them is on the loose?"

"I'm sure *worshipers* is a bit strong. But just in case you still have a living fan left, especially one obsessed with both you and kitchen knives, I want to adjust our itinerary a bit."

"What do you mean?"

"I want to change things up. We can go to all the same spots, but different hotels than the ones published. Except for the castle, of course. I know we have to go there. And I assume it's got fortifications."

Laura put her fork down and stared.

"Reggie, even if you try, you won't find alternative bookings at this late date. And anyway, you've told me yourself what terrible hotel luck you have. Whereas mine has always been wonderful, and none of what you've said gives me any reason to think this will be different."

"But —"

"Are you sure this isn't just an angle to get me to switch the whole thing to a sunnier clime?"

"It's not that at all," said Reggie.

"Well, then — I think you need to learn to just not worry. And if an obsessed whatever does turn up, I mean besides the specific paparazzi that are officially invited, there are more old shotguns in the castle than I can even count. And my aunt is trained on every single one of them."

"Now I'm really worried."

"There, you see? It's all a matter of perspective, when you compare it to a real danger. And make sure my aunt gets a really good look at you when you meet her for the first time. It might even be a good idea to be wearing whatever you'll be wearing in the evening when you try to sneak down the drafty hall from your room to mine."

"You don't mean that we have to stay in separate —"

"Well, once we're in the castle, yes, of course. I told you — there are these family traditions."

"Bloody hell," said Reggie.

11

Reggie dropped Laura off at her home in Chelsea that morning, and then he went on to Baker Street Chambers. He headed for his office, intending to start wrapping things up before his trip.

But Lois caught him in the corridor.

"You're going to kill me," she said.

"Nonsense," said Reggie. "If I were going to kill you, it would have been in the first week you were hired. You've been bloody well perfect since then."

"Thank you, and I hope you'll keep that in mind when I tell you this," she said. "There are two things. First, I'm afraid I got some dates mixed up. I scheduled a motion for you first thing in the morning on Tuesday."

"You don't mean on the Tuesday that —"

"Yes, I'm afraid so. First thing in the morning on the very day after you and Laura get back."

Lois, her cheeks turning just a little pink, reluctantly produced a rolled-up legal brief that she'd been hiding behind her back, and she gave it to Reggie. "I think it's a simple one, though," she said, hoping for a reprieve.

Reggie glanced at it. "It is," he said. "Not to worry. I've still got an hour this afternoon, and if it requires more than that, I'll just take it with me, and I'll prep for it on the way back."

Reggie opened his briefcase, stuffed the brief inside, and closed the briefcase.

"And then there's the other thing," said Lois.

"Yes?" said Reggie.

"I think I'd better just show you," she said.

Lois walked across to the window that overlooked Baker Street. She looked down, grimaced at what she saw, and said, "Yes, there he is. I'm so very sorry, he caught me off guard while I was worrying about my mistake with the scheduling, and he asked if you'd be in at all this morning, and in my weakened state I answered truthfully before I could stop myself."

Reggie joined her at the window and looked down.

Below in the street was Rafferty. He was standing next to his hatchback, which was parked illegally at the curb, and he was pacing back and forth impatiently, hands clasped behind his back.

And now he looked up.

Reggie and Lois both shrank back from the window.

"What's he want now?" said Reggie.

"Something to do with the letters again," said Lois. "Do you want to go out the back through the car park? I'll say I forgot to tell you he was here."

"Won't work," said Reggie. "See the way he's pacing? He must have seen me drive in. He walks up to the corner, looks at the car park entrance to make sure I'm not on my way out, and then he goes back to his vehicle, and then he goes to the corner again. I'll never get past him. I suppose if I timed it perfectly I could just run him over, but then there'd be a fuss."

"I'm so very sorry," said Lois.

"Well," said Reggie. "Perhaps I'll be able to just sneak by him. You can lock up after me."

Reggie took his briefcase with him and went downstairs to the lobby. He picked another suited businessman, crouched down a bit to try to hide behind him, and then trailed behind him out onto Baker Street. Then Reggie started out at a quick pace toward the car park.

"Heath! Glad I caught you!"

Reggie stopped. "I'm leaving the city for a few days, Rafferty. As you know full well."

"Yes, and this will be right on your way. Won't take a moment of your time."

"What are you talking about?"

"We have to retrieve the letters."

"What, you mean the ones we just put on display for the hotel?"

"Yes. They want us to take them back immediately."

"Why is that?" said Reggie. "Surely the exhibit isn't closing already?"

"I'm as annoyed with them as you are, Heath."

"It's not them I'm annoyed with," said Reggie.

"Just last week they were all keen on having the letters," said Rafferty, heatedly, "and now apparently we're just not good enough for them after all."

"Bloody shame," said Reggie. "I was hoping the hotel would just keep the things."

"I need you to help me bring them back," said Rafferty. "As I explained before, we can't have strangers handling them."

Reggie assessed Rafferty's level of stress, which seemed considerable.

"I can spare twenty minutes to help you collect them," said Reggie, finally, checking his watch again. "But then you'll have to drive them back yourself; I'm got some chores of my own."

"Agreed," said Rafferty.

Rafferty drove the hatchback and Reggie followed in his Jag.

This time they managed to park in the front without being challenged. The older doorman came out and tried to open their doors for them, and the younger one went quickly inside and came back a moment later with the hotel manager herself.

She was very happy to see them.

She said, "This is so good of you; thank you for your understanding."

"It is your hotel after all," said Rafferty, in a voice like that of a rejected lover. "The letters will survive without you."

If the hotel manager had a response to that, she managed to keep it to herself. She escorted them once again through the main lobby, with considerably more urgency and purpose than when they had brought the letters in.

That didn't bother Reggie at all.

There was a telly in the downstairs lounge adjacent to the lobby, and as the three of them went up the ramp toward the mezzanine Reggie caught a glimpse of the screen — just as the obligatory soccer match was being interrupted by a news program.

The broadcast headline was about the murder of a fisherman on Canvey Island.

As Reggie looked at the screen, so did the hotel manager, but if the news story mattered in any way to her, she did not show it.

They walked quickly along the corridor.

"Did something fall down?" said Reggie, as they reached the entrance to the letters exhibit.

"Excuse me?" said the woman.

"You've got the entire wall covered in the corridor, except for the spot right next to the letters exhibit. Didn't you have some sort of document on display there before?"

"Oh," she said. "It was damaged. A slight scratch in the glass. We're having it repaired."

They didn't pause; she ushered them right along into the letters exhibit.

"You'll ring me when you're done, please?" said the woman.

"If you like," said Rafferty.

Twenty minutes later, they had all the letters back down off the walls, including the one from the easel display, and nearly all of them stowed back into boxes.

The hotel manager returned.

"Quite done then, are we?" She walked quickly around the perimeter of the room, and she finished her inspection with a glance at the empty easel display at the center.

"So, you managed to get all of them, I see, with no problem?"

"Not to worry," said Rafferty, a bit petulantly. "We didn't damage anything."

"No, of course not," said the woman. "I was just . . . well. I'll just see you out then, shall we?"

She escorted them back along the corridor and down the carpeted ramp into the main lobby, with Reggie pushing the trolley stacked with boxes.

Rafferty brought the hatchback up to the front entrance.

"Let me get some help for you," said the woman, and she pulled the younger doorman from his station to help out. "Charles will load those for you," she said.

"Not necessary," said Rafferty. "We can handle it."

The doorman, no doubt feeling under the gun with the hotel manager standing by, moved to help out anyway. Reggie and Rafferty each loaded boxes into Rafferty's vehicle; the doorman picked up the final box before Reggie could turn back for it.

"No, wait," said Rafferty to the doorman.

But too late. Instead of lifting the box

properly from the bottom, the doorman tried to handle it just by grabbing the corner and a top edge — and the box collapsed.

Framed letters fell out onto the pavement, with a thud and the sound of breaking display glass.

"Bloody hell," said Rafferty.

"I'm very sorry," said the doorman, with a panicked glance back at the hotel manager.

The hotel manager said nothing, but just continued to observe.

"I'm so very, very sorry," said the doorman. He tried desperately to pick up letters and get them back into their frames and, failing that, to just get them stuffed somehow into the boxes already in the hatchback.

"Stop, stop," said Rafferty. "Just let me do it."

"I'm so very sorry," said the doorman again, finally stepping back.

Reggie pushed the boxes in securely, and Rafferty finally got the door shut on them.

"Well," said Rafferty. "No harm done, I suppose. Just a little broken glass."

"I'm so very —"

"Please," said Rafferty. "It's all right."

Clearly, by Rafferty's expression, it wasn't.

But thank God, thought Reggie. At least they were done.

"They're all yours, Rafferty," said Reggie.

Rafferty got in the van and drove out onto Marylebone Street.

Reggie turned to walk back to his Jaguar. As he did so, he saw the doorman trying pathetically to clean up the remnants of the broken box and glass, with the hotel manager still watching intently from the lobby entrance.

Then Reggie stopped. Something caught his eye.

"One moment," he said.

He stooped down toward the broken cardboard box that the doorman was about to carry to the trash, and looked closely — between the flattened sides, the edge of an old, yellowed piece of paper was visible.

"One more," said Reggie. He extracted the letter from the cardboard debris. "Got it."

"I'm so very sorry," said the doorman.

Rafferty had already departed with the other boxes. Reggie took the last remaining letter — it was the one from the easel display, which Laura had read from when they were putting them up — and he put it in his briefcase.

Then he locked the briefcase in the boot of his car.

"I'm so very sorry," said the doorman

once again to Reggie, as though he had sunk the *Titanic,* and he followed that apology with an apprehensive glance back at the hotel manager — who was still watching.

"Relax," said Reggie to them both. "It's just a letter."

Reggie got in his car and drove back to Baker Street. He parked, then looked both ways for Rafferty, didn't see him, and entered the Dorset House lobby and took the lift directly up to chambers. One more nonemergency taken care of.

He had a feeling he was forgetting something minor. But he knew it would come back to him if it was important.

He reached his office. And within seconds, Lois was in the doorway.

"Wembley called while you were out," she said, just a little out of breath from rushing over from her station. "He said it's urgent."

"He always says that," said Reggie.

But of course, sometimes it was true.

Reggie made the return call in his office.

"We got prints back from the murder scene at Canvey Island," said Wembley.

And then for some reason, the detective inspector paused.

"Yes?" said Reggie.

"Aside from Cheeverton's own prints, there was only one other set — and they were everywhere, in the loo, in the kitchen, on a half-eaten bag of little burgers, on the trash, everywhere, in abundance."

"So you're saying you think he had not just a date — but a houseguest."

"Yes," said Wembley. "Our best guess is that she has been living there with him over a number of days, at least."

"She."

"Yes. We ran the prints through the HOLMES database, and we got a match. We've identified her. It's a woman, and it's her prints — and only her prints — on the newspaper clipping. It wasn't his tin box hidden under the floorboard. It was hers."

"I suppose that's good news," said Reggie. "I think I'm more comfortable with it being an obsessed female fan, as opposed to a male stalker."

Wembley did not respond to that immediately.

"Right?" added Reggie.

"As I said, Heath, we've identified her. We know exactly who she is, and we know she's obsessed, but not a fan."

"Well, spit it out, Wembley. Who is she?"

"She's Darla Rennie."

Reggie felt his chest tighten. He said nothing for a moment.

Then he said, "That's not possible."

"It's fact," said Wembley.

"But Darla Rennie is dead!" said Reggie. "She fell between the spans of the Tower Bridge. She drowned in the Thames last September!"

"So we all thought," said Wembley. "And we tried hard to find the body. But not everyone who falls into the Thames drowns, Heath. Darla Rennie is alive. She is at large. And it was her that had Laura's itinerary tucked away under the floorboards."

"Thank you, Wembley," said Reggie.

"And I'm pretty damned sure it was her that stuck a kitchen knife into the fisherman she was living with," added Wembley. "You may recall that she knows how to use one."

Reggie got off the phone.

He recalled quite clearly that Darla Rennie knew how to use a kitchen knife. She had killed a man with one. And that was only one of the felonies she had committed before abducting Laura.

Reggie remembered that all quite clearly.

So now he called Lois into his office.

"Lois, do you know the itinerary for my trip with Laura?"

"Yes, sir, I do. Everyone who reads *The Daily Sun* does."

"Yes. Well. We are going to remedy that. I

182

want you to call around and make some changes to it."

"You mean you want me to change your reservations?"

"Yes."

"To what?"

"To something different. Anything different. Same dates, and the same ultimate destination, but different accommodations."

Lois gave Reggie a puzzled look. Reggie looked expectantly back.

"You mean different from what Laura booked?" said Lois, as if worlds would collide.

"Yes."

Lois shifted uneasily from one foot to the other and looked over her shoulder.

"Are you sure Laura will approve?" she said.

"Lois, who do you work for?" said Reggie.

"You."

"Then do as I say, and get the current itinerary from *The Daily Sun,* and then change all the accommodations that Laura already booked for me and her, and if anyone questions you, they can call me. And change the routes, too."

"But you are traveling by train. There are a limited number of —"

"Well, we're changing that, too. Now we're

going by car. And get us off the obvious main roads."

"I'll try."

"And don't let anyone know. The whole idea is, until we get to the castle for the engagement celebration itself I don't want anyone to know where we are, what route we're taking, or where we're staying."

Lois still looked stumped.

"What's wrong?" said Reggie.

"Sir, you're leaving in two days?"

"Yes? So?"

"Sir, have you ever planned an extended holiday?"

"Lois, I can't remember ever even taking an extended holiday."

"Well, the fact is, it just won't be possible to find alternative accommodations at this late date. Everything will already be booked."

Reggie drummed his fingers on the desk.

"All right then," he said. "Here's a thought. Try the woman who runs the Marylebone Grand Hotel. They're a huge chain; they claim everything travel related from petrol station convenience stores to flagship hotels. They've taken over local inns pretty much everywhere. So they should have something. She seemed to get on with Laura, and she owes us a huge favor for brightening up her little exhibit with our letters and then taking them back again on such short notice. Give her a call."

"I'll try, sir," said Lois. "But it will take some luck. I just hope you're one of those people who are lucky with hotels."

"Of course I am," said Reggie.

12

Late that night, on the top floor of the Marylebone Grand Hotel, Helene was in the suite that she reserved for herself whenever she had to do long hours at the hotel and there was no one with the prestige of a royal or better who would require her to give it up.

Tonight, London was shimmering outside her balcony, the view was spectacular, but she might as well have been on the ground floor, for all the good it was doing her.

She was staring at the World War II photo that she had taken down from the exhibit on the mezzanine.

Helene looked at that photo and tried to remember.

There had always been a special bond between her older brother and her grandfather; some sort of bond that she had never shared. That bond, she knew, was the reason that after all these years, and all her efforts, her brother was the CEO of the entire corporation — and she merely the manager of the hotels.

She had attributed that bond to her brother being older. She had attributed it to gender. She had wondered whether it was due to some sort of special knowledge that she had never acquired.

But now, as she looked at the photo again, it occurred to her for the first time — the difference was the bond that had been created on that day. The bond existed there in the photograph, in the faces of her grandfather and her brother. But it had not existed before.

That meant something, that the bond had not existed before. It meant something important. She tried to remember.

But now the phone rang, and she picked up. It was her brother.

There was no exchange of pleasantries. He asked her a question, and she responded, tensely.

"Mostly," she said into the phone. "I couldn't just pull it down and leave all the other letters up, you know, that would have just called attention to it, and I think that Rafferty person is genuinely paranoid about them. So I had him take them all back. Well, I did try to steal it out from under their noses, but that didn't work out now, did it? The point is, the letter is no longer on the wall, so no one else will see it. And I'm sure it wasn't those Baker Street folks that took the founder's document, so they don't have it to compare signatures with the letter. And anyway, what's the worst that could happen? A little public embarrassment? I know there's no statute of limitations on what Grandfather did one hundred years ago, but he's long since dead. What are they going to do, dig him up and put his decomposed body on display in a prison cell?"

Her brother said something scatological in the kind of angry voice he rarely dared use on her anymore, not since they became adults. But she didn't respond in kind.

"All right," she said. She sighed resignedly. "All right. There might be a way. If the letter still is where I think it is. I'll see what I can do."

She paused for a moment, and then she said: "I took the photograph down, you know. The one from the war, where Papa died? Someone on the publicity staff put it up. It was on display, and you could see — if you looked very closely, you could see a body. Not Papa. The other man who was there."

There was a pause, and then she said,

"Well, it wasn't right to show that in public, so I took it down. I . . . I've been looking at it. There was something that I . . . I've been trying to remember."

He made a response, and then she said, "Well, no, if I knew what I was trying to remember, I'd remember it, wouldn't I? But I was only five. You were nine. So I thought that perhaps you could recall what — Well, all right. Never mind then. I said never mind. . . . Yes, it will be taken care of. Goodbye."

She hung up the phone.

She stared for another long moment at the photograph, picking it up in both hands, as if by the pressure of them she could just coax something out of the black-and-white image.

And then she just put it facedown on the desk.

She didn't bother walking out to the balcony to view the skyline, not even for a moment. She couldn't resolve what was bothering her, and not even the spectacular view would help.

She just closed the drapes, and turned out the light.

13

At the bus stop on Broadway near Tothill Street in London, the R68 bus pulled to the curb and a woman in her mid-twenties stepped down onto the wet pavement. It was raining and she had no umbrella.

But a young man of just about the same age had been sitting behind her on the bus, studying the nape of her neck and the lace of her bra when she would move her left arm occasionally and afford him a glimpse, ever since she had gotten on outside the National Archives in Kew.

It was the third time this week he'd seen her get on at that stop. He'd been thinking for the past hour as they rode how he might best begin a conversation with her, and he supposed he might start by asking her what she was looking for there — he was pretty sure that was what the place was for, looking things up and doing research and the like.

But today she had surprised him. Before she had always taken the bus all the way into Marylebone, but today she got off the bus several stops earlier.

So he had to move quickly; and although this stop was not his own destination, he felt instinctively that it was his last and best chance.

He got off the bus after her, and he opened his own full-size street umbrella and lifted it in one smooth, powerful motion, and swung it protectively above her as if they were in fact long-term traveling companions, and intimate ones at that.

"We can share if you like," he said cheerily, matching her surprisingly quick pace. "You don't want to catch your death."

Just at that moment, as if the universe itself were in tune with his desires, the rain increased. She could hardly decline now; cold water was beginning to run in streams down the ringlets of her black hair. She would have to say yes. And next he would ask her to coffee, where it would be warm and dry.

When she turned to look at him, he saw the brightest emerald eyes he had every seen; he had thought he must be imagining things when he first saw her get on the bus, that they were just a trick of the light — but no, they were real.

She said, "Keep it in your pants, mate," and she pushed the umbrella away.

She walked on quickly down the street, despite the rain. And the young man, though he had wasted his bus fare in making his move, somehow had the good sense not to chase after her.

The young woman walked on to the next block, where there was a taxi stand. She got in the Black Cab at the front of the queue.

"Where to?" said the driver.

She sighed deeply as she sat down, as though she had just now gotten home and safe.

"I do so love these vehicles," she said, making herself comfortable in the spacious backseat. "I even love the smell of them."

"I can't take personal credit for that, miss."

"Well, that's good, I suppose."

"It's just the air freshener."

"And I so admire how you drivers always know where you're going."

"And do you, miss? Know where you're going, I mean?"

"Sometimes. But mostly I find that every day and in every way, I was wrong about something I thought I knew the day before. Especially in the last few months or so. I think there was a time when I was certain about things, but I don't remember it very well. Does that ever happen to you?"

"I don't think so," said the driver. "But my question is — do you know where you want to go right now?"

"Ahh," said the woman. "Yes. Scotland Yard. I hope you don't need directions; I'm not good at them."

"No, miss," said the driver. "I don't, and I can believe that you aren't, given it's only two blocks away. But it's raining, so I'll drive you there anyway. No charge."

14

The rain tapered off, and then started again with a vengeance late in the afternoon. About the time it did, Reggie Heath received another call from Detective Inspector Wembley.

This time, when Reggie heard what Wembley had to say he did not need to be told that it was urgent. He immediately drove through the downpour to Scotland Yard.

He was unable to find a covered space for visitors, and he was forced to use the outdoor car park. He sloshed his way past the revolving NEW SCOTLAND YARD sign to the main entrance, and shook the water from his umbrella.

A sergeant escorted him to the observation area for an interview room on the second floor.

Wembley was already there, waiting. He nodded at Reggie and pointed toward a subject who sat alone in the room on the other side of the glass.

Reggie looked. He blinked, tried to absorb what he saw, and looked again. He stared. His chest tightened involuntarily.

"Bloody hell," said Reggie, under his breath.

"It's her," said Wembley, nodding in the affirmative. "It's Darla Rennie. So she says; we're confirming her prints now, and it sure looks like her to me. What's your opinion?"

Reggie hesitated before answering. He really had no doubt at all, but he just didn't want to believe it. He stared through the one-way window, and then, as if she knew exactly at that moment that he was looking, she turned her head toward the glass and looked directly back.

Still the most startling emerald eyes Reggie had ever seen.

"It's her," said Reggie.

"I thought you'd know," said Wembley. "I believe you had a closer look at her than I did at the time."

The reference was to the events of six months ago, and it wasn't nearly as close a look as some people had been insinuating, Reggie wanted to say. But he didn't. There was no point in acknowledging hinted lies from *The Daily Sun*.

"How did you apprehend her?" said Reggie.

"We didn't. She just walked in this morning, of her own accord."

"Did she say where she has been the past six months?"

"Yes. Shacked up with our murdered fisherman in Canvey. Except of course, she says, during the time at which he was killed. She says she wasn't there when it happened. Says she just found him that way at the house and then got scared and left the scene."

Reggie stared through the one-way window for a long moment, at the petite young woman, seated alone at the hard plastic table.

She looked back directly at Reggie again through the glass.

The look was all wide-eyed innocence.

"Do not let her out," said Reggie, under his breath.

"We don't plan on it," said Wembley.

"When is the bail hearing?"

"In three days."

"Laura and I will be out of town."

"That's fine," said Wembley. "If you add the fisherman to the Black Cab murders, there's not a magistrate in the city that would grant her bail. But when it comes to trial, I expect both you and Miss Rankin will be called to testify to what you know about the Black Cab case."

"We'll be back in plenty of time for that," said Reggie. "And I wish the prosecution all the success in the world. Darla Rennie drowned in the Thames, or Darla Rennie locked away for life, either one is fine with me."

Reggie turned to leave.

"Wait," said Wembley. "One more thing."

Reggie paused at the door.

"She wants to talk to you," said Wembley.

"What?"

"Rennie said she'll tell us everything we want to know. But first she wants to talk to you."

Reggie looked through the window. Darla Rennie wasn't staring back now; she was just sitting there, expectantly, as though she had just come in for a job interview.

"What the hell for?" said Reggie.

"She wouldn't say."

"Suppose I don't want to talk to her?"

Darla Rennie looked for all the world as though at any moment she might just begin whistling a tune and tapping her foot.

"That's your prerogative," said Wembley. "But I think it would help us out. She claims to be a changed woman, Heath. She says that she remembers some things that took place in her life before she fell into the Thames, but not others. She pretty much promised she'd confess what she does remember, but only to you."

"Why?"

Wembley shrugged.

Reggie thought about it just briefly, and then he said, "It's a trick."

"In what way?" said Wembley

"I don't know. But if Darla Rennie asked for it, it's a trick. Maybe she's trying to disqualify me as a witness."

"You aren't *that* important as a witness. And if you get her to confess, we won't need further testimony from you at all. Or Laura, either."

Reggie considered that. If he and Laura could both be spared having anything further to do with Darla Rennie at all, that would be a good thing.

Still — it had to be a trick.

"Have you advised her that anything she says in that room is being recorded?" said Reggie.

"Yes, of course. She's had all the proper warnings."

"You know that she took medications to control her schizophrenia? Did you ask if she's on them now?"

"Does it matter?"

"If she isn't, that could be the trick. She'll claim her confession wasn't voluntary, because she was off her meds and couldn't properly consent. I don't think anyone's ever tried that excuse, but I wouldn't put it past her."

"Well, in fact she is on them. And we have mental health professionals from the Public Health Service who say she's competent. In fact, however bonkers she was when she went into the river, they said their initial opinion right at this minute is that she's perfectly sane and has an excellent grasp on reality. I've already checked with the Crown Prosecution Service, and Langdon said it won't be an issue. So stop making excuses, Heath. Just go in and talk to her. She won't bite — probably — and you'll have it over with."

Surely there was some other objection to be made — but Reggie couldn't think of it.

"All right," he said finally. "But if she looks at me and I turn to stone, you're responsible for shipping my cold remains back to Laura."

Wembley nodded. "If that happens, Scotland Yard will be happy to pay the freight, no matter what it costs."

15

A sergeant opened the door to the interview room and admitted Reggie.

The room was carefully and deliberately sparse, with institutionally neutral pale green walls. There was one heavy plastic table, a chair on one side of it for the interviewee, and two chairs on the other side — one for the interviewer and one for a third party who was usually required to be present but would not be this time, because that's what the Yard had agreed to.

The constable exited, and Reggie was alone in the fishbowl with Darla Rennie.

She looked directly up at Reggie.

Reggie did not want to stare, but knew he could not let her think he was avoiding her glance, either. He looked back.

This woman had Darla Rennie's face, but it had changed. The woman he had known before had an expression that was composed and controlled — as though impenetrably hiding something, though he hadn't recognized that at the time.

Now her expression was composed and relaxed. But of course that was probably an act as well. She must have just gotten better at it.

The last time Reggie had spoken with Darla Rennie, she had been under the delusion that he was Sherlock Holmes, that her long-lost ancestor was the fictional villain known as James Moriarty, and the words she had said to Reggie at that time, just before abducting Laura in a Black Cab, were these: "I will take from you what you value most."

Reggie had one goal now, and that was to make sure she would never get to try to follow through on that threat again.

Reggie pulled out one of the hard chairs and sat down across the table from her.

"Do you know my name?" he said.

"Of course. I asked for you."

She smiled just slightly as she said it.

Reggie did not move. He said, "Tell me who you think I am then."

"You are Reggie Heath, Q.C."

"All right," said Reggie. "Then you no longer believe that I am Sherlock Holmes?"

"No," said the woman.

"You used to believe that," said Reggie.

"So I am told. But I no longer have that delusion."

"Do you know who you, yourself, are then?" asked Reggie.

"Are you asking how well I know myself, or are you asking my identity?"

"Let's start with that second thing," said Reggie.

She started to answer, and then she stopped. She said, "I've had a conversation like this already with the mental health professional. I will be telling you the same thing."

Reggie nodded. "I would still like to hear it," he said.

"Very well. I have researched it to some lengths at the National Archives, and at some other places, and although there are still some things that are uncertain, I can tell you who I am to the extent that my identity is defined by my lineage. My name is Darla Rennie. I am twenty-five years old. I was born in 1973. My parents were Donna and John Rennie, both killed in a car accident two years ago. My mother was an American citizen who came to London in 1962, met my father, married him, and acquired both his name and citizenship. My mother's maiden name was Moriarty. She was the granddaughter of an American named James Moriarty the Second, who came here with the American army during the war and died in a German V-2 attack. His father was James Moriarty, an American who spent some time here in London, and who died in 1893."

"And how," said Reggie, very carefully and distinctly, "did that first James Moriarty die?"

Darla Rennie sighed and looked down at the table for a moment. She seemed to be gathering herself. She raised her head up and gave Reggie a direct and steady look. And then she said this, rattling it off as though it were a legal recital: "You are asking whether I still believe that my great-great-grandfather was the fictional James Moriarty who was killed in a fictional struggle with the fictional Sherlock Holmes at the nonfictional Reichenbach Falls in a nonfictional year more than a century ago. And my answer is no. My great-great-grandfather was indeed named James Moriarty, but he was not killed by Sherlock Holmes at Reichenbach Falls, and you are not Sherlock Holmes, whether fictional or otherwise. I have a firm grasp on all of that. You can ask everyone who has examined me. My delusions are gone."

That statement was more direct and to

the point than Reggie had expected. It took him a moment to absorb it.

"Then why did you ask for me?" he said.

Now Darla shifted slightly in her chair, glanced down at the table, then to the side, then down at the table again for a long moment. Then she sighed, and she looked up directly at Reggie.

"I just wanted to say that I am sorry."

This was unexpected. Ordinary criminals would claim repentance when they were convicted and being sentenced, when they were certain they had no other choice but to pretend it. But Darla Rennie had yet to stand trial.

And she was not ordinary.

"For what?" said Reggie.

"For all the trouble I caused you and Laura Rankin."

"Trouble? Is that how you characterize it?"

"I don't mean to minimize it."

"And what sort of trouble do you think that was? I mean, specifically? Keep in mind of course that you are being recorded."

Darla glanced at the one-way mirror behind her, and then looked again at Reggie.

"Yes, of course," she said. "I am fully aware of the things I've done, and as I told

Inspector Wembley, I will confess to all of it."

Reggie just stared back at her for a moment, waiting for her to add a condition. But she added nothing.

"Very well, then," said Reggie, exhaling, finally. "We're done here, and thank you very much."

The "thank you" was just a reflex courtesy; Reggie would have taken it back if he could. He stood.

"Wait," she said.

Reggie paused.

"I need a lawyer," she said. "I want you to recommend a solicitor, and I want you to represent me when it goes to trial."

"Why in blazes would you want that?" said Reggie.

"Because you are the best," she said, "and because it would mean you have accepted my apology."

"I have accepted nothing from you," said Reggie. "An apology is not sufficient for the things you have done and tried to do. But more to the point, I couldn't represent you if I wanted to. I'm a material witness in your killing of the cabdriver six months ago. The killing that I was accused of, because you framed me for it. Or had you forgotten?"

"I had, actually. But only momentarily.

I've remembered it all now. And I didn't mean that I want you to represent me for any of that."

"What are we talking about then?"

"Did you hear of the killing of a private fisherman down at Canvey? A Mr. Cheeverton?"

Reggie's chest tightened; his pulse quickened just slightly. He had been carefully avoiding this topic of conversation; he indeed wanted to know what she had been doing in Canvey, but he wanted the statement to come from Darla Rennie on her own, not prompted by him. And it wasn't just a legal strategy. It was instinct. He wanted to keep Darla Rennie at the greatest possible distance from Laura and himself.

"Yes, I've heard of it," said Reggie, very carefully.

"I am accused of it."

"I know. Your fingerprints are on the knife that killed him."

"I used that knife in the kitchen."

"Apparently so."

"I mean to help prepare meals."

Reggie looked directly at her and said:

"Your fingerprints are also on a tabloid account of Laura Rankin's travel itinerary for the next week, hidden in the room where you were living. Explain that to me, please."

Quite uncharacteristically, she fidgeted. Then she said:

"When I first came out of the water, I did not know who I was. Mr. Cheeverton knew, but he did not tell me. He would always turn the telly off when the news broadcast came on, and he would never let me see certain sections of the paper he brought home. And so I knew there was something in the news. I began to read very carefully through everything that he did allow into the house. And one day I saw that article — about you and Laura Rankin — and that's when I began to remember. I began to remember what I had done. And I began to track down who I was. And where I am from. There are some things that I still only suspect; there are some things that I want to prove, but cannot — not yet. But it was that article that made me begin to remember who I am — and what I have done. And that's why I kept it."

Reggie considered all that, did not believe much of it, and he said, "Even if the Bar Council would allow it, I wouldn't represent you."

"Why not?"

"Bloody hell, you tried to drive the woman I love off the Tower Bridge!"

She nodded.

"I know," she said. "I mean, I don't deny it. I remember now all the things I did while under the influence of my delusions — not the visceral substance of them, not how any of them felt at the time when I did them, or even clearly why I felt that it was acceptable for me to do them. But the fact that I did them? Yes. I remember that. I don't deny any of it. But I'm back on my meds and I'm better now."

Reggie sat down. He stared across the table at her, trying to suss out what she was doing.

"You're preparing a bloody insanity defense," he said.

"No," she said. "Not anymore."

"What?"

"I tell you honestly, I no longer believe that you are Sherlock Holmes or that I am a descendant of the fictional character Professor Moriarty. That part of me is simply gone."

"Then you're claiming temporary insanity," said Reggie. "And I'm not buying it. Even if everything you just said were true, it would only mean that your delusion is gone. In my book, whatever actions you were willing to commit while under your delusion are also actions that you would be willing to commit with a full grasp of reality. The perception of reality might change. I don't believe the moral choice does. You committed premeditated murder under your delusion. Given comparable circumstances in real life, without the delusion, you would make similar choices. You would kill again, and I will not handle your defense."

Darla Rennie cleared her throat slightly; she looked about the room and down at the table. She raised her head to look at Reggie, then immediately lowered it again.

"Remind me," she said. "Tell me again what it was I did?"

Reggie began to recite her history:

"Your scheme for the Black Cabs caused the deaths of two American tourists."

"That wasn't supposed to happen," she said. And then she quickly added, "But I know it was my fault."

"And then you killed the Black Cab driver who was part of your scheme. You drank a glass of wine with him and then you put a kitchen knife into him."

"Yes. He was trying to blackmail me."

"And you were an accessory in the killing of the second cabbie."

"Yes. Because of what he did. He wasn't supposed to kill the American tourists."

"In other words, he didn't follow instructions, and so you were annoyed with him."

She sighed, looked away, and then back at Reggie:

"You can put it that way if you like," she said. "I'm not denying that one, either."

"Well, God help us all if you get annoyed again." Reggie stood and looked down at her. "You have now confessed," he said.

"I know that," she replied.

"I'm sure you'll find some barrister who'll help you plead whatever you want, but it won't be me, and if there's any justice at all in the British legal system, it won't work."

"Please. Help me," said Darla Rennie.

There was a tone in her voice that Reggie had never heard, and he looked back.

She looked up at him, and she said:

"I nearly died in the river. And I've had months with nothing to do but think about my past actions and what they mean."

"State your point," said Reggie.

"Have you never thought back to something you did long ago and wondered how you could be so clueless, so ignorant of the consequences to other people, that you would have done it? And that you would never do such a thing again, now that you have become aware of it?"

"Yes," said Reggie. "But we're not talking about the crime of me standing up my first date at an adolescent dinner party out of sheer terror. The things that you did are at another level. You're claiming your delusions are gone. Perhaps that's true, but I've no way of knowing that you won't go off your meds again. You also claim a life-changing experience. Repentance. I'm not the judge of that, but the first test of your sincerity is that you accept the responsibility and consequences for your actions."

She nodded.

"I know," she said. "I confess to all of it. I will not plead insanity or diminished capacity in any way. I will make no excuses and present no witnesses at sentencing. I will simply plead guilty and accept my sentence without complaint, knowing full well that I deserve whatever punishment the court dispenses."

Reggie paused.

"Well," he said. "All right, then. Good to know. But I still can't represent you."

It was time to restore the distance between them. He turned once again toward the door.

"I did not do it," she said.

"I don't care."

"I didn't kill the fisherman," she said. "I did all the other things, and I will accept my punishment for them. I know I will not go free. But I did not kill the fisherman.

Perhaps I would have done, if he had attempted to do what I know he was thinking about doing. But he didn't, and so I didn't."

Reggie shook his head. "I still can't help you. You must get someone else."

Reggie exited the interview room and closed the door behind him. He went back to the observation area, where Wembley and an official from the Crown Prosecution Service had been watching.

Reggie joined them, and they all watched through the one-way window as a constable came in and escorted a quiet Darla Rennie from the interview room.

"Nice work," said Wembley. "She admitted to each of her individual crimes. All on tape. All with the proper legal cautions. I knew there was a reason why we called you."

"Be careful," said Reggie. "She admitted to the Black Cab crimes, but you already had the evidence to convict her on those, so she undoubtedly knows that there's no point in denying them. And none of her promises about how she's going to plead at sentencing are legally binding. And she didn't admit to anything regarding the fisherman in Canvey."

"We'll get her on that one as well, when Forensics is done. Her only hope on that was self-defense, and now that she's admitted that he did not in fact assault her, we'll get her for that murder, too."

"Do whatever you need to do," said Reggie. "But don't let Darla Rennie back out on the street."

16

Reggie returned to Baker Street Chambers. He had an early dinner date with Laura, he was running late, and he had not yet had time to even consider what he would tell her about what had just transpired at Scotland Yard.

And then, as he entered chambers, he saw her sitting there at his desk — which was good. But he read the expression on her face — and he knew that he had already bolluxed it up.

And it wasn't that he was late for dinner. Laura had already adjusted to that. She'd gotten yesterday's bag of mini-burgers from the hotel out of his cooler and had it open there on his desk.

"I thought we had agreed," said Laura.

"We did," said Reggie. And then, "About what?"

"Lois gave me this just now," said Laura. She stood, and held up a sheet of paper.

"Apparently, it is our new travel itinerary."

"Ahh. Yes," said Reggie. He had forgotten that he had done that. The shock of actually seeing Darla Rennie at Scotland Yard had quite pushed it out of his mind. "I asked Lois to see if she could make a few changes. Nothing major, though, I'm sure."

"Reggie, I had us booked on a nice, leisurely train trip through Cornwall," said Laura. "I had us in the top-floor suite of a quaint little bed-and-breakfast, with a view of the garden and the lake and the apple orchard."

"Yes," said Reggie. He began to worry.

"You have us driving back roads through the Dartmoor National Park, with a stay in the Marylebone Super Slumber — which was formerly a combination convenience store and petrol station, and which now has four lovely one-hundred-and-fifty-square-foot studio units, one of which was still available, which will be ours, and will be the one closest to the motorway on-ramp. Which is convenient, I suppose, since we are now driving, rather than rocking and rolling happily along on the train."

"Yes. Well, you see — how do you know we have the room closest to the motorway on-ramp?"

"I know these things because I think to

ask. This is why I have good luck with hotels and you have bad. It's because I plan ahead and then I ask."

"Yes," said Reggie. He had always known this about Laura, this careful-planning thing. He was not sure whether he loved her because of it or in spite of it, and undeniably it was sometimes useful — but either way, it was putting him on the spot at the moment.

"Yes," he said again. "But there is a reason."

"A reason to book close to the on-ramp?"

"No, I mean there was a reason why I asked Lois to change the reservations."

"Yes, I know — a clipping of our itinerary at a murder site. But we discussed that. It's nothing at all to worry about. And we agreed that we would proceed as planned."

"Yes," said Reggie. "But that was before we knew who the clipping belonged to."

"Well, all right, then," said Laura. "I'll ask if I must. Who did it belong to?"

Reggie hesitated, then said:

"Darla Rennie."

Laura stared at Reggie for a moment.

"That young woman is dead," said Laura.

"No," said Reggie. "She fell from the bridge, but she did not die. She survived."

Laura sat down.

"When did we discover this?"

"The Yard found her fingerprints everywhere in the house — in the loo, on the kitchen utensils, on fast-food wrappers . . . and on the clipping of our itinerary. So I asked Lois to change the itinerary. And we got professional help to do it, too — the manager from the Marylebone Grand Hotel. She pulled strings to get our reservations at this late date."

Laura thought about all this for a moment.

"All right," she said finally, nodding. "If I have to stay at the Super Slumber to avoid a felonious twenty-five-year-old obsessed with my fiancé, I'm willing to do that."

"I think the relevant thing is that she tried to drive you off the Tower Bridge and into the Thames."

"Well, yes — but it was you she was obsessed with, Reggie, not me. I'd have been fine if she didn't want to jump your bones. I know a rival when I see the claws come out, and she was one. Or was trying to be. It's a good thing I'm so secure, or I'd be worried now that she'd be ringing you up for a pint and a shag."

Reggie tried not to confess that Darla Rennie had indeed, in effect, rung him up.

"You'll be happy to know that she's in

custody at Scotland Yard at this moment," he said instead. "And for more serious crimes than allegedly wanting to jump my bones."

"Under arrest, then?"

"For the murder of the fisherman and for everything she did before she went for her little swim in the river."

"Well, that is good to know. The Yard is sure they have the right person?"

"It's her. I've seen her myself."

"You mean she *did* ring you?"

Reggie stammered for a moment, then found his voice:

"No," he said. "She did not ring me. Well . . . at least not technically. It was the Yard that rang me."

Laura absorbed that.

"Well, all right, then," she said. "I don't know why, but for some reason I was just thinking that if Darla Rennie ever managed to swim back up from the murky depths the first thing she would do is try to look you up."

"Well," said Reggie. "She . . . she did in fact ask Wembley to contact me."

"I knew it!" Laura actually jumped up out of her chair.

"But only for legal representation."

"Oh, sure. Is that her standard line?"

"I said no, of course," said Reggie quickly. "And I persuaded her to confess. To everything except killing the fisherman in Canvey. She's denying that, for all the good it will do her."

"Are we sure that charge will stick?"

"Her fingerprints are on the murder weapon, and plunging a kitchen knife into a troublesome but unsuspecting male is an M.O. she's used before."

"But why," said Laura, "would Darla Rennie admit to all the murderous rot she did with the Black Cabs — and then deny killing this fisherman in Canvey?"

"I don't know," said Reggie.

"Perhaps she didn't do that last thing?" said Laura.

Reggie shrugged. Emphatically. He sat back in his chair and said, "Not our problem."

"That's certainly true," said Laura.

"She claims an alibi," said Reggie. "She says that she was in fact at the Marylebone Grand Hotel at the time the murder occurred. But she has no corroboration. The hotel has CCTV, and Hotel Security turned the tapes over to the Yard. They couldn't find her on the video. It's not a perfect system; there are some blind spots. But even so —"

"What was she supposedly doing at the hotel?"

"Visiting the exhibit, she says."

"Or stalking us," said Laura.

"She had no way of knowing we were there. So if she was at the hotel, it was for some other reason. But as I said, there's nothing to indicate that is where she was when the crime was committed."

"Hmm," said Laura, and she sat back down. Then she said:

"Well, then. From a travel perspective, this is actually good news. If it was Darla Rennie who was hiding our itinerary under floorboards, and she's now in custody and will remain so, then we no longer need to worry about a crazed stalker. We can go back to my original travel bookings."

Reggie nodded. "I'll have Lois cancel what she set up through the Marylebone Grand manager."

"Let's celebrate," said Laura. She opened the bag of mini-burgers, took one of the little sandwiches out, and began to unfold its bright red-and-white wrapper.

Reggie was staring at her.

"What?" said Laura. "I've seen you eat much worse things. We're British, for God's sake. Just wait until you get to my aunt's castle, if you want see a meat dish that's truly stomach curdling."

"It's not what you're eating," said Reggie. "I'm trying to remember where I've seen those wrappers before."

"At the hotel, of course," said Laura. "That's where I got them. They're just for the exhibit; I've never seen one anywhere else."

"Yes," said Reggie. "But I have. At the murder scene in Canvey."

Laura stopped eating. She looked at the wrapper, and then at Reggie.

"The hamburger wrappers at the dead fisherman's house are like this?"

"Yes," said Reggie.

"The hamburger wrappers that have Darla Rennie's fingerprints on them?"

"Yes."

Laura stopped eating. She sighed. She put her burger wrapper back in the bag. She put the bag of burgers back on the desk. She stared at them for a moment, and then she said:

"Do you know what that means?"

"No," said Reggie, not quite honestly. He actually did have a suspicion what it might mean, but he didn't want to go there.

Laura went there anyway:

"Does Forensics have a time of death for the poor fisherman?" she said.

Reggie nodded. "The body was discovered at six in the evening, and Forensics put the time of death as one to two hours before that."

Laura considered that, and then said:

"Darla Rennie can't have done it then, can she?"

"How do you mean?"

"These little burgers and their unique wrappers went on sale at the hotel exhibit just when we arrived, at four in the afternoon. They were never available before that — see, there's even a date on the wrappers. But it takes almost an hour and a half to get from Marylebone to the far end of Canvey Island. So if the time of death was between four and five, then Darla Rennie could not have done it — she would still have been en route from the hotel. She could not have got to the house before five-thirty."

"Hmm," said Reggie. "At the earliest, given she can't drive worth a damn, and buses take longer. But if she was at the hotel, why didn't we see her?"

"We might have missed her while we were in the exhibit room, hanging the letters," said Laura. "If you had a white board, I could draw it out for you. I know you're not good at itineraries."

"No need, I get it. But if she brought her sandwiches to the house after the fisherman was killed, then she must surely have discovered the body."

"Perhaps she did discover it — and then just fled?"

"So she claims," said Reggie. Then he cleared his throat and sat back to think about it for a moment.

"You realize," he said, "that you are suggesting a forensic alibi for Darla Rennie?"

"I don't think the problem is me suggesting it. I think the problem is that it's right there in front of us."

"So what do you want to do?" said Reggie

"What we must," said Laura. "We have no choice, do we?"

"There's always a choice," said Reggie. "We can choose to keep silent, and in all likelihood, she'll be convicted of the fisherman's killing as well as the others."

"Well, yes, but that means she'll be convicted of a crime that you and I know she didn't do."

"That's true," said Reggie. "But keep in mind the sort of crimes she did commit. What she tried to do to you before. And keep in mind that now that I've refused to represent her in court, she's likely to be even more annoyed."

"Well, none of that really matters, does it?" said Laura. "If we know something that proves her innocent of this one — regardless of all the other bad things she did do — we have to say, don't we?"

Reggie did not respond to that. He knew the proper answer. He knew what should be done.

He just didn't want to do it.

"I don't like the risk," he said. "The possibility she might get out and hurt . . . someone else."

"Well, who are you thinking she would be likely to —"

Laura stopped. She peered closely at Reggie. He tried to avoid eye contact.

Laura knew what that meant.

"Make the call," she said. "We're not putting this on me."

Reggie nodded. He picked up the phone and was about to ring Inspector Wembley at Scotland Yard.

And then, before Reggie put the call through, Laura put a hand on his arm.

"They won't just let her loose, will they?" she said. "Just because she didn't do this one thing? They'll hold her for all the other things that she did do?"

"Well," said Reggie. "They will certainly charge her with her other crimes."

"Good," said Laura. "And she won't just get out on bail?"

Reggie hesitated.

"She won't just get out on bail?" said Laura, again.

"No," said Reggie. "Well . . . not likely, anyway, given the severity of her crimes. And they will always deny bail if the accused is considered a danger to herself or others."

"Good," said Laura.

"But then, when I spoke to her at the station, she seemed — well — quite lucid. Nondelusional. Reasonable, even. Almost . . . persuasive."

"You're not saying she will be released?"

"No, not at all. I mean, if the mental health professionals in the National Institute of Health, and the justices of the Crown Court, and the barristers in the Crown Prosecution Service are all doing their job properly — they won't let her out."

Laura pondered the likelihood of that level of competence from all the officials in all those institutions, and many or most of them being men, in dealing with Darla Rennie. And then she said:

"Oh, bloody hell. We have to tell Wembley her alibi anyway, and that's all there is to it. So make the call. We'll use the changed itinerary, just as a precaution, and I'm going to go home and finish packing before I change my mind."

Reggie made the call.

17

At midmorning on Saturday, in front of Laura's house in Chelsea, in air that was crisp and clear, Reggie looked one last time into the boot of the Jaguar. In his opinion, everything necessary for the trip was now packed tightly inside.

There was not a lot of storage space in this aerodynamic and completely impractical vehicle, and it occurred to Reggie that his changing life circumstances might soon demand a change in daily transportation.

But for the moment, they would make do with what they had: One large suitcase for Laura, pushed as far back into the boot as possible, which wasn't far. One medium suitcase for Laura, squeezed in between the larger suitcase and the wiring of the rear taillight, just barely. One duffel bag for Reggie, mashed in on top of and around the edges of the others.

A small day case for Laura was tucked in

behind the passenger seat. The only thing remaining was Reggie's briefcase.

Reggie remembered the hearing that had been moved to Tuesday. Before stashing the briefcase into the boot, he sat down in the driver's seat, with the briefcase in his lap, and he opened it to make sure he had what he'd need.

Laura put a hand on his arm.

"You promised. You said not one moment of our trip would be waylaid by law chambers activities."

"I know," said Reggie. "But it's just a small brief — and I won't touch the bloody thing, I won't even take it out to look at it, until our trip is over and we are in the car and on our way back."

"Well, I'm not riding with you if you're going to be reading a legal pleading while you drive."

"Of course not," said Reggie. "I'll be in the passenger seat."

"So you're saying that I will get to drive your lovely XJS all the way back, through the twisty curvy country roads of Dartmoor?"

"Yes."

"With the top down?"

"Subject to weather conditions, yes."

"And at speeds that I deem manageable,

no matter how terrified you get?"

"Subject to regulations enforced by the local constabulary, yes."

"All right, then," said Laura. "You have a deal."

Reggie tucked the briefing document securely into its compartment, and was about to close the briefcase — then Laura stopped him.

"What's this?" she said.

Reggie looked. There was one document in his briefcase — old and yellowed — that should not have been there.

"Oh, bloody hell," he said. "I forgot I had it. When we were bringing the letters back from the hotel, I had to pick this one up off the street. I was going to just toss the thing, but then Lois told me the woman from the hotel called this morning just to find out if we'd got it safely back into the archives."

"It's historical, Reggie; of course you can't toss it. And Rafferty would get positively violent. Just keep it in there, and we'll return it when we get back."

"Fair enough," said Reggie. He closed the briefcase and got out to stuff it into the boot of the car. He shut the boot lid twice to make sure it had latched — and now they were ready.

Reggie got in on the driver's side.

"I told you it would all fit," said Laura.

"And you were right," said Reggie.

The Jaguar started on the very first try, and they pulled out into the road.

18

In the criminal evaluation wing of the National Institute of Health, Dr. Miner pondered the brain mapping of the highest profile case he had seen in his twenty years at the institute.

He had two sets of images taped on the wall — one taken of the young woman when her schizophrenia had first been diagnosed two years ago and one taken just in the last few days, six months after the trauma of her falling into the Thames River from the Tower Bridge.

The protocols did not allow for using brain images as a conclusive diagnostic tool for a behavioral condition, certainly not for purposes of sentencing. But there was already an image available from her care under a previous physician, taken just to eliminate the possibility of a tumor or identifiable physical brain trauma. And a current image had been taken to assess whether she had sustained any injuries in the recent fall from the Tower Bridge.

From a certain angle, and in a certain light, it seemed to Dr. Miner that perhaps blood flow within regions of the woman's brain had changed. Was this significant? He didn't know. And if it was a significant change, was it good or bad? He knew of documented instances of brain trauma having a negative effect on a person's later behavior.

But he had never heard of one where it worked in reverse.

Was it possible? Could the impact of the fall, or the prolonged effects of near drowning in the cold river, have somehow unblocked a blood vessel to a critical area? Could some abnormal mass of tissue have been destroyed, allowing the recovery and healthy growth of the normal area?

She was still on her meds, of course. But aside from that, was there an identifiable, provable, physiological change in the young woman's brain that would evolve her from the delusional schizophrenic that she had been to the calm, collected, bright, and completely normal woman that she now appeared to be? If so, it would be a first. Treatment for the disease was always lifelong.

Dr. Miner's job was to evaluate her for

purposes of either incarceration or confinement to a mental facility. But at the moment, that wasn't the first thing on his mind.

He was beginning to think of the journal article he would write about her, and where he would submit it, and the awards and recognition he would win.

He could be on talk shows. He could be sitting across from Oprah, discussing the nature of free will, the difference between good and evil, and how they related to the physiology of the brain. It would be great fun.

Of course, the young woman's future was at stake. There was also that.

And possibly also the well-being of people who might encounter her in the future, should she be released.

If she was still suffering from a mental condition and that was the reason she had committed her crimes, then she would be committed now to a facility for treatment, for an indefinite period that would probably turn out to be life.

But if she was no longer suffering from such a condition — if it could be irrefutably proven that the condition was the cause of her criminal acts and the condition was gone and could not return — then all bets were off. No one in an official capacity would be certain exactly what to do. It was not just a medical question; it was a legal one as well.

It was not unusual, of course, for an accused to claim repentance, to express regret, to undergo a miraculous conversion in the holding cell in the hope of gaining an advantage in sentencing. More often than not it was likely to be a sham, in Dr. Miner's opinion.

But Darla Rennie had not attempted a plea of temporary insanity. She had simply pled to the Crown's charges. No defense, no plea for any considerations at sentencing. Nothing at all. And that was unusual.

So much so that Dr. Miner had tried a little experiment — a test of her state of mind.

His office had a waiting room, much like the waiting room in any doctor's office — an upholstered sitting bench and a couple of chairs, indoor plants in the corners, old magazines on a coffee table, and, sometimes, copies of more-or-less recent daily papers.

Because the individuals Dr. Miner evaluated were in criminal custody, this room had a locking door and there were guards on staff, one at the front desk, and others available when needed. But aside from that, there wasn't much to keep someone in who was determined to get out. Even the evaluation room itself had a window to the outside world, with a view of trees, and an open gate, and the road — a view of freedom for the taking.

So on the first day that she was there, Dr. Miner had extended an unstated invitation to Darla Rennie to escape. After first arranging with a guard to be stationed out of sight down the corridor, the doctor had exited the evaluation room into the corridor, leaving the door visibly unlocked, and then he'd gone back into the adjoining room to watch through the mirror and see what Darla would do.

He watched as she turned her head toward the door. Then she looked out the window, at the trees stirring in the breeze, and then back at the unlatched door again.

And then she had remained seated, exactly where she was.

He tried another variation on it the following day, and again she ignored the opportunity.

So today he would do the last of those tests.

She was in the room now, reading today's *The Daily Sun.* And now he was about to go in and tell her that today was the last day of her evaluation. That he had completed all the tests and observations that were possible, that in his professional judgment she was perfectly sane and (though this would be a lie) probably had always been so — and that he would notify the correctional authority of that finding.

Which meant, he knew, and he knew she did as well, that upon leaving the mental evaluation facility she would be taken to Broadmoor, to begin a very long prison sentence.

It was hard to imagine this young woman as a murderer. Dr. Miner had made sure there were no sharp or pointed objects around, not in the waiting room, and not even in plain sight in his own office, just in case. Even so, it was hard to imagine.

But could she kill with a glance? Probably. Or more likely, a man would do his own self in, looking into those emerald green eyes and thinking there might be something there for him.

Dr. Miner didn't think that. He had been married thirty-five years, he was comfortably overweight and balding, he had gotten over the fantasies of office affairs long ago, and he knew how young women looked at him — or, rather, through him. He was not someone to be fooled on that score any longer.

He did, however, want to go on *Oprah.*

Dr. Miner took the brain images down from the wall now and put them into the case folder with his other documented findings.

He opened the door to the waiting room and looked in.

And then, in a panic, he dashed from the waiting room into the corridor.

Darla Rennie was gone.

Dr. Miner ran to the back door and looked out — no one in sight.

He ran back down to the front desk. The guard there initiated the alarm, and then they both ran out to the front gate.

No luck. The guard at the gate hadn't seen anyone, and he said so, as he hastily stuffed his lunch and sports paper under his chair.

The guard rang Scotland Yard to let them know.

Dr. Miner trudged back to his waiting room.

On the coffee table was today's *The Daily Sun,* open to the celebrity gossip pages.

The doctor was too discouraged to even look at it. His own visions of fame were rapidly fading. Instead of appearing on *Oprah,* he'd more likely get grilled in the media for letting a murderer loose.

He went into his office and shut the door behind him. He sat down behind his desk and put his face in his hands, waiting for Scotland Yard to call and his dreams of glory to be over.

Several moments went by.

And then Dr. Miner heard a sound from an adjacent room — something bumped, in the storage room on the other side of his office wall.

He raised his head out of his hands.

Could it be? Had Darla Rennie returned?

That room was kept locked, and it was still locked when he had looked for her in the corridor. But it was not a heavy lock. She could have picked it and gotten in, and locked it from the inside.

Or she might have been hidden somewhere outside and then come back into that room, now that Dr. Miner thought of it — because this was the room where they stored the clothes and few personal belongings that patients were allowed to have with them when they arrived.

Dr. Miner left his office and went into the corridor. He tried the latch on the storage room door. It was still locked.

Perhaps he had been imagining things. It might have been wishful thinking.

But he had a key, and he used it. He unlocked the door and pushed it open.

The room was silent — and dark.

He stepped inside and looked for the light switch.

It took him just one second too long to find it.

19

To get out of London, Reggie and Laura took the M5, as crowded and urban as any motorway in England.

Twenty minutes later they downsized slightly onto the M30. And then, two hours farther out, they turned off onto the scenic route through Dartmoor.

They drove for some fifteen minutes on a two-lane road, past farmland, hedges, and meadows. And then, with the air getting cold and the day getting late, Laura said:

"Are you sure this is the route?"

"Yes," said Reggie.

"Perhaps we should find someone to ask?"

"We have a map," said Reggie.

"Well, yes, but —"

"And I have complete faith in your ability to read it."

"I don't. Nor in yours while you're driving."

"Well, I suppose, if we see a petrol station, we should fuel up anyway. But I haven't seen one in the last ten miles —"

"There's one," said Laura, "straight ahead."

There was, indeed. And it was really about time; who knew how long it would be before there would be another?

"Last facility for twenty miles, it says," remarked Laura, looking ahead at the station's road sign.

Reggie pulled in.

It was a self-service, UNDER NEW MANAGEMENT, according to the placard in front. There was no attendant at the pump, but there was a convenience store, and a garage and tow truck in the back.

Laura went into the store for a consult on the map, and Reggie was about to fuel the car up when an attendant, late twenties, came out from inside the garage, wiping his hands on a greasy blue rag.

"I can help you with that!" he shouted.

"No need!" Reggie shouted back, but the attendant came over anyway.

"They can be tricky, sometimes," he said.

"I think I've got the hang of it," said Reggie. "Done it once or twice before."

The attendant studied Reggie's style of holding a petrol nozzle in a tank, and nodded sagely, as though he agreed that Reggie

241

might just possess the requisite skill.

And then he began to walk a 360 around the car.

"Had one of these, once," volunteered the attendant.

Reggie nodded.

"The carburetor can be finicky," said the attendant.

"This one's fine," said Reggie.

"Got her loaded up for a trip, do you?"

Reggie glanced over. The attendant was peering through the glass into the car.

"Nice interior," said the attendant.

"It came with the vehicle," said Reggie, hanging up the fueling nozzle.

"You pay inside," said the attendant. "If you like, I can give your car a once-over in the garage while you're doing that. The inspection's free. Have it done in a jif. Your tires look a little low."

"No, thanks," said Reggie. "The tires are fine."

Reggie made sure the Jag was locked, and then he went inside to pay. He joined Laura inside the convenience store, where she was finishing up a chat with the clerk. She had the map out, and bags of spicy crisps and juice from the store.

"They have an annoying attendant here," said Reggie.

"It's good we stopped, then," she said, handing Reggie one of the bags of crisps. "You know how you get when you're hungry."

Reggie and Laura got back in the Jag and pulled out onto the road.

In the rearview mirror, Reggie could see the attendant standing in front of the garage, still wiping his hands with the greasy rag as he watched them drive away.

They continued on the two-lane road, through rolling, rocky hills, passing the occasional sheep and wild ponies, but seeing few cars on the road.

Laura had the window down, her hair was undone with wind, glinting red and gold in the sun as they sped along, and for a while Reggie forgot any notion of someday soon trading his car in for something more practical.

Just then the first raindrops began to splat on the windshield — individually at first, then in teams, and then, as Laura gave up and rolled up her window, in a torrent.

No matter. A bit of rain on a country drive. That's what country drives and rain were for. So that you could tell the difference between that and lying on a sunny beach in the South Seas.

And then — so far along into the national

park that they weren't even passing sheep anymore, and with not a farmhouse or cottage in sight — Reggie felt just the slightest rotating vibration from the passenger side of the car.

And then a faint sound to accompany it, in aggravating rhythm.

And he knew immediately what it had to be, even before Laura said anything — but he just couldn't believe it, because he had bought a complete new set of tires just two weeks before, in preparation.

"Is that what I think it is?"

"Yes," said Reggie. "We have a flat."

Reggie pulled the car to the side of road — at least to the extent possible. The water had carved out a muddy little stream, and it wasn't possible to get completely clear of the narrow road without dropping the front wheel into that gully.

Reggie started to get out of the car.

"It's pouring buckets," said Laura. "Let's just call the Automobile Association."

She picked up her mobile and tried.

No reception. Reggie tried with his, with the same result.

"Well, here we are then," he said. "I'm sure this won't take a minute."

"I'll help," said Laura.

"No need," said Reggie. "I've got it."

Reggie got out of the car and into the rain; he opened the boot, and dug beneath the packed-in luggage to find the compartment that enclosed the spare. He began to search for the spanner and jack, which were buried underneath all the luggage. Rain poured in all the while.

And then, with the afternoon growing very late, headlights appeared on the road behind them.

A large vehicle slowed and pulled over.

It was the tow truck from the petrol station.

Reggie stood up from trying to get the tools out of the boot. He turned and saw the garage attendant he had spoken to earlier get out of the truck.

The man walked over to Reggie, but he didn't bring his tools with him.

"Little trouble on the road, mate?"

"As you can see," said Reggie.

"Hmm," said the man. He made no move to take a closer look, or to do much of anything. He just stood there, studying Reggie, and the open boot of the Jaguar, and the general situation as though he had never seen anyone with a flat tire before.

"So," he said after a moment. "A big-time London barrister, are you then?"

"Why do you say that?" said Reggie.

The man looked caught off guard, just for an instant, by that obvious question. And then he said, "I know London barrister luggage when I see it."

Reggie didn't buy that explanation. But at the moment, he didn't much care.

"Can you change it for us?"

The man shrugged. "Looks complicated," he said. "Might be it needs to go back to the shop."

"It's just a flat," said Reggie.

"Never know what might come up," said the garageman. "A lot easier to do in town."

Reggie reached for his wallet. He knew he was going to be charged a premium. Probably the garage attendant intended to make a week's salary here and now. Under the circumstances, Reggie was willing to pay it, if it would get them under way any quicker.

"There's a spare in the boot, and I know it's a good one. I'll move the luggage myself so you can get at it. How much to change the tire right here?" he said.

"Not in London now, are you? These are the moors, you know."

"Look," said Reggie. "It's a simple question."

"Not in a court, either, unless courts have changed their appearance since I was last in one."

Reggie guessed that probably had not been too long ago and by "in one" the fellow probably meant standing in the dock.

"Can you change this tire or not?" said Reggie.

"Well now, there's the question of what I can do, and then there's the question of what I will do. What I will do is what I've already said: crank your vehicle up onto the flatbed for you, and drive both you and this lovely woman, who it appears to me has shown great patience with you, into the next town, where you can both go to the pub and get a nice serving of fish-and-chips — and quite honestly, she looks hungry to me, mate, if you don't mind me saying so — while the garage fixes your vehicle. I'll even come in and hoist one with you and the lady; the first round is on me."

In an earlier day, or in just a slightly different setting, or with just the slightest difference in phrasing in the words coming out of this lout's mouth, Reggie would have flattened him. He was ready to do so now.

But the rain was pouring down, and he was trying to stay focused on his objective — which was to get off the road and out of the rain — and mainly, most important, to get Laura in a warm bed for the remainder of the evening, safely, away from crazed stalkers and Darla Rennie and the paparazzi and anyone else who might be inclined to interfere. No complications. No drama. Just that.

And so Reggie merely growled:

"The car doesn't need fixing. All we bloody need is for you to change the bloody tire. Are you going to do that?"

"Well, it's raining, mate, can't you tell? So I'll do what I said and take you and the car and the lady into town — or you can change the bloody tire yourself. You choose."

"Just get the fuck out of the way," said Reggie.

For a moment, it looked as though the tow driver might not do that. For just a moment, it looked like they would indeed come to blows. Reggie could see in the bloke's eyes that he was ready to do so, as ready for it as Reggie himself now was.

"Suit yourself," said the driver, and then he stepped aside, and with just one quick glance back over his shoulder he stomped back to the tow truck.

Reggie watched in just a bit of surprise. It was not standard procedure for the tow driver to refuse to do the repair. He had to know that Reggie would later call and complain to his employer. And it was not a sensible course of action, if the driver had simply been intending to run a road repair scam, to have pushed it so close to a confrontation. There was no advantage to be gained in doing that.

Reggie knelt in the mud to change the tire. Laura stood in the rain, trying to hold the umbrella over both Reggie and herself and the baggage, as he finally wrestled the spare out of the boot.

"What was all that about?" said Laura. "Why was he so insistent on driving us into town?"

"I've no idea," said Reggie. "Hold it a little to the left, please?"

20

It was dusk when Reggie torqued the last bolt into place.

There were no streetlamps; there were in fact no lights visible of any kind in any direction.

Still standing with the umbrella in the rain, Laura asked if she should get the torch out of the boot.

"No," said Reggie. "Nearly done."

And he was, but it was a bloody good thing. He was pretty sure there was indeed a torch in the boot, but he also couldn't remember the last time he had checked the batteries in it.

He pounded the wheel cover back into place.

"Piece of cake," he said.

Soaked and muddy, they put the tools away, tried to shake the water off the umbrella, and got back into the car.

Reggie turned the key. The starter

cranked, at a high pitch. Then nothing.

Reggie glanced over at Laura. If she was concerned, she wasn't showing it. She stowed the umbrella behind the seats.

Reggie turned the key again; the starter whined — and then the engine caught on, spit twice through the tailpipe, and roared into life.

Laura smiled slightly.

"That's nice, isn't it?" she said.

Reggie nodded, and they drove out onto the road.

Forty minutes later they spotted the turnoff for the Marylebone Super Slumber hotel.

The rain was letting up. The yellow and white lights of the hotel broke the darkness.

They drove up securely, on a fine gravel road, to a building that had once been a large country farmhouse but now, to all appearances, was completely renovated. The white paint on the exterior walls fairly glowed with ethereal light. Candles and tablecloths were visible through the windows on the first floor.

It was wonderful.

A young male bellhop came out as Reggie and Laura were just opening the car doors. He took the bags from the boot and loaded them onto a cart. Then he hovered around

251

Laura like a puppy, trying to think of additional services to perform, until Reggie got out of the car with his briefcase.

"Let me help you with that," said the bellhop.

"Thanks, I've got it," said Reggie.

"I'll just put it on the cart with the others," said the bellhop, reaching for it.

"No, thank you, I carry my own briefcase," said Reggie, wrestling it back.

The bellhop stood back, as if thwarted in the one thing that he truly had to do, but he quickly recovered.

"Right, then," he said cheerily. He turned back to Laura, grabbed hold of the cart with the luggage, and then, as if it were in doubt, told them to come this way.

They proceeded into the lobby, which was country-house modern, with elegant use of wood and stone, sparkling clean, and perfectly lit.

"This will do then, won't it?" said Reggie.

Laura nodded. "It's perfect. I take back every negative thing I ever said about your hotel luck."

The desk clerk checked them in, remarking that they had been given the highly desirable top-floor suite, at the special request of the hotel chain manager herself.

They took the lift up to the third floor;

the bellboy brought their luggage, got his tip, and departed.

It was not a suite; it was just one large bedroom, but it was a very large one, and with a pink-tile bath and loo attached, a mirror for the entire length of the his-and-hers sinks, and a king-sized bed with so many plush decorative pillows one could swim in them.

Laura went to the window, pulled open the heavy, golden drapes, and looked out.

"In the morning," she said, "I expect we'll see wild ponies on the rocky crags and a golden sunrise over the moor. But tonight we're on our own for entertainment."

Reggie sat on the bed and picked up the hotel phone.

"Shall I make dinner reservations for eight?" he said.

"You shall not," said Laura. "You shall have room service deliver a bottle of champagne and then go away. I mean room service go away, not you. After they deliver the champagne. Which they'd better do damn quick."

Laura was climbing from the window side of the bed, where she had been standing, to the phone side of the bed, where Reggie was sitting, tossing pillows out of her way as she came toward him.

21

The fire alarm went off at three in the morning.

Reggie knew it must be three, instinctively, because he knew that whenever people tell of bad things that happen in the middle of the night, 3:00 A.M. is what they really mean.

Not midnight. At midnight, good things often happen, and very good things had been happening at this particular midnight, he was still recovering from them, and he was — until that jarring sound — in the most profound sleep from them.

He leaped out of bed. Well, not quite. He felt as though he had leaped, but he had only just managed to get his bare feet on the floor.

The alarm was not the pleasant, bell-ringing noise used for fire drills in public school, but a shrill, syncopated shriek — and it filled the room.

Laura was sitting up next to him. She smelled enticing, and shrieking fire alarm or not, Reggie took a moment to inhale.

"How is it," said Laura, "that the world always seems to know when I'm naked?"

The alarm continued to insistently shriek as they hunted up their most available clothes. Reggie quickly pulled on his boxers. Laura immediately put on Reggie's long-tailed shirt, and was looking about for something to complete the ensemble when someone pounded hard on the door.

Reggie opened it. The bellhop was there.

"Fire alarm! You must get out now!"

"Where is it?" said Reggie.

"What?" said the bellhop, who seemed to have lost his focus for some reason.

"The fire."

The bellhop didn't answer that question; he just stared at Laura, who hadn't quite gotten the shirt buttoned yet.

"There is a robe in the bath! I'll help you find it!" he said, and he eagerly tried to enter the room.

"No, you won't," said Reggie, pushing him back into the corridor. "Thank you for the warning. We'll be right along."

With Laura in the bath getting her robe, Reggie, still in just his boxers, took a moment to pick up his briefcase.

"Leave your belongings," said the bellhop, back in the doorway. "There's no time."

"I've already got it," said Reggie.

"I'll hold this for you, so you can go back in and get dressed," said the bellhop, reaching to take the briefcase.

"You said there's no time," said Reggie, holding on to it just from habit.

"It's very cold downstairs," said the bellhop. "You really should —"

Laura came out of the bath now in her bathrobe, and carrying Reggie's as well. She tossed it to him.

"You can never tell Reggie anything," she said. "He doesn't even worry about shrinkage. Are we all ready then?"

"This way," said the bellhop, even though he didn't seem quite satisfied with things, and Reggie and Laura dutifully followed him down the corridor to the stairs.

A dozen guests of the hotel had assembled in the lobby.

"We're the last ones down," said the bellhop, as though they had badly lost a contest.

"Well, to be fair, we were on the top floor," said Laura.

Now the on-duty manager — a well-tailored man of about fifty — walked out to the center of the lobby and called for attention.

Everyone would be allowed back in their rooms, he said, as soon as the staff had completed their security sweep of all the floors.

"Does that mean that there was not in fact a fire?" said Reggie.

The manager turned and took note of Reggie — and then exchanged an insider's glance with the bellhop.

"Oh no," whispered Laura to Reggie. "You've gotten on the troublemaker list."

The manager didn't want to respond directly to a question from a troublemaker, so he deliberately turned to address everyone else in the room.

"The system is new," said the manager. "And there is some slight possibility of an occasional false alarm. But the good news is, we have completed the check and it is now perfectly safe to return to your rooms."

And then, before the crowd of guests could actually disperse, the manager looked directly at Reggie.

"And I can tell you unequivocally that this was not a drill," he said, quite loudly. "In future, we would hope that *all* guests would follow both the hotel rules and their own good sense, and not attempt to retrieve their

belongings in the event of a fire. No possession is worth your life. Even if you do have
the largest room on the top floor. Thank
you very much for your patience, and enjoy
your stay."

The assembled crowd followed the hotel
manager's lead, and all of them stared for a
brief, accusatory moment at Reggie and the
briefcase for which he had, it seemed, inap-
propriately risked his life.

"Well," said Laura, whispering in Reggie's
ear. "I hope you're proud of yourself."

"I'm just glad I wore the bloody robe,"
said Reggie.

After a few moments, the crowd of hotel
guests dispersed. Reggie and Laura made
their way back to their room.

Reggie opened the door, and Laura went
in first.

And then she immediately paused, just
inside the doorway.

"Something's wrong," she said.

And something was. Her suitcase was
open and all of its contents dumped on the
bed. All of the drawers to the little hotel
dresser were open, and the closet had clearly
been rifled.

Laura quickly checked each area in turn.

"Nothing seems to have been taken," said
Laura. "But they tossed everything. Does

that mean they didn't find what they were looking for?"

"Maybe what they took was pictures," said Reggie. "Maybe it was the paparazzi."

The bellhop arrived to help out.

"Yes," he said. "Might well have been. I've seen some very high-end cameras check in."

"Nonsense," said Laura. "Even the paparazzi don't make money by publishing photos of just a person's belongings. They might throw a false fire alarm to get us downstairs half-dressed, if they thought they could get away with it. But they'd get nothing from tossing our room."

"I can move you to another room, if you like."

"No," said Laura. "Thank you, but right at the moment, all we're interested in is a couple of hours' sleep."

The bellhop lingered — hoping to provide additional assistance, it seemed at first — but then Reggie tipped him, and he departed.

A few hours later — too few — Reggie and Laura came downstairs for breakfast. They walked zombie-like to the buffet room.

"Food or sleep," said Laura, as they picked up their plates. "Food or sleep. I hate it when I have to choose between life's necessities."

But there was bacon, greasy and nicely overcooked. Baked beans. Stewed tomatoes, still warm, with the scent of them wafting up.

Reggie loaded his plate and sat with Laura at a table by the window.

He had his briefcase with him. He put it on the empty chair next to him and opened it up, flat, with the contents of both sides exposed.

Laura raised an eyebrow.

"Not to worry," said Reggie. "It's not work. I just want a look at the itinerary."

Reggie sorted through several documents, moving them from one side of the briefcase to the other.

"Found it," said Reggie, lifting a sheet of paper from the briefcase. "And I think you'll like this next one. It's supposed to have some sort of special room."

He showed her the list of destinations.

"Lois said the hotel manager made this list for us herself," said Reggie. "You can see her notes there."

Laura looked at the notes and nodded approvingly. "She says that the special restored railway car is undergoing repair — but I hear all the other rooms are wonderful as well. I couldn't have done better myself."

As Laura said that, the cook came out

from the kitchen. He walked very closely past them with a tray of bacon so new that the grease bubbles were still popping. He slowed his pace as he passed their table, and the scent of more fresh breakfast was enough for Reggie to think about getting back in the line. He started to get up from the table.

"They certainly keep the buffet well stocked," said Laura. "It was full just a moment ago, and now here they are topping it off again."

Now the desk clerk appeared at the entrance to the dining room. He looked about for a moment, and then came directly to their table.

"Are you Mr. Heath?"

Reggie admitted it.

"We have a phone call for you, sir."

Laura gave Reggie a questioning look.

"I've no idea," he said. "Only Lois knows where we are, and I told her to hold all calls." Reggie started to exit the dining room with the clerk, but then looked down and saw that he still had the briefcase open on the chair. "Watch that for me?" he said to Laura.

"Of course."

Reggie went to the front desk and picked up the phone.

It was Wembley.

"You're damned hard to get a hold of, Heath," he said.

"That's intentional," said Reggie.

"I'll give you the summary version," said Wembley. "Darla Rennie has escaped. And she's killed again."

Reggie absorbed that for a moment.

"Heath? You still there?"

"How in hell did that happen?" said Reggie.

"Slight breach of protocol at the mental health institute. According to the guards, she must have just got up and walked out of the examination room, and when her psychiatrist caught up with her in the storage closet she whacked him a couple of times on the head with a blunt instrument. O'Shea is on her way there now."

"Bloody hell, Wembley, the woman's bonkers and that's the best they can do?"

"My words to them exactly."

"When?"

"Yesterday afternoon."

"Are you looking —"

"Of course we're looking for her. That's why I rang you. I've notified the police in Dartmoor, but they can't do much more than keep an eye out, and it's a lot of territory to cover. I've got the fisherman's place in Canvey under surveillance, in case she tries to go back there. No leads on that, by the way. So if she didn't kill him — which we've all assumed must be the case, since you provided her that hamburger wrapper alibi — we've no idea who did."

"So your point is," said Reggie, "if Laura and I had kept our mouths shut, Darla Rennie would have been charged with the fisherman's murder, would still be in jail pending arraignment rather than going directly to the mental facility for evaluation on the earlier crimes, and would not now be on the loose to stalk us."

"I'm not making a point at all, Heath. I'm just telling you how things stand. And we think her original delusion is back — assuming it was ever gone. Apparently she was reading another gossip column about your fiancée."

"Thank you for the heads-up," said Reggie.

He got off the phone and returned to Laura at their table.

"It's the most amazing thing," she said, as he sat down. "In the time that you were gone, the busboy has come by no less than three times, asking if he could clear my plates. And I think it was perfectly clear that I was still eating."

"Clear your plates?" said Reggie. "Is that what the next generation is calling it?"

"I've no idea what you mean. Anyway," she said, picking up the now-closed briefcase from the empty chair, and handing it to him, "I noticed you still have that Sherlock Holmes letter in there, mixed up with everything else."

Reggie had to think about that for a moment.

"You mean the one from the hotel?" he said.

"Yes. I shut it back up tight inside. If you lose it, Mr. Rafferty will have your head."

"I think we have more pressing concerns," said Reggie.

Laura delayed a bite of breakfast and looked up.

"The phone was Wembley," said Reggie. "Darla Rennie has escaped custody. She is at large."

Laura took a moment to look at Reggie and absorb the significance of that.

Then she reached for the maple syrup.

"Well, it's a shame," she said. "But we're not letting it spoil our holiday. I'll be fine."

"Well, you're fine, of course," said Reggie. "But it's me I'm worried about."

Reggie thought about it for a moment further, as Laura continued with the French toast. And then Reggie stood.

"I need to make another call," he said.

"Who?" said Laura.

"I think I need to make sure Nigel made it across the pond."

"Of course he did. Why wouldn't he?"

"No reason," said Reggie. "But I think I'll just check."

22

Nigel Heath arrived at Butler's Wharf by cab in the early morning, having spent the previous fourteen hours on a flight from LAX to Heathrow.

It was a red-eye with a stopover, which Nigel had selected because it was affordable — cheaper by half than anything quicker and more direct.

So he'd hardly slept, but he was in excellent spirits even so.

It was no small thing to be allowed to house-sit his brother Reggie's penthouse for a few days. Reggie had always been stingy with such invitations in the past. He was mellowing a bit now — under Laura's influence, in Nigel's opinion; as part of a couple, Reggie was beginning to allow for things that had not occurred to him when he was so completely single, and that included extending an invitation to his brother to stay in his expensive, fancy digs when Reggie himself was out of town.

And at the moment, Reggie and Laura were both very much out of town. Even out of mobile phone range — Nigel had already tried from the airport.

That was fine. He would have the place to himself for a bit, before journeying to Laura's aunt's castle himself, to participate in the engagement festivities.

He was a little concerned that he might need to come up with a toast for that soiree. He knew he had to have one for the wedding; he wasn't sure about a mere engagement party. He had asked Mara if she knew what the protocol was, but she had responded that she didn't understand the British at all.

Which was not entirely true, of course — she seemed to understand Nigel himself rather well. That was true from the moment they met in Los Angeles, and it was still true now that they were living there together.

If a toast was needed, he supposed he could come up with some sort of joke about being Reggie's best man at the wedding and the better man at the party. Or something to that effect. Which might be amusing to the people who knew them both well. Nigel was fine in pubs, but he found these formal occasions a bit intimidating. Special forks, special plates, special foods. Things that should be said or not said. It was all very high-pressure.

Right now, he was just looking forward to going out on the penthouse deck and settling in with a pint of Guinness and a fine view of the city lights.

The cab departed, and Nigel went to the glass-walled exterior lift — the one that went from the ground level of the old dock directly and exclusively to Reggie's penthouse.

Nigel opened the security panel next to the lift, and punched in the code.

Nothing happened. It should have beeped. It should have flashed green. It should have announced that the code was accepted and that access was granted.

He tried it again.

Still no announcement, but this time Nigel noticed the LED display.

SECURITY DISENGAGED, it said, with the red letters flashing faintly against the black display. ALARM OFF.

That was odd. Reggie would never leave it that way.

Nigel pressed the button to call the lift. A hydraulic motor whined into action, and the lift from Reggie's penthouse began to descend toward Nigel at ground level.

So Reggie had gone off on his engagement trip without activating the security system. Very odd indeed.

Nigel got in and took the lift to the top of the building. He stepped from the lift into the unlocked foyer of the penthouse. He called out, "Reggie?"

He didn't expect an answer; Reggie wasn't supposed to be there. But Reggie being present was the only explanation Nigel had for all the security measures being down.

"You here?"

No answer.

Nigel walked into the wide, glass-walled dining area, which he knew had been foremost in Reggie's mind in buying the place. It looked out over the Thames, it let in the moonlight, and you couldn't ask for a better Saturday night date setting. It was where most of Reggie's courtship of Laura had taken place.

The dining-courting room looked fine. Nothing out of place there. Nigel walked on into the kitchen.

Here, too, everything was fine — Reggie had a cleaning service, and he was not sloppy in any case. There was nothing lying around on the counter, nor would there be, with Reggie gone on holiday.

The kitchen had its own little square Formica breakfast table, with four plain, minimalist chairs, which to a stranger would have seemed just a little out of place in the otherwise elegant furnishings of Reggie's penthouse.

But the table had belonged to their parents. It was what they could afford when Reggie and Nigel were growing up in the East End, and Nigel understood why Reggie had kept it.

Their father had died ten years ago, of heart failure precipitated by business failure. Their mother had followed shortly after. It had marked the first point in Nigel's life when he had begun to suspect that optimism might not always be justified. That life was not fair. That often the people who belong together might not ever find each other, and that when they did the world might grow envious and resentful, and try to drive them apart.

Or, failing that, just somehow kill them.

Nigel — in his last year of university at the time — had resolved then that the next time he saw such an injustice again begin to take shape on a truly happy couple, barring the basic ravages of old age, of course, because there was only so much that one could do, he would do his damnedest to prevent it.

And he had not forgotten that resolve.

He moved on from the kitchen now and checked the bedroom. It was perfect, and improved from what Nigel had seen of Reggie's digs in earlier years. The loo as well was as it should be. There were some of Reggie's things in the cabinet, and even more of Laura's.

Finally, Nigel went into the office — or the den, really — it wasn't that large a room, and Nigel knew that Reggie didn't use it that much; generally if he worked late, he would remain at chambers to do so.

The room had a window — but not with the wonderful Thames view that the dining room had. This window was just an exchange of views with the windows in another residential building across the street.

There was a chair and a desk, built-in track lighting in the ceiling, a tower-style personal computer below the desk, a separate display monitor on the desk, and next to that a small lamp.

The room was dark, and Nigel flipped the wall switch.

The overhead lights came on — and nothing else. Not the computer. Not the monitor. Not the desk lamp.

Nigel reached down and flicked the individual switch for the lamp. It came on. So did the computer and the monitor when he tried them. They started up with the expected log-on screen — no information to be gained there.

But still it was odd. Nigel knew that Reggie liked his electrical devices simple and obedient and, unlike Nigel, he was not particularly concerned with how much electricity he used. When he flipped the wall switch for the overhead lights, he wanted everything else to come on as well, no matter how many kilowatts he was consuming.

But someone had turned all of these devices off individually.

And probably not for low energy consumption.

More likely just to avoid attracting attention from anyone in the building across the street.

Nigel picked up Reggie's desk phone, and he rang Lois at chambers. It was a bit early in the morning, but she might be there.

She picked up.

"Nigel! Are you back?"

Nigel acknowledged that he was, but just for Laura and Reggie's engagement party.

This was the third time that Nigel had returned to London since moving to Los Angeles two years ago, and each time Lois, and also Rafferty on the leasing committee, would ask if he was back for good, and each time he would say no.

He made a point of mentioning to Lois that Mara would be coming out with him when it came time for the actual wedding. Then he got to the reason for his call:

"I'm at Reggie's place now. I think it's been burgled. Or at least searched — I can't tell if anything's been taken, but someone has been here and tried to hide that they were."

"Oh, dear. Intruders there, too?"

"What do you mean, 'too'?"

"Mr. Rafferty is almost certain that someone has gotten into the letter storage room on the top floor on Baker Street. He won't say how he knows this — apparently he's changed the locks and established some sort of secret tracking mechanism since that thing with the Texans last year — but he says he's certain that someone did break in and rifle things, though they tried to disguise it, and apparently did not actually take anything."

"Bloody hell," said Nigel. "You'd think I could go away for a few months and everything be fine."

"Yes, you'd think," said Lois.

Now the phone that Nigel was using —

Reggie's phone — began to beep annoyingly.

"I'll get back to you," said Nigel. "I think Reggie is getting another call."

Nigel picked up the incoming call. It was Reggie.

"How was your flight?" said Reggie.

"Crying babies," said Nigel. "And a crying adult, too, when I saw what the meal service was. But I'm glad you called. The place looks great, but I have a question or two about your security system here."

"You got in all right?"

"Obviously. But that's my point. The system was off. I've looked around, and nothing has been taken that I can see, but I think someone has been here."

There was a long pause now from Reggie. Longer than Nigel would have expected.

"Darla Rennie is alive," said Reggie, finally.

Now there was a pause from Nigel.

"We have a bad connection," said Nigel. "Whatever you just said — I think you should probably say it again."

"I said Darla Rennie is alive."

Nigel's chest tightened. "Darla Rennie drowned in the Thames," he said.

"No such luck," said Reggie.

"She survived the fall? And the river?"

"Apparently. She's been living with a fisherman from the Thames Estuary. He was found stabbed a few nights ago, with her fingerprints on the murder weapon. And under the floorboards was a newspaper clipping. Just one — the itinerary of our engagement trip to Laura's aunt's castle. And Rennie's fingerprints were on that clipping."

"Bloody hell," said Nigel.

"The good news was that she turned herself in. The Yard had her in custody."

Nigel said, "Why are you stating good news in the past tense?"

"Wembley said she killed the psychiatrist who was evaluating her."

"So she's still homicidally bonkers."

"And then she escaped."

"Bloody hell," said Nigel again. "Does the Yard have any idea of her whereabouts?"

"Wembley's best guess — and mine — is that she'll go back to doing what she was doing before."

Nigel thought about that for a long moment.

"I see," said Nigel. He knew what the implications were.

"I can't track her down myself," said Reggie. "I have to stay with Laura."

"Of course," said Nigel. "So you need someone to —"

"Nigel, I need you to find Darla Rennie — before she finds us."

"Understood," said Nigel.

Nigel got off the phone with Reggie, and then he called Inspector Wembley at Scotland Yard.

"I didn't know you were in town, Heath," said the inspector.

"I'm supposed to be on my way to an engagement party," said Nigel.

"I think she's too good for him," said Wembley.

"That's your opinion," said Nigel, not entirely certain whether Wembley really meant it. "I understand that Darla Rennie is at large?"

"Yes," said Wembley.

"What are you doing to track her down?"

"Right at the moment, talking to you, Heath. Make it worth my while. You knew her, didn't you? A couple of years ago?"

"In a way. We were in group therapy together. The careers group, they called it, but it was really the career failures group. I was there with the intent of abandoning my solicitor's license and punishing myself for winning a tort case that my clients deserved to lose. She was there cultivating a deep resentment of Black Cabs and a delusion of my brother being Sherlock Holmes. We had to confess all sorts of things in the group. She confessed to being a genius, a sort of schizophrenic savant, but having no sense of directions whatsoever, hence her failure as a Black Cab driver."

"Anything else?"

"You've been in a room with her, haven't you, Wembley?"

"Yes, if you mean the interview room."

"Well, then, you already know. She's as seductive as hell. Which would be fine in and of itself, if only she were not also completely unbalanced and known to kill people."

"Good point," said Wembley.

Then, out of the blue, Wembley said:

"Did you manage a romp and tickle when you were with her at therapy?"

"No," said Nigel, surprised by the question, but answering anyway. "Almost did. We made an appointment to meet between therapy sessions, but she was late — or lost, or something — and I gave up waiting. Missed her by that much."

"What about your brother? Did he do her when he got involved in that Black Cab case?"

"No," said Nigel, now getting annoyed.

"How do you know?"

"I know my brother," said Nigel, "and I

know there hasn't been anyone else after he met Laura Rankin. Regardless of what he might have wanted people to believe in his single days."

"I only ask," said Wembley, "because when I requested that he come down to the Yard to talk to Darla Rennie, he seemed just a little nervous about it."

Nigel said, "I think you'll find that of the three of us — myself, Reggie, and Laura — the only one who is not completely terrified of Darla Rennie is Laura."

"Yes," said Wembley. "Well, even so, I've notified the local authorities in Dartmoor National Park to be on the lookout, in case she tries to waylay them on their little drive. But it's a large area. And of course she might not even go after Laura at all; she might just decide to try to keep her freedom and flee the country. In the meantime, we're pursuing all leads."

Nigel thought about that for a moment.

"Pursuing all leads means you don't have any that are worthwhile, doesn't it?"

"It means what I said," replied Wembley, tightly. "We're doing the best we can. O'Shea is at the crime scene at the mental health facility right now. I've given her permission to talk to you, if you want to call later."

"O'Shea is good," said Nigel.

"Damn right she is. You know, it's your brother's own fault that Darla Rennie got out, Heath."

"How so?"

"He and Laura rang me up with an alibi for her for the murder of the fisherman; their theory is she couldn't have done it, because these blasted hamburger wrappers are unique and prove she was at the Marylebone Grand Hotel at the time."

"Hamburger wrappers?"

"Darla Rennie entered the house, saw the body, dropped the bag of burgers and wrappers, and then ran — according to her story. I thought it was nonsense. But based on what your brother and Laura told me, I had the alibi checked out — and it turns out that, just as they said, the hamburgers in those wrappers were unique to the event taking place at the hotel, and could only have been purchased at the hotel itself, at the same time Cheeverton was being murdered at Canvey Island. And they had Darla Rennie's fingerprints on them. It's a shame. If it weren't for the damn junk-food wrappers, she'd have no alibi. The security tapes from the hotel don't show her being there at all. CCTV can have blind spots, of course — but the point is, there's no other record of her being there except the damn wrappers. If it weren't for them, she'd still be charged with the Canvey killing, and she'd still be safely in jail."

"All right," said Nigel. "But I can't imagine the Darla Rennie I knew running from the sight of a body."

"She claimed that she's no longer the Darla Rennie you knew. She claimed that she's no longer delusional. And that she no longer kills people."

"Nice if it's true," said Nigel. "But I'm not betting my brother's life on it. Or Laura's. I'm sure your team is doing all they can, but I'm going to look for Rennie on my own. I trust you don't mind."

"I'll lend you a copy of her file," said Wembley. "Find her if you can. And if you can disprove her alibi while you're at it, more power to you. I guarantee you, we won't let her get out the next time."

23

By the time Reggie and Laura departed their hotel that morning, the drizzle had turned into rain.

It hadn't been easy getting out of the hotel. The news about Darla Rennie at breakfast had been distracting, and the phone calls with Wembley and Nigel had taken some time.

And then the hotel manager had second thoughts, apparently, about how Reggie and Laura had been treated the night before. He greeted them personally as they were checking out.

"I've been instructed to offer you free accommodations," he said, "at the Dartmoor Deluxe. It's one of our most special properties, just at the western edge of the national park, and a wonderful stopping point if you are heading to Land's End, or Penzance, or any points southwest."

"Thank you," said Reggie. "But tonight

was our only stay in Dartmoor. We only have a few hours' drive now to our destination."

"The weather is looking inclement," said the manager. "It might take you longer than you think. The road is always uncertain. You never know what might happen."

"I'm sure it won't take us the entire day," said Reggie.

"No, no, of course not," said the manager. "And that's why I've been instructed to offer you a very special stay — for an hour or two on your afternoon drive, just as a break to freshen up, or the full night if you want it, whatever you like, completely free of charge."

"Well . . ."

"That's very kind of you," said Laura. "Do we need a coupon or anything?"

"Absolutely not. Just drop in, say your name, and our staff will do the rest."

"All right then," said Laura. "No promises, but if we need a break, we'll keep the Dartmoor Deluxe in mind."

And then, finally, they were on the road.

After an hour in the increasingly cold and windblown rain, they drove past the small sign announcing that they were officially now in the Dartmoor National Park. Farming fields gave way to a patchy mix of olive green heather, tan-colored scrub grass, and gray-white stones with black moss on their sides. The sheep and occasional farmhouses turned to wild ponies and rocky cairns.

If you had lunch in a basket, the sun was shining, and you were a few hundred meters from your house, thought Laura, it was nice country for a picnic.

But at the moment, it was simply isolated and bleak.

The conversation waned a bit; Laura leaned her seat back and closed her eyes, and Reggie began to test the Jaguar on the curves, just for the entertainment.

And also because he had noticed the temperature gauge beginning to climb just a bit. Sometimes an increase in speed helped the fans cool the motor.

"Wait," said Laura suddenly. "Slow down."

"What's wrong?"

"Stop for a moment."

Reggie did so, pulling the car to the left on the road, but not actually off of it, because there wasn't enough of a shoulder for that.

"I saw someone," said Laura.

"You mean back the road a quarter mile?"

"Yes. You saw him, too?"

"Some farmer-type bloke standing at the

edge of the road, in a heavy coat with a hood and with his hands clasped behind his back?"

"Well, yes, exactly. I don't think I've seen a single other person, or a farmhouse, or anything civilized at all for the past ten miles."

"And?"

"Well, shouldn't we go back and see if he needs something?"

"What is it you think he needs?" said Reggie.

"I don't know. But what would he be doing out here all alone in the rain?"

"Waiting for a bus?"

"Reggie, there are no buses on this road."

"For a truck, then. Or a tractor."

"We're too far into the reserve for that."

"Was he waving his arms wildly and screaming for help?"

"Well . . . no. But I think he raised his head as we drove by."

"He won't fit in the back, and he wouldn't like it if we tied him to the roof."

"Reggie, I don't mean give him a ride, but shouldn't we go back and see if he needs something?"

Reggie sighed, restarted the engine, and put the car into reverse.

"All right," he said, "if you insist. But my

guess is, if he needs anything regarding us at all, it's to take the long-handled axe that he's hiding behind his back and hit us over the head with it and drag us back to his cave to feed to his irradiated mutant urchins."

"You've seen too many American movies."

"Agreed. But I'm just glad he'll be swinging his weapon on your side of the car first and not mine."

24

Nigel had no car. Whenever he returned to London, he always got around either on foot, or by tube, or, on the rare occasion when he could afford it or was forced to splurge, by Black Cab. There was seldom a need for anything else.

Today he took a Black Cab directly to Scotland Yard to pick up the file from Wembley.

Then he went to the tube station, got on the Hammersmith line to Barking, and from there he caught a bus to Canvey Island.

Had Darla Rennie's delusions in fact returned, and was she once more targeting Reggie and Laura? It seemed likely; Nigel could think of no other reason for her to have been hiding the published itinerary of their trip under the floorboards of the fisherman's house.

But if it was true, then the woman had a problem: Reggie had changed that itinerary.

He and Laura would not be at the stops originally listed in the paper. And if Darla Rennie attempted to find them just by driving out to Dartmoor and looking for them — well, that would be nearly impossible . . . and foolish. Especially given that she had no sense of direction.

And as delusional as she might be, Darla Rennie was no fool. She would not put herself in the position of driving aimlessly in Dartmoor, and Nigel knew he would not find her by doing that himself.

So he rode on the bus to Canvey Island, studying the file from Wembley as he rode.

Nearly two hours later, the bus rolled through the town's little center and dropped Nigel at the corner of Long Road and High Street. Nigel got directions from the driver, and began walking toward Oyster Creek, which ran between Canvey and Southend-by-Sea and emptied into the Thames Estuary.

At the foot of Long Road, Nigel found a paved footpath, with a narrow grassy strip on one side and a sloped muddy bank on the other, running parallel to the creek.

Nigel had to choose his direction: He could go to his right, toward the Smallgains Marina, where Cheeverton's boat was supposed to be moored. That was not his

287

preferred choice; boats were not in his comfort zone.

Or he could go to his left, toward Cheeverton's house, where the body was discovered. But he knew O'Shea from Scotland Yard forensics had already been all over the house, and he saw no issues regarding those findings in the file. There wouldn't be much to accomplish there.

And then he saw a third choice: the High Water Pub, just at the corner of Long Street, only yards away from where Nigel was standing, and right in the path of anyone — say, Cheeverton himself — who ever had occasion to walk from Smallgains Marina to the house where Cheeverton had lived.

Between the boat and the pub, Nigel's choice was easy. He entered the pub.

Nigel's eyes adjusted to the indoor light, and he looked about.

It was not a fancy pub, but it had the essentials. There was a center bar, some tables in front, and a few booths at the far wall and in the corner. There was a jukebox and local bulletin board on the wall immediately to his right.

On a small table next to that wall, between the bulletin board and the shelves that adjoined the bar, was a white-and-red sack of some sort of fast food.

The place was nearly empty; the afternoon crowd had not yet begun to arrive.

Nigel went up to the bar, and the bar woman came right over to greet him.

"What are those?" said Nigel, pointing at the red-and-white sack.

"Hamburgers. Trust me, you don't want one. They're a few days old."

"That's an unusual wrapper. Were those bought around here?"

She shook her head. "My daughter was up in London on a historical tour for a children's class. They toured an exhibit at a hotel and then bought a bunch of these before they got on the bus to come home. They had leftovers, so I kept them for Mr. Sizemore over there in the corner. He'll make fish bait out of them."

In the corner booth, a grizzled, seventyish fisherman, Sizemore apparently, had nearly finished his pint.

"Fish will eat stale cooked hamburger?" said Nigel, to the bar woman.

The man in the corner spoke up.

"Carp will. And sometimes flounder. If you'd been swimming along the bottom muck of the Thames your whole life, you'd be willing to eat them, too. Anyway, we don't separate the meat. We roll the bun and burger up into little gooey balls with some grease, put a hook in 'em, and throw 'em in the water. I don't know why it works, and I don't care."

The bar woman nodded, and she said to Nigel, "You can have one if you want."

"I'm no longer hungry," said Nigel. "But do you mind if I take one of the wrappers?"

She raised an eyebrow.

"Whatever floats your boat," she said.

Nigel took one of the wrappers and looked more closely.

It was red and white, and it had the name of the Marylebone Grand Hotel on it, and the date of their special exhibit.

So much for Darla Rennie's alibi. There was no proof now that she went into the hotel that day at all. She could have been in the pub, happened to pick up a couple of these, taken them home, and still been in town to kill the fisherman.

So she was as potentially murderous as ever.

Nigel had one photo of Darla Rennie in the file from Scotland Yard. It was her original booking photo, from her first arrest at Scotland Yard for the Black Cab murders. That made it not quite current, but it would have to do. He took it out and showed it to the bar woman.

"Have you seen this woman in the pub recently?"

The bar woman looked at the photo and whistled softly.

"Can't say that I've seen her," she said. "But you might come back and ask one of the young lads later. I'm sure they'd have noticed."

The grizzled fisherman came over now.

"Let me have a look," he said.

The bar woman whispered to Nigel, "Go ahead, show him. No one's called Sizemore a lad in forty years, but I'm sure he still thinks he is."

The man shot a suspicious glance toward the bar woman, and then he looked at the photo. He nodded.

"I've seen her," he said. "She wasn't dressed like that. But it was her, just like I told the bloke that was here before."

"Someone else was asking? Police?"

"Didn't say," said the man, shaking his head. "Might have been. But maybe not. Too well dressed. Tall man, gray suit."

"When?"

The man cleared his throat and sat down on a stool at the bar.

"Bring us a couple of pints, please?" said Nigel to the bar woman. She began to pour them.

"A couple of nights ago, I think," said the man to Nigel.

"And when did you last see this woman? Was she here at the pub, during the day?"

"Can't say that I saw her in the pub," said the man, picking up his fresh pint. "I'm usually out on the water during the day, and that's where I saw her. A couple of months ago. Just once. Cheeverton sent her below right quick, but I got a look. You don't forget a chippy like that."

"So where you saw her was on Cheeverton's boat?"

The man nodded and took a long draught of the beer.

"Nowhere else?"

The man shook his head. "Just in the photos. The one the other bloke showed me was a little blurry, in some big hotel lobby or the like, and she was wearing a wig or something, but it was her all right. You can't mistake those eyes, know what I mean?"

"You mean blurry like a surveillance photo?" said Nigel. "From a security camera?"

"How would I know? All I know is, she's the one I saw on the boat."

Sizemore turned away now and went back to his booth.

Nigel took several of the hamburger wrappers, paid for the beers, and headed for the door.

He exited the pub, got to the footpath, again faced his original choice — boat or house — and this time he walked to the marina.

Nigel didn't know much about boats; generally speaking, he appreciated them more from a distance. And as he approached the marina, he tried to convince himself that there was no reason to look at this one.

But he couldn't. He reached the dock and began walking between the rows of shining watercraft.

He found Cheeverton's — and as little as he knew about boats, he knew immediately that this one had seen better days.

It wasn't as sleek in form or nearly as new as most of the other boats in the marina. Its brass fittings were tarnished, and thick layers of heavy oil-based marine enamel had built up over the edges, from many years of repainting.

That's what you would do, thought Nigel, if you knew the boat was your livelihood, but you couldn't afford any higher degree of maintenance.

The access point from the dock onto Cheeverton's boat was marked out with two parallel rows of yellow police tape.

The tape warned anyone who happened by to stay out, but it didn't provide much of an actual physical barrier. All one had to do was push down on one line of tape, push up on the other, and step over and under onto the boat.

Nigel did that.

He put one foot tentatively from the dock onto the boat, and immediately he was reminded why he was not very familiar with these things.

His queasy stomach told him. He didn't even have to be out on the water; just the hint of it was enough. The residual fumes from boat motors and odors of fish bait were enough.

Nigel took a couple of deep breaths, told his body to pay no attention to the surface that was about to move under its feet, and stepped fully onto the deck of the boat.

The boat rocked. Nigel put one hand on the top of the cabin to steady himself, and he looked toward the stern.

He saw two compartments. The smaller of them would be the bait tank. That one didn't matter, and he wasn't going to look in it.

The larger compartment, some six feet in length and two wide, was for the day's catch.

Nigel walked uneasily back toward it,

294

knelt to keep his balance, and opened the hatch door.

He looked inside. He saw melting ice in the steel-sided compartment.

Then he took out his mobile and rang Inspector O'Shea of Forensics.

"Heath? You're in town?" she said.

"I'm at Cheeverton's boat," said Nigel. "Had no trouble getting onto it — I mean, no more than usual for me. It's been taped off, but I got by it easily enough. And it looks to me like someone might have pushed the tape around before me."

"Any obvious mischief?" said O'Shea.

"Not that I can see, so far," said Nigel.

"Well, if you do see something broken in, notify the locals. We completed our investigation there in any case. The boat wasn't the crime scene. Cheeverton was killed at his house. So what's on your mind, Heath?"

"I see there's an ice tank," said Nigel.

"Of course there is," said O'Shea. "It's a fishing boat."

"The tank is big enough for a body," said Nigel. "Even a fully grown adult male like Cheeverton, if you pushed on it enough. Now, I don't see any blood on the ice, but that could have been replaced. So what I'm wondering is —"

"Please," said O'Shea. "Give me a little

credit. We checked the boat thoroughly for human blood, and it was no easy thing, with all the biological substances you find on the deck of a fishing boat. And we looked in the tank; we tested the ice; we tested his clothes; we accounted for the possibility that the body might have been wrapped in something, stored in the icy catch hold, and then transported to the house and dumped there. It didn't happen that way, Heath. He wasn't killed on the boat."

"I see," said Nigel. "So you have no doubts at all about the time of death?"

"No. Why?"

"Because I've got some doubts about Darla Rennie's alibi," said Nigel.

"Don't blame me for that one," said O'Shea. "It was your brother and Laura Rankin came up with it."

"Everyone keeps saying that," said Nigel. "But I don't see what else they were to do, once they'd realized it. But let's assume it's true, for the moment. If Darla Rennie didn't kill the fisherman, someone else did. So do you have any other suspects?"

"That's Wembley's arena, not mine. But I think the problem is motive. Who'd want to kill him?"

"Perhaps he was just in the way. Perhaps the real target was the person living with him — Darla Rennie herself."

"Uh-huh. Well, I know of a lot of people who didn't think highly of Darla Rennie. One of them is a close relative of yours. Problem is, when the murder was committed, none of those people knew that she was even alive, much less that she was living with this fisherman in Canvey. So do you have anything else for me, Heath, or can I get back to my regular duties?"

"You're at the mental health facility?"

"Yes, and no, not as a patient."

"Anything there that will help me find Rennie?"

"Her evaluating psychologist was bashed over the head with a blunt object in the storage room and died from severe head trauma. Does that help?"

"No. What exactly was he bashed with?"

"A hammer, probably, but we haven't found the murder weapon yet. And we haven't found her fingerprints."

"Anything else?"

"This is probably not important," said O'Shea, causing Nigel's pulse to quicken just a little, "but I thought one thing was interesting. The staff here say Dr. Miner was very particular about the reading material he allowed in his waiting room. He'd have your typically out-of-date magazines on various topics, and at least one current daily paper, and he liked to draw conclusions about his patients according to what they would choose to look at. And so between one patient and the next, he would always go back into the room and put all the reading choices back in their original, neutral positions. Now, Darla Rennie was his last patient, and of course he wasn't able to come back and put her selection back in position after he got bashed on the head."

"I get it," said Nigel. "So what was Darla Rennie reading before she made her escape?"

"*The Daily Sun*," said O'Shea. "She had it open to the celebrity column. Which is interesting, because —"

"Because Darla Rennie clipped an earlier column with Reggie and Laura's original itinerary and concealed it under the floorboards in the house."

"Yes," said O'Shea. "Of course, the doctor wasn't foolish enough to give her scissors. So she didn't clip this one. But she did have it open to the same columnist again, just on a different day. The blurb is short. Shall I read it?"

"Please," said Nigel.

O'Shea read it, with some exaggeration, in what Nigel realized after a moment was intended by O'Shea to be a gossip columnist's voice:

" 'Laura Rankin Changes It Up: Not happy with her original engagement trip itinerary, the actress has enlisted none other than the manager of the entire Marylebone Grand Hotel chain to plan a new one for her. Details? Very hush-hush. But we're sure she'll still end up at the castle on Sunday (else tongues will begin to wag).' "

"So Darla Rennie read that column on the day she broke out?" said Nigel.

"It would appear so," said O'Shea.

"Good to know," said Nigel. "Thank you."

Nigel got off the phone and moved from the ice tank at the stern to the cabin entrance at the center of the boat.

The cabin door had been sealed earlier with the police warning tape.

The door was still shut — but the tape was broken.

Nigel opened the door and went inside.

If the boat had been ransacked, the upper portion of the cabin interior didn't show it. It wasn't sparkling, but it wasn't trashed. The radio was still in place, and it was the only thing both valuable and portable, so if someone had broken in for theft, they hadn't gotten much.

Nigel steadied himself again, reminded

himself that he was only on a little boat in a marina, not at sea, and he went down the several narrow steps to the tiny sleeping quarters belowdecks.

He saw a cot. No blanket. There was a small, stainless-steel sink, and then a narrow entrance to the onboard loo.

Nothing remarkable.

And then, as Nigel turned to leave, he opened the cabin door again, and this time the incoming daylight revealed an irregularity on the surface of the cabin floor.

The flooring was made of heavily varnished, polished wood slats. Ordinary gray dust — even though it was only the slightest accumulation, about as much as might have settled in the three days since the fisherman had been killed — was immediately apparent where the sunlight struck it now at an angle. And that slight dust was everywhere, distributed evenly on the floor.

Except on one specific slat.

Nigel knelt down. He took a credit card from his wallet, inserted the edge of it into the narrow crack between two adjoining wood slats, and carefully gave it just the slightest levered pressure.

The slat moved. Nigel lifted it out.

There was unvarnished, solid wood underneath the top slats. There was no hidden compartment, not a planned built-in one, anyway. There was very little space to conceal much of anything, at least nothing that was much thicker than a sheet of paper.

But it would have been a foolish place to put something so thin and light when the boat was still in use. It would have migrated, and could have slid anywhere underneath the floor.

Unless it was fixed in place with something. Nigel put his face down almost nose to the floor to look.

Yes. A tiny hole in the rough wood base underneath the slats. Just one. From a thumbtack, or something like it.

Someone had concealed something — probably a document — within the last week or so, and then someone had come back for it, even more recently, after the murder.

Nigel stood. The little boat rocked dizzily back and forth.

But it was all right. He knew everything now that he needed to know from Canvey.

He could leave the boat, return to London, and get on a nice, stable train.

25

In the Dartmoor National Park, rain was pouring down. The pathetically scruffy-looking man still stood at the side of the road, motionless in the mud, rainwater running down from the sleeves of his overcoat and from the hood that concealed his face.

"We have to at least see if he is in trouble," said Laura.

Reggie backed the Jaguar up toward the man, narrowly avoiding a shallow ditch on the side of the road.

The man in the rain did not move, but just remained standing with his hands behind his back.

Laura began to roll her window down.

"Don't," said Reggie, but too late. The window was down. Laura's face was clearly visible and exposed, to this man whose face was hidden by the hood of his bulky coat and who was obviously holding something behind his back.

"Cheers," said Laura to the man. "Do you need assistance? Is there anything that we can —"

The man leaped forward, across the little ditch, landing with his feet planted directly in front of Laura's door. His shoulders moved suddenly, his right arm swung from one side, his left from the other, and both hands came together, centered, to point a device directly at Laura's face.

The flash went off, then another, and then another, as the camera fired in rapid automatic bursts.

Reggie put the car in gear and floored the accelerator. The front wheels spun for a moment and then got traction; the rear wheels fishtailed, but luckily did not go into the ditch — and the Jaguar screamed down the road, leaving a spray of mud and water in its wake.

Laura rolled up her window. For about thirty seconds they drove in silence.

Then:

"Well," said Laura. She wiped a couple of residual muddy water drops from her face.

Reggie said nothing.

"Go ahead," said Laura. "Say it."

"I will not," said Reggie.

"Last chance," said Laura. "You don't get to put it in the bank and use it later."

"All right," said Reggie. "If you insist." He waited, tried to keep it in anyway, but couldn't: "I told you so."

Laura nodded affirmatively and looked straight ahead.

"Yes," she said. "You did."

They drove on for another hour. It was still daylight, but rain was hitting the windshield in sheets, and visibility was almost nil. For a long stretch, there were no lights visible anywhere — not in the moors to either side, not on the now-invisible horizon, and not in the overcast sky above.

They were, Reggie estimated, still almost two hours from the castle.

Laura dozed. Reggie blinked.

And then the engine rattled.

The sound was faint. Reggie hoped he had only imagined it.

And then it happened again. He checked the temperature gauge.

The red needle was past the midway point — and climbing.

Reggie began to wonder whether he should wake Laura and warn her — or just let the impending car disaster unfold.

But then, mercifully, in the distance ahead and just to the left, there were points of light. A neon sign.

THE DARTMOOR DELUXE. Just as the

hotel people had promised.

Reggie took the first turnoff he saw, and hoped he had guessed right.

He had. Over the next mile the sign grew closer. And now he pulled off the main road and onto the drive toward the hotel.

The sound of the tires on asphalt changed to the sound of the tires on a gravel-paved roundabout in front of the hotel, and it woke Laura.

She sat up.

"Oh," she said. "A break, then?"

"I'm afraid so," said Reggie. "I need to see about the car. I'm sure we can still make it to your aunt's place by seven — but I guess we're lucky the hotel set something aside for us."

This was clearly just a small hotel, a converted farmhouse of some eight or ten rooms, and probably with limited staff.

"I suppose," said Laura, "that the kitchen will be closed?"

"I'll be happy if they just have a room, as they said," said Reggie, "but I'm glad you brought the crisps."

They got out and shut the car doors, and the desk clerk, a man of about forty, came out to meet them.

"Ahh," he said. "You're Laura Rankin, aren't you?"

Laura acknowledged that, as Reggie opened the boot to get their bags.

"Your room is all ready for you, and if you need something from the kitchen, just ask," said the clerk, and then he offered to carry Reggie's briefcase.

"I can manage it," said Reggie, "but you're welcome to bring what's in the boot if you like."

"Yes, of course," said the clerk. He grabbed the two bags out of the boot. And then he said, pointing at the briefcase:

"I can put that in the safe, if you like."

"Thanks, no," said Reggie. "We'll only be an hour or two, I expect, and then we'll be on our way."

"Is your car all right?" said the clerk. "I thought I heard something."

"I think it just needs to cool off," said Reggie. "But can you get a mechanic out to take a look?"

"Absolutely," said the clerk. "I'll arrange it."

"My, it looks warm and cozy in there," Laura whispered to Reggie, as they walked up to the main entrance. "We must be running on my hotel luck now, not yours."

"This way, then," said the clerk, and Reggie and Laura both looked back over their shoulders.

The man wasn't following them up to the entrance. He had both their bags in hand, and he was motioning in another direction.

"You've got the special suite," he said, pointing the bags toward a small stone-and-mortar structure some fifty yards to the back and side of the main building. "It used to be a shepherd's hut. Very private. Specially designed and appointed, for the newly wed or new to bed, and other special occasions for special people. Right this way."

Reggie and Laura turned reluctantly away from the main entrance.

"We're running on my luck after all," said Reggie.

They walked on across the crunching gravel. The rain had taken a short break, but the air had turned bitterly cold.

The desk clerk opened the door of the former shepherd's hut, and turned on the inside lights for them.

"Well," said Laura, looking about. "Indeed, it has been renovated, hasn't it?"

And it had. Reggie looked about and nodded. All the modern conveniences were present, just as if someone had taken the interior of an en suite mid-range London hotel room and plunked it down inside old stone walls.

"This is really not bad at all," said Laura.

Then she added, "It's a bit chilly though."

"Yes," said the clerk, already on his way out. "But it will warm up right enough when you turn the furnace on. The thermostat is right there on the wall. Cheers."

Laura opened a bag and began to unpack.

Reggie went to the thermostat and increased the setting to something closer to normal room temperature.

Several shivery minutes went by.

The furnace — not a forced-air built-in, but a gas-fueled aftermarket unit, attached to the wall in the front room — made no sound or acknowledgement of any kind. Reggie knelt down for a closer look to be sure, and then he picked up the phone and called the front desk.

"The pilot doesn't appear to be on," said Reggie.

"Oh, not to worry," said the desk clerk. "You'll see the pilot switch at the bottom right. You can't miss it. It's completely safe, and so easy a child could do it. Just push in, then turn, and it will come right on, and then you set the furnace as toasty as you like."

"But," said Laura, "I think I smell gas."

"We think we smell gas," said Reggie into the phone.

"Nonsense," said the desk clerk. "That's

just the aroma from the peat bog. People always make that mistake and think they smell something. But no need to worry. Just get down next to the furnace and follow the instructions I gave. Don't be afraid of it."

"I'm not afraid of it," said Reggie. "I just think that you should —"

"The furnace engineer came all the way out from Marylebone Grand Hotel head-quarters and checked it just this afternoon," said the night clerk. "So it's in perfect working order. And it's easy. My grandmother could do it."

"Then I suggest you send your grand-mother right over, because we can't make it work, and we're bloody freezing!"

There was a short pause, and then:

"Right then," said the night clerk. "I'll be there as soon as I can. It might be a few, because we just had a sudden influx."

"Make it soon," said Reggie, not bother-ing to ask what sort of influx that could be, "or we'll be camping in your lobby."

"Oh, can't do that, I'm afraid. Company rules. But we'll get your thermostat squared away, right enough."

Reggie went back to the furnace, got down on all fours, and tried to peer inside.

"You're not going to try to do it yourself, are you?" said Laura.

"I can turn on a furnace," said Reggie.

"I think this is one of those special portable kinds," said Laura. She was putting her coat on as she said it.

"Where are you going?" said Reggie.

"Either I'm going back to the car to get my small bag or I'm stepping out for a moment so that when you blow yourself up I won't be standing next to you."

"You'll be singing a different tune," said Reggie, "when you come back and see how warm and toasty I've made the place."

Reggie crouched down, peered in at the dark inner workings of the furnace, and prepared to push and twist the pilot switch one more time.

Laura stopped short of the door. She had hoped that Reggie would actually step away from the furnace and come with her outside to get her bag and then she could maneuver him into the lobby until a professional arrived.

But Reggie had called her bluff.

And so she couldn't possibly leave. She remained standing there within a few feet of him and what she felt in her gut was going to be a disaster.

She held her breath and said a silent prayer.

"Reggie," said Laura, having finished her

silent prayer.

"Reggie," she said again.

"What?" he said, looking up from the pilot.

"I swear that I smell gas. I am leaving right now," she said, "and you are coming with me."

26

At the lobby, the clerk was trying to settle back into his nap after the conversation with Reggie, because there truly was no influx of customers.

And then he jumped up suddenly from his chair and came to attention.

Someone unexpected had just entered, and she was much more important than a customer.

It was Helene Redfern herself. The clerk recognized her from the corporate training videos, from a photo hung on the wall just behind him — and from the attitude with which she approached.

She seemed more than a little annoyed, and she did not bother with pleasantries. He knew he was in trouble.

"When guests pull up in this weather, I expect you to go out to meet them," she said.

"Yes, ma'am, I'm sorry. I . . . I wasn't

expecting anyone else this evening."

"Do you mean that all the reserved guests have arrived?"

"Yes, ma'am."

"Including the special ones I told you about yesterday on the phone — Laura Rankin and Reggie Heath?"

"Yes, just a few minutes ago. And I did come right out to meet them."

"Did you offer to help with their bags?"

"Of course."

"Did you offer to put his briefcase in the safe?"

"I did, ma'am, but he wouldn't turn loose of it."

"I see," said Helene. She stood in the lobby for a moment, considering what to do, as the chauffeur brought in her own bags from the limo.

"Have any reporters checked in?" she asked.

"Reporters?"

"Are there any media people hanging about?"

"I . . . I don't think so. Why?"

"Never mind," said Helene. "How did Laura Rankin and Reggie Heath seem when they came in?"

"I . . . I'm not sure what you mean," he said.

"Were they talking about anything in particular? In a hurry to get to a phone, anything like that?"

The desk clerk hesitated, then said, "He seemed cranky and worried about his car, and she seemed anxious to get someplace warm. I escorted them to the shepherd's hut, and I explained to him how to light the pilot, though he seemed rather dense."

"So they still have the briefcase in their possession? With them in the hut, not in the car?"

"Yes, ma'am. He took it out of the vehicle and into the hut with him. He wouldn't let me touch it. I saw it in the hut."

Helene nodded and turned away.

And then she turned back.

"Why was the pilot out?" she said. "Isn't the furnace working properly?"

"Oh, yes, ma'am. When the engineer you sent this afternoon checked it, he said it was fine."

"I didn't send an engineer this afternoon," said Helene. She stared at the desk clerk. "I sent no one out at all."

The desk clerk shrugged. "A man showed up in a Marylebone Grand Hotel truck, and he said he came to fix the furnace."

"But no one here made a call for him to come?"

"No, ma'am."

"Odd. Well, did you light the furnace for them?"

"No, ma'am. The engineer said it was new company policy — that all guests light the pilot themselves."

"Nonsense," she said. "We would never —"

And then she stopped.

"He only worked on that one furnace? The one in the shepherd's hut?"

"Yes, ma'am."

Helene turned from the clerk, exited the hotel lobby, and stepped outside into the cold air.

The wind coming from the direction of the hut brought a whiff of gas.

She paused. She didn't want to think it was so, but she had a suspicion of what was about to happen.

For a brief moment, what ran through her mind was that it was too late now to turn things back anyway. It was her brother's doing after all, not her own. He was responsible for it, not her, and her doing nothing now would ultimately rebound in her favor. It would be to her own advantage right now to just turn around and walk back into the lobby, collect her limo driver, and leave the premises immediately.

She decided to do that. She stepped back into the lobby. She approached the intimidated clerk, and she was about to tell him to get her bags back into her vehicle.

And then, in her direct line of sight, over the clerk's shoulder, was that photograph again — from the bombed-out pub in 1944. Apparently it had been distributed to all the hotel branches for the centennial.

She stared at the photo. Even since she had seen it in the hotel earlier, it had been bothering her.

Not just the fact that, if you looked closely, you could see a glimpse of a body behind the fallen snooker table.

What was bothering her was how her childhood memory seemed to be shifting.

For all her life she had believed — perhaps because all the adults around her had told her it was so — that it was her father who had carried her out from beneath the rubble to the street, before the upper floor collapsed.

But she had never been able to square that thought with other memories — the sight of her father's body, lying still and motionless on the floor of the pub in front of her, as she sat dazed against the wall, and in that exact same moment the sensation of two strong hands gripping her below the armpits, and then of being lifted, and then carried, out of the dust and chaos.

If those memories were true, then it was not her father who carried her out.

She stared at the photo now, at the glimpse of the tan uniform visible on the body of the man behind the snooker table, and she knew. She remembered. It came flooding back.

It was the American captain. Who she didn't even know. Who her father had just then met. It was the American captain; he had carried her out.

And then he had immediately gone back in.

She had turned, crying, wanting to run back in herself, for her father — but a passerby restrained her. So she could only watch, as the American went back in — and then her grandfather, too — and then her brother.

And then — after what seemed like an eternity had passed — her grandfather and her brother came back out.

But no one else.

Not her father. Not the American.

And then — a deafening roar, a shudder, a flood of particles in the air, and the second floor, under the weight of the heavy slate snooker table, had come crashing down in front of her.

Helene remembered it all very clearly now. All of it. In sequence.

And with that memory fresh in her mind, she stepped outside again.

She smelled the explosive gas from the shepherd's hut.

And she began to run toward it.

27

Nigel took the bus from Canvey Island to Barking, and then the tube from there to Paddington Station in London.

If you wanted to go from Canvey Island to Darby House in Newquay and didn't want to drive — and he was sure Darla Rennie didn't want to — this was the way you would go.

And if your arrival time was dictated only by the need to be there before Reggie and Laura themselves arrived at the castle — which might well be all that Darla Rennie required — you might even be taking this exact train.

With that in mind, after taking his seat, and just as the train was pulling out of the station, Nigel took a stroll through the other cars.

He didn't see her. But of course there are ways to duck out of sight on a train.

And for that matter, she might even have

thought ahead — anticipated that Nigel, or the Yard, or someone else might be in pursuit of her and checking at Paddington, in which case she might well get on at another station.

But for the moment, Nigel didn't see her. He returned to his seat.

It was possible Darla Rennie was one train ahead of him. He hoped not. But even if she was, given the limitations of the roads through Dartmoor, Nigel expected to arrive a few hours before Reggie and Laura would — and that's what mattered. Rennie could make no attempt on them until they got there. And that would give Nigel time.

An hour and twenty minutes later, in Exeter, Nigel had to change trains. He checked the departure board and scrambled quickly, just in time to get on a train just then pulling out for Newquay.

He waited for an older couple with an umbrella and travel cases to get on ahead of him. Then he moved quickly toward the back of the car, bumping shoulders just briefly with a gray-suited man who had chosen a location in front.

Nigel noticed something unusual in the encounter, but he kept moving.

Nigel found a seat in back, with an empty seat next to it and another empty one across. It was a good location, with a view of anyone else who might enter the car. He settled in.

The flight from Los Angeles had been long and bumpy; Nigel had not slept on the red-eye, and he had not slept since arriving. He did not intend to sleep now. But the rhythm of the train was soothing. He faded.

And then he woke.

"Sorry," said the woman who was now sitting across from him. "I didn't want to disturb you. But a snack service was being provided, and I didn't think you'd want to miss it. I think I recall from careers therapy that you would want the chicken salad and American-style coffee."

Nigel recognized her voice, and then he saw the emerald green eyes — set with perfect symmetry in a pale face, all of it surrounded by the hood of a dark velour sweater.

From a distance, he would not have been able to pick her out, given what she wore. She might have even been on the same train as him the whole way.

The freshly poured coffee was on the fold-out table in front of Nigel, steam still rising from it, and the aroma called to him. But he didn't move. He tried to register as little surprise as possible.

"You didn't disturb me," he said. And then he quickly took a gulp of the coffee, even though it was still a bit too hot.

"Oh," she said. "My mistake. I thought I did, once."

"Where are you heading?" said Nigel.

"The same place you are, I presume," said Darla Rennie.

"What are your intentions there?"

"Regarding?"

"Regarding anything."

"I'm not going there to jump your bones," she said, "if that's what you're asking."

"It isn't."

"I'm sorry I was late for that little rendezvous we had scheduled that evening after therapy," she said. "What was it, more than two years ago now? I presume you just went ahead and started without me?"

She crossed her legs, brushing against Nigel's in the process.

"That was some time ago," said Nigel, ignoring that contact. "Do you remember everything you've done in the interim?"

Darla Rennie looked down and stirred her tea. Then she looked up.

"Yes," she said. "I know the things I've done."

"People say you've taken a nasty bump

and had a spot of amnesia. Do you now know who you are?"

"I know who I've been. And I know now who I was supposed to be."

"Do you know who Reggie Heath is?"

"I know exactly who he is. And I know what he has done."

That didn't sound good.

"Are you on your meds?" asked Nigel.

"Yes," she said. "And I know I need them."

"Six months ago — before you fell into the Thames — you wanted revenge for the death of your great-great-grandfather," said Nigel. "Which is carrying a grudge for much too long, if you ask me. Are you still intent on it?"

"Why else would I be on this train?" she said.

Nigel took a deep breath and looked toward the front of the car. The man in the gray suit was still there.

"The man in the front of the car," said Nigel. "Is he traveling with you?"

"The tall one in the expensive gray suit?" said Darla.

"Yes," said Nigel, "the one with a gun under his jacket."

"I've never met him," said Darla Rennie.

"Good," said Nigel. "My guess is that he's Scotland Yard, undercover. I believe I will call him over."

"You shouldn't."

"Why not?"

"I think you're wrong about him being Scotland Yard," said Darla Rennie. "In any case, be aware that he no longer has his gun." As she said that, she placed a 9mm Beretta on the table in front of her, with the point of it in Nigel's direction.

"Not with you, and not with Scotland Yard," said Nigel. "Who, then?"

Darla Rennie didn't answer. They were rounding a bend now, and the train sounded its whistle.

"We're almost there," she said. "And there's something I think you should know."

She brought a cardboard box, somewhat smaller and flatter than a shoe box, out of her bag and placed it on the table between them, next to the gun. And then she took the gun back and held it in her lap.

"That is a Scotland Yard evidence box," said Nigel.

"Of course it is," said Darla Rennie.

"I'm impressed. How did you get it?"

She shrugged. "The tricky part about Scotland Yard is just getting in and out the first time," she said. "I learned everything I needed to know when I turned myself in. If you're observant once inside, you pick up quickly enough where things are, what procedures are followed, what disguise to use, and how to get about. When all of this is done, it will probably be a bit of an embarrassment to them that I could just walk back in again, when they're all out in a lather looking for me. But in my opinion, Scotland Yard has been deserving of a bit of embarrassment, for a very long time."

Nigel thought that last remark was curious.

"How so?" he said.

She glanced out the window now, and so did Nigel.

They were approaching a tunnel.

"If you really want to understand me," she said, turning back to the box, "you can look in here."

She kept her hands on the box, her fingertips caressing the taped edges. "You might want to. As I recall from our therapy days together, it bothers you when you win your case and then find out that the parties involved were not who they seemed."

Finally — reluctantly — she opened the box.

Nigel restrained his impulse to lean forward to see what was inside; she was becoming skittish, and he didn't want to botch the opportunity. He waited.

Darla Rennie reached inside the box and took out a one-page document. She kept the written side of it to herself, folded it once, and tucked it into an inside pocket of her coat.

"I need to keep this one. For now."

Now, finally, she pushed the open box slightly toward Nigel.

Nigel cautiously put his hands on both sides of the box, and prepared to draw it in closer for a look.

Now there was a very slight change in the lighting of the car. A barely perceptible flicker.

Instinctively, Nigel looked first at Darla Rennie — whose look of surprise showed that she had noticed the change as well.

And then he looked toward the far end of the car, where the tall man in the gray suit had been standing.

The man was no longer standing there.

And now the train entered the tunnel.

Everything went completely dark. And silent. Nigel heard no voices, at least nothing distinguishable, just the whirring rush of the train and the echoes of it as it entered the tunnel.

The train car's lights should not have gone out. Something was wrong.

Instinctively, Nigel clamped his hands

down on the box.

It occurred to him that perhaps he should have been taking possession of the gun instead. But it was too late for that choice now.

The train whirred past small yellow lights in the wall of the tunnel, creating a strobe-like effect in the otherwise pitch-black. Nigel sensed movement in the aisle of the train, one person, perhaps two, and, just a moment after it was certainly a moot point, a whiff of Darla Rennie's perfume. She was in motion.

The train came out of the tunnel. And Darla Rennie was gone. The gun was gone. The letter she had taken from the box was gone, but Nigel still had the box and its other contents tightly in his possession.

Nigel stood up into the aisle and looked in both directions, but he could see no sign of Darla Rennie — or of the individual who had been standing at the opposite end of the car.

The train was beginning to slow. A conductor's voice crackled over the PA system.

Nigel stood, with the cardboard evidence box securely under his arm. There would be no time to search for her again on the train; the best chance would be to spot her when she disembarked. He began moving toward the front.

The train came to a complete stop; the doors opened, and Nigel jostled his way immediately out onto the platform, into chilly, foggy coastal air.

He stood against the platform wall, and watched.

It was not a large station — just an outdoor platform, with a sheltered ticket booth and snack bar. And she had to be disembarking here. It would make no sense for her to stay on the train and go on past to the next stop.

But even so, he couldn't find her. The fog was so thick that visibility was only a few yards, and there were more people disembarking, in both directions, than he had expected.

Too many people in hats and overcoats were milling about. Darla Rennie might be among them, or she might be holding back until the very last moment, waiting for him to leave. Or she might have already gotten out ahead of him unseen.

He couldn't take the chance of waiting; if she was heading directly to the castle, it was important that he get there before her. He went quickly down the stairs from the train platform to the taxi ranks at the street.

Two vehicles ahead were already pulling

out. A third taxi had just pulled in to off-load passengers, and Nigel had to wait until they got their luggage out.

Finally he managed to get into the cab. He tossed his small duffel bag into the back-seat, held on to the cardboard box, and told the driver to take him to Darby House castle.

28

Nigel's taxi approached Darby House on a long, pebble-paved driveway, lined with tall sycamores.

Out to the far left, beyond the lawns, the edges of a small forest were visible, probably the estate's deer park that Nigel had heard about.

To the right were lawns, then a stone gardener's cottage, and then a mile or so of rocky, sparse moorland — ending, Nigel understood, in the cliffs above the Atlantic Ocean.

Darby House was straight ahead. There was no wall or fence around the interior portion of the estate, but there was a gate on the narrow road, and on this day, Nigel was glad to see, the gate was closed and manned.

His taxi came to a stop, and a uniformed guard, carrying a clipboard, came out from a little temporary shelter that had been set up next to the gate.

"Good evening," said the man cheerily. "Do you mind very much if I ask your name?"

"I'm Nigel Heath. I'm expected."

"Ahh, yes," said the man, looking at the list on the clipboard. "Indeed you are. Go right on through then. You'll see the round-about at the fountain."

"Wait," said Nigel, before the taxi driver could proceed. "You're not checking for picture IDs then?"

"Well, no," said the guard. "We've got nothing to compare them to if we did."

"And you've not been checking in the boots of vehicles?"

"No. Truth is, we weren't really expecting that security would be needed here, except to weed out the intrusive photographers, and the groundskeeper was going to handle that himself. But if you like, I can hold you here at the gate until the lady of the manor sends someone down to vouch for you."

"No," said Nigel. "I'm rather confident that I myself am not a threat. But have you seen a petite young woman, jet-black hair and eyes the color of those lawns over there?"

"No, sir," said the man. "Though I believe there are dating agencies where, if you specify those particulars, they will do their best."

"Carry on then," said Nigel. "But if you see her, ring the house and ask for me before you let her in."

The guard held the gate open, and the taxi drove on through.

The cab proceeded on up the drive, around the central fountain, and came to a stop at the front door of the castle.

Nigel guessed that the structure probably comprised some fifty rooms, on three levels. Although it retained its original structure, it did not radiate a history of broadswords and crossbows in the way that the larger coastal castles and ruins did; it had been built relatively recently, in the seventeenth century probably, and renovated even more recently, with pleasant peach-colored plaster and paint covering the original heavy stonework.

Best to be civilized and not frighten visiting Americans, Nigel supposed, if one wants to use tour groups to pay for the castle's upkeep.

There was staff to maintain it of course, and Nigel was greeted at the door by a butler.

The man introduced himself as Spenser. He looked to be as old as the sycamores that lined the driveway, but was not nearly so tall. Nigel had never seen a short butler; he had always presumed that height was one of their job requirements, necessary for supervising subordinate staff and intimidating guests.

This butler was balding, but with a comb-over that combined the few remaining strands together with some sort of molding gel, perhaps even candle wax, in a way that was so obvious that it screamed defiance — it knew it was a comb-over, and was proud of it.

The defiantly combed butler also had a surprisingly strong grip. He tried to take Nigel's mac, and the duffel bag, and the cardboard box. Nigel surrendered the duffel bag and mac, but held on to the box.

"I will take you to Lady Darby," said the butler, in a clear, imperious voice that had all the stature the man needed.

The butler escorted Nigel to the back of the castle, to a sitting room overlooking the back lawn, where Laura's aunt Mabel — formally Lady Darby, outside of the family — was having tea, with two guests who had arrived early.

"You must be Reggie's brother Nigel," said Laura's aunt.

"Because Laura said I'd be the really

good-looking one?" suggested Nigel.

"Well, that, too, I'm sure, but Laura said you'd be traveling informally and have the sort of stressed, smoggy-looking tan that people tend to get these days in Los Angeles."

"Fair enough," said Nigel.

Aunt Mabel looked to be about seventy years of age, perhaps a little more. She was tall, with a slightly equine face and a leisurely pace in her speech that, to Nigel, indicated intelligence and a comfortable attitude toward life.

She introduced Nigel now to the two tea guests — Lady Ashton-Tate, an actress in her sixties who was now edging her career more toward causes and had become friendly with Laura since an encounter involving plastic ducks, conservation of red squirrels, and a bomb plot the previous year; and Lord Tate, who had apparently threatened to take Reggie down to the river and teach him how to fly fish for trout, if only Reggie would arrive in time.

"Then Laura and my brother are not yet here?" said Nigel.

"No," said Aunt Mabel. "But not to worry. There's plenty of time before dinner."

"I'm looking forward to it," said Nigel. "But may I use your phone?"

The butler showed Nigel the phone in the first-floor study. Nigel waited until the man left the room, and then he rang Scotland Yard.

"I've seen Darla Rennie," said Nigel, the moment Wembley got on the phone.

"Where?"

"On the train to Newquay. She's in the vicinity, and the only security here is one local constable greeting guests as they drive up. Unless you put someone on the train, undercover. An authorized firearms officer perhaps?"

"No," said Wembley. "I didn't. No one from my division is carrying in that vicinity. You are at the castle now?"

"Yes."

"And your brother and Laura are there?"

"No. They haven't arrived."

There was a pause, as Wembley put the phone down and checked with one of his subordinates. Then he was back.

"You're certain it was Darla Rennie you saw?"

"I spoke to her myself, Wembley. And she's armed."

Now there was another pause, and this time Wembley wasn't consulting anyone. He was absorbing the gravity of this news.

"I'll try to get someone out there," he said.

"But I hope the weather holds. There's a storm coming in off the North Atlantic, and those smaller roads become impassable. With the wind, sometimes you can't even get a helicopter in."

Nigel hung up the phone. That was the best response from the Yard that he expected, but he was still concerned that it might come too bloody late.

Nigel sat down at a mahogany table in the center of the study and prepared to examine the contents of the cardboard box.

But now the door opened and the butler poked his head in.

Nigel wasn't sure of the etiquette. Wasn't the fellow supposed to have knocked?

"Yes?" said Nigel.

"If you are finished with your phone call," said the man, "shall I tell Lady Darby that you will be joining her for tea?"

"Thank you, but no," said Nigel, closing up the box. "Can I have my mac back? I'd like to take a walk around the grounds."

"Not the entire grounds, I hope," said the butler. "That would take a full day."

"I just want to stretch my legs a bit."

"I hope you don't plan on going onto the moors, sir," said the butler. "We have a spot of weather coming up."

"Well," said Nigel, "at least you're not

warning me of a full moon and weird howl-ings in the night."

The butler gave Nigel a blank look — at first. And then he said, "Of course not, sir. That would be so last century."

"Thank you," said Nigel. "I promise I won't venture beyond the lawns."

"Shall I stow that away for you, sir?" said the butler, as Nigel exited the study. Spenser seemed to be offering to exchange Nigel's mac for the Scotland Yard evidence box.

"No," said Nigel, "I'll just take it with me."

Nigel waved to Aunt Mabel and her friends as the butler escorted him past the sitting room, and then out one of the back doors and onto the estate's walking path.

"I was hoping you'd have a moat," said Nigel.

"We used to," said the butler. "It's filled in now with compost and bulbed plants. But I can ask the landscapers to change it all back for your next visit, if you like."

"Thanks much," said Nigel. "I'll let you know."

The butler went back toward the house. Nigel looked about.

The lawns and low garden hedges ex-tended more than a hundred yards in all directions.

To the north was the windbreak of sycamores lining the road on which Nigel had driven in, which would obscure any vehicles arriving from that direction until they reached the gated path. That was unfortunate, though at night headlamps would be visible.

To the east and south was a hedge that marked the edge of the moors.

Nigel took to the path due west. In ten minutes, at a fast pace, he reached the one-room stone gardener's cottage.

Nigel stood in front of the cottage and looked back at the castle. The sun was setting behind him; it wasn't quite dusk yet, but the castle was beginning to fall into shadows. The air was growing rapidly colder and the wind was picking up.

It didn't seem likely that Darla Rennie would try to sneak across from the forested side. Not with her sense of direction. And she wouldn't scale the cliffs or come across the moors. A commando approach just didn't seem likely.

So one way or the other, Darla Rennie would have to come right in through that front gate and up to the front door. At least that was Nigel's best guess.

At the moment, there was still enough light to watch for that from here. And he had an hour before the grand dinner was supposed to start.

Nigel went into the cottage and sat at a rough-hewn table in the center, with a line of sight through the window toward the gate. He put the cardboard evidence box on the table and, finally now with a bit of confidence that he could do so privately, he opened it.

A musty odor of decayed paper escaped, and Nigel knew immediately that what was inside the box was far older than the box itself. Darla Rennie must have transferred the materials from an older box to this new one before removing them from the Scotland Yard archive.

Nigel gingerly touched the edges of the two items in the box — a single sheet and something thicker and bound, underneath that sheet.

He carefully removed the sheet from the top, and then — when he saw what was beneath it — he set that sheet aside for a moment.

At the bottom of the box was a copy of *The Strand Magazine*. Nigel had seen one once before in a museum. This one looked very much like it — a century or so old, and showing the effects of time, even though carefully stored.

One top corner of one page had been

tweaked down — many years ago, certainly, because it would have broken the paper to do so now — as an apparent marker.

Nigel carefully turned to that page and saw the title of the story:

"The Final Problem," by Arthur Conan Doyle.

Fair enough. And in a way, not all that surprising that Darla Rennie would be carrying that around. Especially if, as was appearing to be the case, she still was under the delusion that her ancestor was the fictional Moriarty, and that he had been killed by Sherlock Holmes, and that, somehow, Reggie was Holmes.

A little surprising, though, that this copy had apparently come from Scotland Yard.

Nigel set the little magazine back into the box and turned his attention to the sheet that had been covering it.

It was just one single sheet. The sheet was still intact — the edges had not disintegrated, and it had been stored without folding, so there was no crease breaking it apart — but it was nevertheless yellowed with age. It was as old as the magazine it accompanied.

The words were typewritten, with the blunt impressions and slightly uneven lines of a very old machine, and the ribbon ink had faded.

Even so, the words were legible enough:

To whom it may concern:

If not desperate times, these are certainly dangerous ones in London. Nothing less would account for the measures that I, on behalf of Scotland Yard, have taken. I acknowledge those measures now and affix my signature to this document, so that if anyone should inquire in future, the pain endured and the bravery shown by the individual here named will be known.

Let it be known, then, that the individual known as James Moriarty, killed this last December 17th, was in fact the American agent James Smith, in the employ of the Special Branch of Scotland Yard, and that all the actions that he is reputed to have taken under the name James Moriarty were in fact in service to this country and in the interests of justice. And that he did not die in the manner reported in the newspapers, but that he was in fact murdered in the Docklands by the fiend known as Redgil. It is the request of his widow that this information shall be retained by Scotland Yard in perpetuity, to be acknowledged and revealed at any future time at which anyone with good reason should ask for it, so that any such person who shall have reason to care will know that the man known as James Moriarty lived his life with courage and in honor.

Signed this day, December 20, 1893
by Inspector Charles Standifer, Special
Branch, Scotland Yard

Darla Rennie had stolen this document from the Scotland Yard archives. She had gone to great lengths to do so.

Why?

Nigel wanted just a moment to think about that, but he didn't get it. Some flash of light, piercing the dusk from somewhere outside the cottage, flickered past the window.

Nigel picked up the box, went to the doorway of the cottage, and looked to the east, toward the main house. Bright yellow light was pouring out now from the windows on the second floor. The dining room was being prepared.

He looked to the north, toward the gate. Someone's limo was pulling up there. A much smaller vehicle, almost certainly the car of a paparazzo, was behind it. And the headlights of more approaching cars were flickering through the gaps between the trees.

There was little time. Nigel put both documents back into the box and took it with him as he walked back to the house.

The wind was increasing, and raindrops began to fall. Wembley's paranoia about the weather might turn out to be well-founded.

Nigel went to the front entrance and rapped on the door.

It opened immediately, and there was the butler again.

"Good evening, and welcome to —" he began; then he stopped. "Oh. It's you."

"Yes," said Nigel.

"I'm glad that you avoided the moors," said the butler, though rather grimly.

"So am I. Question for you: Do you have a guest list?"

"Of course."

"May I see it?"

The butler frowned, because of course this was an irregular request — but then he relented, Nigel being the brother of one of the guests of honor. He turned away, went to a small room next to the cloakroom, and then he returned with a list, complete with a clipboard and a highlighter for marking names off.

Nigel began scanning through the names.

"Who are these two you marked in red?" said Nigel.

"Known paparazzi," said the butler. "They will be allowed certain specific photo opportunities. Especially with Lady Ashton-Tate, if they are so interested."

"Have they already arrived?"

"Yes."

"Did you check their credentials?"

"They were unmistakable, sir."

"And who are these in yellow?"

"Other guests who have already arrived."

Nigel perused those.

"You recognized all of them — as being who they claimed?"

"Yes, sir. I am nothing if not fastidious in my study of the society pages."

"And the names that are not highlighted are the guests still to arrive?"

"Yes."

"I see a name has been crossed off," said Nigel.

"That was Lord Buxton, sir. The publishing magnate."

"Yes," said Nigel. "I know who Buxton is."

"Miss Rankin said that he was sulking and not likely to attend. We were in danger of having an unbalanced seating arrangement, but now we have someone to take his place.

Lady Darby was insistent that we have at least one magnate, of some type. And one called just yesterday and said he would be in the area. So now those places are filled. Lady Darby does very much appreciate the occasional serendipity."

"Who's the stand-in?"

"Harold Redfern," said the butler. "The hotel magnate. And his sister."

"What, the fellow couldn't find a proper date?"

The butler raised an eyebrow at Nigel, who had arrived at the castle quite obviously alone.

"Don't give me that look," said Nigel. "I'd have had a date, if the airline was offering a twofer, but it wasn't. But she'll be here when it comes time for the wedding. Mara will be the maid of honor, in fact."

"Of course, sir."

"Seriously," said Nigel. "I absolutely have a life. It just isn't in London so much anymore."

"Of course, sir. I was not intimating anything to the contrary. But be aware that the hotel magnate's sister accompanies him to this occasion because they are business partners. Apparently the hotels are a family operation."

"Two magnates for the invite of one,

then," said Nigel. "A bargain rate."

"My very words when I heard," said the butler.

"All right," said Nigel, satisfied with the names remaining. "I guess you understand how important it is that no one who is not on the list be admitted?"

"That is always important, sir."

"Well, even more so this time. What about a band? Were musicians retained for this event? A string quartet, or something?"

"That was necessary, sir, given that we have no karaoke machine."

"And you verified them as well?"

"They are all second-great-nieces and -nephews, or cohabitors of second-great-nieces and -nephews, of Lady Darby. I know them as if they were my own, and I am almost that fond of them."

"All right then," said Nigel. "I suppose I'd better find my room and get ready for dinner. You'll let me know when Reggie and Laura arrive?"

"Of course. And I will show you the way."

Nigel followed the butler toward the main stairs, in the center of the great hall. They passed a small room, where an open door revealed half a dozen men in drivers' uniforms, smoking and playing cards.

One of them, the tallest of the several

men, glanced up briefly as Nigel and the butler passed by.

The butler escorted Nigel up the stairs, and then along the third-floor corridor.

The walls were wood panel on the lower half, painted plaster on the upper, and every few feet or so in the upper half — almost as if in a museum — there was an oil portrait, or a small tapestry, or some grim and impressive artifact, usually framed and behind glass, but sometimes not.

It didn't surprise Nigel, now that he thought about it, given that the castle was beginning to host tour groups.

"What's this?" said Nigel, at the top of the stairs.

"It's a broadsword, sir. The lady says it belonged to the first Earl of Darby, whose father built the castle, or at least the first edition of it, in the sixteenth century."

"I see it's chipped. Saw some action, did he?"

"No, sir. My understanding is that the blade was quite pristine until the third earl used it to chop wood."

They walked on down the hall, but then Nigel paused again.

"And this one?"

The butler sighed, probably because it was so obvious, but Nigel was fascinated, and had to ask.

"A crossbow, sir."

"A family history to it, or is it just generic?"

"Purely for show, sir. For the tour groups. It was purchased at a reenactors' faire."

Nigel nodded, and then hurried on as the butler proceeded impatiently down the hall. Nigel tried to ask about other items on the wall, but the gentleman's replies got shorter and shorter.

"Wait, just a moment. This one?"

"Dueling pistols, sir, and yes, they were fired, and no, no one died except for the poor fellow who was holding the horses."

"And this one?"

"A shotgun, used by the current Lady Darby's father to annoy quail before the family became acquainted with the Ashton-Tates at a dinner party and everyone became devoted to barbless fly-fishing and saving red squirrels."

"And this —"

"Those are candlesticks, sir, please don't tell the lady, I removed them from the library for polishing, and I've been stowing them in that little display ledge until I have time to get them done. And here is your room, sir, thank you very much, dinner is at seven, and I advise you not to miss it, because if you want something later from the kitchen you will have to pull on that velvet rope, and I assure you that no one is likely to come. Oh, and what they say about the third floor is true — if you don't want to use a chamber pot, you'll need to go down the stairs to the shared loo on the second floor."

29

A short while later, dinner was ready to begin. Nigel managed to get there on time, in jacket and tie. A tuxedo, fortunately, was optional.

The dining room was formal and bright. The light from the overhead lamps prismed through crystal chandeliers, and reflected off the silver and white linen and translucent china. As the guests were escorted to their seats, a conversational dinner murmur and clinking of utensils began to grow.

As the butler escorted Nigel to his seat, Aunt Mabel came over for a word.

"I've seated you at the far end," she said, indicating the end of the table farthest from where she and Reggie and Laura would be seated. "It's intentional. I hope you don't mind."

"No," said Nigel. "But any particular reason I should be aware of?"

"I was obliged to send Lord Buxton an

invite, for some social and political reasons that I find too embarrassing to explain, but mainly because he owns half the media and Laura's publicity agent insisted on it. I hoped he would decline, given his past attempts toward Laura; one hates to have rejected suitors sulking at an engagement party. But in case he did not, I put his seat at the far end, and I put you there to contain him."

Nigel nodded.

"Some people never find each other at all," continued Aunt Mabel. "And some people find each other just in the nick of time. When I see that second thing happen, I don't like anything to come along to ruin it. So my thought was that if you should notice Buxton trying to put a tarnish on my niece's lovely glow, you would tell him to drop by the library after dinner and have a brandy with me, after which I would whack him with the fireplace poker if need be."

"A sound plan," said Nigel.

"Yes," said Aunt Mabel. "Mercifully, Buxton had the good sense to decline. He did send a reporter or two, for a media event after, whom we are accommodating at the insistence of Laura's publicity agent. But one must have a magnate of some kind at the dinner table, just for social variety. And so in our seating arrangement, we replaced Lord Buxton, and whichever German lingerie model he planned on bringing, with a hotel-chain owner who volunteered at the last moment."

"Yes," said Nigel. "The butler told me."

"You'll also have a paparazzo and a token Tory Member of Parliament to contend with. I hope you don't mind."

"Piece of cake," said Nigel.

"And now," said Aunt Mabel, "I am beginning to wonder just where the guests of honor could be. Laura is always so punctual. And she loves a good meal."

"I'm sure they'll be along," said Nigel, though he was getting worried. He considered and rejected the idea of alerting Aunt Mabel to the danger from Darla Rennie. If anything, disrupting the dinner would make it more difficult to keep an eye out.

Nigel took his seat as Aunt Mabel went back to the head of the table.

Across from Nigel was the hotel magnate that Aunt Mabel had warned of. The man was tall, in his early sixties perhaps, with a lean face and a faint red birthmark that ran along the side of his right jaw.

Next to him there was an empty chair, where presumably his sister would sit when she arrived.

Dinner was about to begin — it was well past the scheduled starting time, even though the two chairs next to Aunt Mabel were still empty.

Aunt Mabel, beginning to look discomfited but unable to delay the start of things any longer, tapped a silver fork rather aggressively on a crystal wineglass. Everyone stopped murmuring.

"Ladies and gentlemen, welcome all. As some of you may have noticed, our guests of honor have not yet arrived. I do try to make the weather cooperate for these little soirees, but sometimes it displays a mind of its own."

There was a polite collective chuckle from the hungry guests.

Nigel wished the weather were a reasonable explanation. But it wasn't. At least not yet. It hadn't stopped any of the other guests from arriving. Except for perhaps the hotel magnate's sister.

Nigel checked his watch: It was twenty minutes after.

"And time, tide, and creamy tomato bisque wait for no man. Or woman," Aunt Mabel continued. "So we will proceed with our first course, and when Laura and Reggie do arrive, we shall rap them on the knuckles with a reminder of what they have missed,

and perhaps next time they become engaged
— or whatever — they shall know to arrive
on time."

There was slight laughter again after the
engagement or whatever remark, and then
the table resumed its general murmur, as
two staff people — a middle-aged, portly
woman in charge and a gray-haired, slightly
built woman wearing unflattering eyeglasses
and obeying commands — entered the
room and began the service.

As a bowl was set in front of Nigel, he
had the distinct feeling that someone was
staring at him. He looked up and across the
table.

The man seated across — Redfern, the
hotel magnate — was indeed staring directly
at Nigel.

"Heath, isn't it?" said Redfern, in a voice
that was sharp and direct.

"Yes," said Nigel. "I don't think we've
met."

"No," said the man. "But I learned when
I arrived that I would have the privilege of
sitting directly across from Reggie Heath's
brother. But quite far away from the main
celebrities, I see. Reggie Heath and Laura
Rankin are to be at the other end, are they
not? Is there a reason for the distance? A
recognition of sibling rivalry, I suppose?"

"No," said Nigel. "Laura's aunt Mabel — Lady Darby, to you — is fond of Heaths, and she thought it would be fair to distribute us about evenly."

"Ahh," said the man. "Well. I am Redfern."

"The hotel magnate," said Nigel.

"Really? Is that how I am referred to? The magnate?" The man laughed, with a pretense of humility, but just a pretense — Nigel knew he was boasting.

"For purposes of dinner table seating, I think that's the case," said Nigel. "And I believe you have a sibling who shares that honor?" Nigel nodded toward the empty seat next to Redfern.

"You are well-informed, Mr. Heath. I do. But my sister will be late. She was called away on an urgent . . . maintenance issue on one of our properties."

"Oh. So you let her be the one to get her hands dirty. Nicely done."

Nigel said this lightly, and then was surprised at the man's initial reaction — which was a frown, then a pause and a loss of eye contact, and then a recovery and a casual denial.

"Not at all," he said. "She was simply nearby, and I wasn't."

"Of course," said Nigel, knowing he had

touched a nerve, and wondering what sort of nerve it was.

Now the staff was back. The soup was taken away by the portly woman, and the slighter, gray-haired woman came around with the salad.

Just for an instant, Nigel caught the scent of something familiar — he twisted in his chair to look in back of him — and could not locate it.

Surely the serving staff was not wearing such a perfume.

But now the first course was done, the second was beginning, and Reggie and Laura had still not arrived.

"Something wrong?" said the hotel magnate.

"No," said Nigel. "I just . . ." And now he paused. He wasn't sure why — it might have been the tone of voice, or it might have been something in the man's expression — but suddenly Nigel did not want to reveal more than he needed, and he said, not seriously, "I was hoping for seconds on soup."

"I take it you're unclear on the concept of a formal dinner?"

Nigel sat up in his chair and looked directly across at Redfern. Was the man prying for some reason?

Or was he just obnoxious and trying to

start a verbal dinner-party war?

Nigel was about to respond appropriately — but now the petite gray-haired server with the unstylish spectacles was bringing the beef bourgignon.

She avoided looking directly at Nigel as she set his serving down. But when she put a plate in front of Redfern, she seemed to linger — staring at the man when he wasn't looking.

Then she caught Nigel noticing, and she quickly moved on.

One course after another played out this way — until now, finally, the only remaining course would be dessert.

Nigel was certain now. It wasn't really a bad disguise, but given a long enough look, and enough time to study over it, pretty much anyone would see through it. Darla Rennie's appearance was that distinctive; she could not disguise it completely from someone who knew the face and was genuinely looking for it.

Nigel had no doubts about the gray-haired server at all, and he knew that after she served the dessert he would have to not let her out of his sight. He couldn't take the chance that she might escape again.

But this had made him wonder about something else.

"Mr. Redfern?" said Nigel.

"Yes, Mr. Heath?"

"I would imagine your hotels have security cameras?"

"Of course. State of the art. I mean, in the appropriate public access locations, of course, not in our guests' rooms." He laughed. "Or in the loo, either."

"And especially the Marylebone Grand Hotel itself, so recently renovated, and celebrating its centennial? You would certainly have your state-of-the-art CCTV in place there?"

Now Redfern gave Nigel a direct look, and an indirect answer.

"The Marylebone Grand is state of the art in every way," he said.

"I only ask," said Nigel, "because Scotland Yard was trying to determine if one particular person had been there recently. You may have seen the news reports. About this woman named Darla Rennie? And the fisherman killed in Canvey?"

Redfern stared back at Nigel.

"I mention it," said Nigel, "because the Yard looked at the CCTV tapes from your hotel — which I presume your security service provided — and they couldn't find any image of Darla Rennie at the Marylebone Grand Hotel on that specific day and time. Or at any time, in fact. Even though we are pretty sure she was there at some point; the question is just exactly when."

"So?" said Redfern.

"But she was in fact caught on CCTV. Because someone was showing her surveillance picture down in the pubs in Canvey — just before the killing. So what I'm wondering is this: Is there any reason why anyone from your hotel would have been showing her picture around earlier — but excising it from the CCTV tapes that your hotel turned over to Scotland Yard?"

"No," said Redfern. "There isn't. If there was a photo, it came from somewhere else. Not from our cameras. Why would I or any of my staff excise a photo from our security tapes, Mr. Heath?"

"I've no idea," said Nigel. "So when I ask Scotland Yard to take a closer look to see if the tapes were altered — something they wouldn't routinely be looking for, because they wouldn't expect it — I'm sure that will bear you out."

Redfern glared across at Nigel. As he did, the gray-haired serving woman entered the dining room, pushing the cart of tiramisu, and beginning to distribute it from a tray.

"Is this a family trait," said Redfern, "you and your brother, and things that don't concern you?"

Nigel pondered the significance of that question, and was considering a response.

But now the butler entered — and not with any sort of dinner-serving apparatus, but with a somber look on his face, a look that he tried to keep to himself, avoiding eye contact with all the guests at the table, and walking directly to Laura's aunt Mabel.

He leaned in, trying to be subtle about it, and mostly succeeding. In fact, Nigel noticed, the only two people in the room paying attention to the butler's portentous attitude were himself and Mr. Redfern.

The butler whispered something in the ear of Aunt Mabel.

Her expression immediately became, just for an instant, as somber as the butler's. She put down her fork. Then she recovered, managed a quick smile to those immediately around her as she removed her napkin from her lap, excused herself, and stood.

Aunt Mabel, followed by the butler, both with faces like surgeons delivering bad news in hospital, began a purposeful walk from Aunt Mabel's end of the table toward the end where Nigel, the Tory MP, and Mr. Redfern were seated.

Aunt Mabel and the butler were walking on Nigel's side of the table, and the closer they got the more ominous their bearing seemed. Given the things that he knew were going on, Nigel was certain this could not be anything but bad news, and he finally abandoned decorum and turned to look as they approached.

From the corner of his eye, he thought he detected a very unexpected expression on Redfern's face. Something like a concealed smirk. Nigel had no idea what that might mean and, at the moment, didn't care.

And then — when Aunt Mabel and the butler had finally reached Nigel's table position, just one seat from the very end of the table — they kept on walking. To the end of the table, and then around it.

And then they stopped.

Aunt Mabel was now standing to the side and just behind Mr. Redfern, with the butler respectfully a step back. The gray-haired serving woman was standing stone still with the cart of tiramisu a few steps back.

Aunt Mabel leaned in and whispered something in Mr. Redfern's ear.

Redfern's expression changed. Blood drained from his face, causing the slight pink birthmark on his jaw to stand out in relief.

He nodded to what she was saying, but he

remained in his seat. He whispered something back to Aunt Mabel. Nigel tried to catch it, but couldn't.

Aunt Mabel shook her head, leaned in, and whispered something again.

Now Redfern stood, brushing Aunt Mabel rudely back. The blood returned to his face. He looked at no one, said nothing to anyone, and stormed from the dining room.

And at the same moment, a tray of tiramisu went crashing to the floor.

Nigel stood. He had to choose a suspect, and a direction. Darla Rennie — the gray-haired serving woman — had dropped her tray, and was bolting for the kitchen.

Nigel ran after her — into the kitchen, dodging the two cooks and the supervising maid, and then through the kitchen and into a stairwell, and then up the stairwell, into a subordinate serving station on the third floor, and then through that serving station onto the third-floor corridor.

Darla Rennie stopped. She whirled to face Nigel, and she pointed the Beretta at him.

"Let me go," she said.

"I can't," said Nigel. And then he asked her what he'd been wanting to ask since the train. "When you said you knew exactly what my brother had done — what did you mean?"

"I meant that he told the truth," she said. "About my alibi. Despite everything he feared."

Now she glanced down at the interior stairs that led up from the floors below. She turned and began running again toward the end of the corridor.

She was heading toward a corner balcony, from which Nigel knew exterior stairs led to the ground level. He continued in pursuit — and then he stopped.

Midway between Nigel and the point at which Darla Rennie was escaping at the far end was the main interior stairwell. And from the top of those stairs, Redfern's driver now stepped into the corridor.

Farther down the stairwell, moving slowly and apparently unafraid, Spenser the butler was ascending the stairs as well.

Nigel recognized the driver now; he'd seen him earlier, in the room with the other limo drivers.

But Nigel had also seen him on the train, and on the train he'd had a gun, at least at first. Which meant he wasn't Redfern's driver at all — he was Redfern's private investigator. Or Redfern's enforcer. Or worse. He might well be the person who'd been asking about Darla Rennie at the pub.

Which meant he might, at least possibly,

also be the person who had killed the fisherman Darla Rennie was living with.

But all that was just adrenaline-fueled speculation on Nigel's part. The proof would be in what the man did now.

For a moment, the man's intent was unclear. He looked first in Nigel's direction, then at the fleeing Darla Rennie. Then at Nigel again.

And then he looked at the wall next to him — at the display case for the first old weapon that the butler had described to Nigel earlier.

The driver smashed his elbow through the glass of the display case — and then he withdrew the broadsword.

And then he came at Nigel.

Nigel decided that the man's intentions were no longer in doubt.

"Spenser!" shouted Nigel.

Spenser had now reached the top step.

"Sir?"

"Crossbow, pistols, shotgun — which of these bloody weapons work?"

Spenser pondered the question, as the driver moved toward Nigel.

Finally — "Candlesticks, sir!" shouted Spenser.

Nigel ran forward, head-on toward the driver — and reached the candlestick shelf

just in time. He grabbed one without slow-
ing, and then he dropped down onto the
slick hardwood floor as the man began to
raise the heavy two-handed sword.

Nigel ducked and slid for the last two
yards.

He swung the candlestick for the driver's
left kneecap, and he made contact.

There was a scream. The driver went
down.

Nigel ran onto the balcony, and then
down the stairs after Darla Rennie.

30

In the dining room, dessert had not gone
smoothly.

Aunt Mabel knew what had caused Mr.
Redfern to leave so abruptly; she had, after
all, delivered the unfortunate news to him.

He had not handled it well, not with
proper decorum at all. It was certainly sad
news about his sister. But one would have
thought that he would have shared in Mabel's relief at hearing the corresponding
good news about Laura and Reggie —
especially after Redfern had taken the
trouble to ask about them.

Where Redfern had gone after storming
from the dining room Aunt Mabel did not
know. His car was still on the premises, and
she had sent the butler to look for him.

Why Nigel Heath had chased the serving
maid into the kitchen was even more per-
plexing. Aunt Mabel did not know precisely
what was going on, but she knew it was

more than met the eye. At least she hoped
it was.

In any case, it was time for the dinner to
come to an end.

She went to the head of the table and
tapped her fork on her champagne glass.

The chaotic murmuring in the room froze
in anticipation.

"I hope you have all enjoyed the tiramisu,"
said Aunt Mabel. "At least all of you who
were able to get some. Thank you all for
braving the most unfortunate weather
conditions to attend. Really, I know it's been
a proper gale outside for most of the
evening. Under normal circumstances, I
would at this point be inviting you all to
join us in the ballroom, or in the study for
brandy for those of you who neither dance
nor move well. But I have been informed
that at this very moment, the rain has
stopped, the moon is out, and the winds
have at last subsided. For those of you who
wish to stay the night, we have accommodations and you are most welcome, but be
aware that only the lower two floors have
plumbing and the third floor requires chamber pots. For those of you who have ar-
rangements of your own nearby — be aware
that right now is probably your best window
of opportunity, and if you choose to forgo

the customary brandy or cigar in the study, no one will be offended, least of all the happily engaged couple, who may well, when they finally arrive, have other things on their mind. Thank you all very much."

This speech had the desired effect. The guests who had not already done so began to exit toward the first-floor foyer.

31

At the back of the castle, Nigel ran down the exterior stairs after Darla Rennie.

The rain had stopped, at least temporarily. There was a gap in the clouds, and the moon glowed through it.

Nigel could not see Darla Rennie. But the only direction that made sense was toward the west — toward the stone gardener's cottage — and he ran in that direction.

He reached the cottage and ran inside.

She wasn't there. Her gray wig and server's uniform were discarded on the table.

And now Nigel heard the back door of the cottage slam in the wind. He looked through the window and saw her — Darla Rennie was running across the moor, toward the west, on the cliff side of the estate.

Nigel ran out in pursuit.

He was running on ground that was alternately rocky and soft with winter yellow moss and thistles.

In the distance was the black-coated figure of Darla Rennie, running toward the cliffs.

"Darla Rennie!" shouted Nigel as he ran. "Darla Rennie, I know who you are!"

That didn't seem to help. She didn't slow.

"Darla Rennie!" shouted Nigel again. "Darla Rennie — you know who you are!"

That may have helped; at least it seemed to, at first, because she paused.

But then Nigel realized that she had come to the edge of the cliff.

And now another figure appeared, striding rapidly along the cliff's edge from the north.

It was Redfern.

Nigel was within about fifty yards of Darla Rennie now; so was Redfern; he had slowed to a walk, but was moving steadily closer to her.

She turned toward Nigel, with the gun in her hand.

"Stop!" she said.

Nigel stopped.

"You are Darla Rennie," said Nigel. "You are not Moriarty. You were never Moriarty."

"I know who I am," she said.

"And your ancestor was never Moriarty. He was a brave man who simply took the name."

"I know that now," said Darla Rennie. "I

370

know who my ancestor was, and I was glad to learn it. But I am still myself, regardless of who went before me. I cannot change that, and I cannot change what I have done."

"Not true," said Nigel. "Perhaps you cannot change what you have done. But people change who they are on a daily basis."

"Bollocks," said Redfern.

He was now within just a few yards of Darla Rennie, both of them standing on the cliff's edge. He took another step closer, and she turned the gun from Nigel toward Redfern.

"No one changes," said Redfern to Nigel. "You are as naïve as she is delusional. I've known exactly who I am since I was nine years old, and it's made me the man I am today."

Redfern took another step toward Darla Rennie.

"Give me the document," he said.

Darla looked directly at Redfern. She reached inside her coat, and she took out a one-page document.

"I know who you are," she said to Redfern, "and I know what you did. Come and take it, you sonofabitch."

Whether it was intentional or not Nigel couldn't tell — but Darla Rennie lowered the gun when she took out the document.

And Redfern took the opportunity. He lunged toward her, reaching with one hand for the gun, and with the other for the sheet of paper.

Redfern missed the document — Darla let go of it at the last instant — but he grabbed her gun arm. She responded by grabbing his collar.

And before Nigel could move, they both were gone over the edge of the cliff.

Nigel ran forward. The sheet of paper caught in an updraft, blew back toward him, and he grabbed it.

Nigel stood and looked down from the edge.

The moon was still out. White waves crashed clearly on dark rocks below.

And this time, there could be no doubt. He was looking at two broken lives and bodies on the rocks below.

32

It was after midnight. The sycamores lining the driveway were still whipping back and forth in the wind, but the clouds overhead remained parted.

One after another, limousines pulled out from the castle, their tires cutting crisply through the thin layer of water on the pebble-paved roundabout.

Aunt Mabel and the butler came to the front door. She waved to each of the long town cars as they rolled out.

"Do you suppose," Aunt Mabel said to the butler, "that it was my reference to chamber pots?"

And then, as the last limo rolled out, she looked once more out toward the road.

And she saw them — a pair of headlights, very close together, unlike all the departing vehicles, turning from the muddy two-lane road and onto the castle's driveway.

It was not the sort of vehicle she was

expecting, and she waited in the doorway as it drew closer.

It was a tiny Fiat. None of her friends had one, not even the environmentally conscious ones. It was the sort of vehicle favored by the paparazzi, for maneuverability and access to intimate destinations, she presumed.

It was a two-seater. Well, not formally a two-seater — she knew it had a backseat, but not one big enough to accommodate an actual adult.

The vehicle pulled to a stop in front of the castle door. Lady Darby nodded to the butler, and he went out to assist.

The driver's door opened. A scruffy man in a hooded sweatshirt stepped out.

The butler ignored him and opened the passenger door.

"Thank you," said Laura, as she got out. "How are you, Spenser?" she said to the butler.

"I'm quite well, miss," he said. "And very pleased to see you."

The butler was ready to escort her toward the door, but she wasn't ready to head in that direction.

"No, wait," she said. "There's more."

Now one arm became visible, extending from the backseat, getting a grip onto the door frame, and now the other hand got a grip on the passenger seat back — and Reggie Heath extricated himself from the backseat of the tiny Fiat.

He stood. He flexed his back and neck and shoulders and took a moment to straighten out. Then he reached back into the car and pulled out his briefcase.

He came forward to join Laura.

The butler was now finally ready, he thought, to escort them both into the castle.

"Wait," said the scruffy man in the hooded overcoat. He took a camera from the driver's side of the car, and nodded expectantly in Laura and Reggie's direction.

Laura and Reggie obliged. They paused, put their arms around each other, and posed in front of the castle step for the paparazzo.

The camera clicked and flashed several times and from several different angles.

"Got it," said the man. "Cheers."

The paparazzo got back in his car and drove back out to the road.

Now, finally, Reggie and Laura turned toward the front door.

"Should I have tipped him or something?" said Aunt Mabel, as the paparazzo drove out of sight.

"No need," said Laura. "I just promised him a sort of future scoop."

"Well, that's fine, so long as he didn't demand your firstborn or such."

Laura raised an eyebrow at that, but quickly returned it to neutral.

Both she and Reggie were drenched in rainwater and mud. His coat and Laura's hair both looked to Aunt Mabel as though they might actually be singed.

"You poor things," she said, "what you've been through. Which do you want first — dry clothes, or brandy?"

"Brandy," said Laura.

Moments later, the butler set four large brandies on a table in the study, in front of a roaring fire.

Aunt Mabel, Laura, and Reggie waited — and then, as the butler left the room, Nigel entered. He carried the Scotland Yard evidence box under his arm, but other than that, he was pretty much fresh from his pursuit on the moors.

Aunt Mabel looked at each of them in turn.

"You are all three of you a mess," she said. "You can have your brandies now, but I'll expect you all to change before breakfast."

Now the butler returned.

"Inspector Wembley has arrived," said the butler.

"Well, tell him to set up a perimeter, or whatever it is they do," said Aunt Mabel. "I believe he's missed most of it. So he can wait now until we've had our brandy."

The butler exited to deliver that message.

Laura and Reggie looked across at Nigel.

"How was your flight?" said Laura.

"Wonderful, by comparison," said Nigel. "How was your drive?"

"Laura plans the next one," said Reggie.

"All right then," said Nigel. "Let's share."

He placed his Scotland Yard evidence box on the table.

"What I have," said Nigel, "is an 1893 letter signed by an Inspector Standifer of Scotland Yard Special Branch, stating that an American agent in his employ had taken on the name of James Moriarty for undercover purposes — and that his widow had chosen to keep it, and wanted that fact recorded for any possible descendants, one of whom we all have come to know as Darla Rennie. This was in the Scotland Yard archives for the past hundred years or so, until she managed to smuggle it out."

Nigel put that document on the table.

Now Reggie opened his briefcase.

"What I have," said Reggie, "is an 1893 letter written to Sherlock Holmes by a felon named Redgil, in which Redgil in effect confesses to torturing and murdering that same American agent. Which was stored safely away from prying eyes in the Baker Street archives, until it became part of the hotel exhibit."

Nigel nodded. "As expected," he said. "Handwritten, and signed, by Redgil himself."

Now Nigel took out the document that he had grabbed above the cliff.

"And that signature will match this one — from a couple of years later, in which a man calling himself Redfern established the first Marylebone Grand Hotel, using, clearly, the counterfeit money he had obtained during the process of murdering the American agent. All of which would have been a considerable embarrassment to *his* descendants, the siblings Harold Redfern and Helene Redfern. Which, I gather, was the reason for some of the apparent inconveniences on your trip. The Redferns were concerned about what would happen if someone other than Darla Rennie succeeded in matching up those signatures and revealed them to the press, say at a media event already scheduled at Darby House."

"Murder for that?" said Laura, "Over a little corporate embarrassment?"

"One thing leads to another," said Reggie.

"Well," said Nigel, after a moment, "I think one of the Redferns had more of a motivation than that. Helene Redfern had a hand in the attempts to get the letter from Reggie's briefcase. But I think that's where she drew a line. We know that she died trying to go back and warn you both about the gas."

"It's a shame we didn't cross paths with her," said Laura. "We'd gone back toward the car, so we didn't see her come from the lobby."

Nigel nodded. "The two Redferns shared a lineage and a history, but I don't think it was quite exactly the same history. I think the nine-year-old Harold Redfern helped his grandfather kill the American captain, in the chaos and rubble after the V-2 bomb attack. It's clear that Darla Rennie thought so."

Now Nigel picked up all the documents and bundled them together.

"Darla Rennie wasn't stalking you two," he said. "She was back on her meds and that delusion was gone. But she was in fact tracking down Harold Redfern; something she started doing from the moment she knew who her own ancestors actually were. After surviving the river, she had started reconstructing her own history — not just who she had been, but where she had come from. She started at the National Archives, where she found a reference to the document at Scotland Yard that recorded the actual identity of her great-great-grandfather. Then she went to the exhibit at the Marylebone Grand Hotel. And there it was, all laid out in front of her — the murder letter from the original Redgil, the founder's document for the hotel, showing the same signature as on the incriminating letter; and the war photograph, showing where her great-grandfather had died — and who was around him when it happened."

"There's a good lesson there for family dynasties," said Laura. "If you start your corporate empire by torturing and murdering someone, be sure to advise your descendants not to brag about it later."

"Yes," said Nigel. "But unfortunately, at the same time that Darla Rennie was discovering the documents exhibited at the hotel, the hotel security chief was discovering her. She'd been there too often, and too conspicuously, and that made Redfern realize that they had actually put evidence of a murder on display. So Redfern's security man tracked Darla Rennie to Canvey Island, found out where she lived, and went there intending no doubt to retrieve the incriminating signed document she had stolen — or perhaps to do worse. But Cheeverton came back to the house early, surprised him there — and got killed for his trouble. And I think Dr. Miner had a similar encounter at the institute, although we'll have to wait for O'Shea's report on that. But we know that Redfern's security man has been trailing Darla Rennie all the while she has been in pursuit of Redfern — and I think he was just as willing to kill as his employer."

There was silence for a moment.

Then Laura said, "We're lucky, I suppose, that Darla Rennie switched from avenging a fictional ancestor to avenging her real ones."

Reggie put the bundled documents back into the Scotland Yard evidence box.

"When she found the letter from Scotland Yard about who her great-great-grandfather really was, I suspect that had a positive effect on her," said Reggie. "But when she saw the murderous letter that Redgil wrote to Sherlock Holmes — well, that was another matter."

"One needs to be careful about the past," said Laura. "We all get at least one clean slate."

Nigel closed the box.

"I suppose Wembley will be getting anxious," said Nigel. "How about Aunt Mabel and I deal with him now, and leave you two alone for a bit?"

33

Several hours later, sometime well after midnight was Nigel's guess, but nowhere near a reasonable hour in the morning, it became necessary to determine whether the rumors about lack of plumbing on the third floor were in fact true. Too much brandy, possibly, or too much water chaser as an afterthought.

He got up out of bed and took a look around.

Yes, it was true. The choices were either a chamber pot or go downstairs one level to the shared loo on the second floor.

And tired as he was, Nigel was not going to use the chamber pot.

He stumbled out the door and into the corridor. He had a rough idea which direction to take, at least, and he took it.

Several wrong turns later, and then finally a correct one, he found the shared loo — or someone's loo, anyway — made use of it, and then headed back in search of his own room.

He was in the corridor now that overlooked the grand ballroom. Or else it was *the* ballroom; he wasn't sure there was actually more than one. But a ballroom was what it was.

Nigel heard a sound. He looked down into the ballroom.

There was a high turret window overhead, letting in moonlight that was finally shining unimpeded. In the ballroom, it shone on two figures, wrapped closely together, dancing, so slowly that the motion was almost imperceptible, in silence.

Laura's eyes were closed, her head resting on Reggie's chest. Reggie stood as tall and relaxed as Nigel had ever seen him.

Nigel nodded in the affirmative, and then continued on. He had a plane to catch in the morning.